"I would like y ... my children."

Thunder roared. Cymbals crashed. Trumpets blared.

And that was only what was going on in Mitch's head. He'd had no idea he'd react this way until Elaine spoke the fateful words.

"There's no point in marrying beforehand, because neither of us is interested in getting married to begin with."

Mitch felt his brow dip into frown territory. That was news to him. "Go on."

"I think the best approach is to wait. See if I get pregnant and if I do, then and only then explore marriage." She paused for his reaction. "I just thought it would be a good idea not to put so much pressure on each other. You have to make love something like every other day for seven days to increase the odds of getting pregnant."

"It does sound like a lot of hard work," he mused. He reached for his scone and buttered it.

"Fortunately I'm a workaholic."

Dear Reader,

It's October, the time of year when crisper temperatures and waning daylight turns our attention to more indoor pursuits—such as reading! And we at Silhouette Special Edition are happy to supply you with the material. We begin with *Marrying Molly,* the next in bestselling author Christine Rimmer's BRAVO FAMILY TIES series. A small-town mayor who swore she'd break the family tradition of becoming a mother *before* she becomes a wife finds herself nonetheless in the very same predicament. And the father-to-be? The very man who's out to get her job....

THE PARKS EMPIRE series continues with Lois Faye Dyer's *The Prince's Bride,* in which a wedding planner called on to plan the wedding of an exotic prince learns that *she's* the bride-to-be! Next, in *The Devil You Know,* Laurie Paige continues her popular SEVEN DEVILS miniseries with the story of a woman determined to turn her marriage of convenience into the real thing. Patricia Kay begins her miniseries THE HATHAWAYS OF MORGAN CREEK, the story of a Texas baking dynasty (that's right, *baking!*), with *Nanny in Hiding,* in which a young mother on the run from her abusive ex seeks shelter in the home of Bryce Hathaway—and finds so much more. In *Wrong Twin, Right Man* by Laurie Campbell, a man who feels he failed his late wife terribly gets another chance to make it up—to her twin sister. At least he *thinks* she's her twin.... And in Wendy Warren's *Making Babies,* a newly divorced woman whose ex-husband denied her the baby she always wanted, finds a willing candidate—in the guilt-ridden lawyer who represented the creep in his divorce!

Enjoy all six of these reads, and come back again next month to see what's up in Silhouette Special Edition.

Take care,

Gail Chasan
Senior Editor

Please address questions and book requests to:
Silhouette Reader Service
U.S.: 3010 Walden Ave., P.O. Box 1325, Buffalo, NY 14269
Canadian: P.O. Box 609, Fort Erie, Ont. L2A 5X3

Making Babies

WENDY WARREN

Silhouette

SPECIAL EDITION®

Published by Silhouette Books

America's Publisher of Contemporary Romance

For my daughter,
Elisabeth Elana Laura Blough,
link to the past and the future,
key to joy in the present.
Your daddy and I adore you.
"Our hearts spoke your name, and God heard."

SILHOUETTE BOOKS

ISBN 0-373-24644-7

MAKING BABIES

Copyright © 2004 by Wendy Warren

This edition published by arrangement with Harlequin Books S.A.

® and TM are trademarks of Harlequin Books S.A., used under license.
Trademarks indicated with ® are registered in the United States Patent
and Trademark Office, the Canadian Trade Marks Office and in other
countries.

Visit Silhouette Books at www.eHarlequin.com

Printed in U.S.A.

Books by Wendy Warren

Silhouette Special Edition

Dakota Bride #1463
Making Babies #1644

Previously written under the name Lauryn Chandler

Silhouette Romance

Mr. Wright #936
Romantics Anonymous #981
Oh, Baby! #1033
Her Very Own Husband #1148
Just Say I Do #1236
The Drifter's Gift #1268
The Oldest Virgin in Oakdale #1609

WENDY WARREN

lives with her husband, Tim, a dog, a cat and their recent—and most exciting!—addition, baby daughter Elisabeth, near the Pacific Northwest's beautiful Willamette River. Their house was previously owned by a woman named Cinderella, who bequeathed them a gardenful of flowers they try desperately (and occasionally successfully) not to kill, and a pink General Electric oven, circa 1958, that makes the kitchen look like an *I Love Lucy* rerun.

A two-time recipient of Romance Writers of America's RITA® Award for Best Traditional Romance, Wendy loves to read and write the kind of books that remind her of the old movies she grew up watching with her mom— stories about decent people looking for the love that can make an ordinary life heroic. Wendy was an *Affaire de Coeur* finalist for Best Up and Coming Romance Author of 1997. When not writing, she likes to take long walks with her dog, settle in for cozy chats with good friends and sneak tofu into her husband's dinner. She always enjoys hearing from readers, and may be reached at P.O. Box 1208, Ashland, OR 97520.

Elaine's Fertility Goddess Shake

1 cup plus 2 tbsp of the best chocolate or vanilla-caramel ice cream you can find
1/2 cup organic soy milk, regular or vanilla—chilled
1 small ripe banana
1 tbsp organic peanut, almond or cashew butter
1 couch
1 romance novel

Put 1 cup ice cream into a blender. Put 2 tbsp into your mouth. Add 1/2 cup soy milk (to the blender) then the banana and nut butter. Process until smooth. Pour into a tall, frosted glass.

Sit on the couch, pick up your novel, sip your drink and think sexy thoughts. You'll be a goddess in no time.☺

Chapter One

Pencil erasers tasted like gum mixed with sand. Elaine Lowry knew this for a fact because she'd just chewed through one while staring at a large flat appointment book lying open on the desk in front of her.

For two days each week, Elaine worked in the outer office of Harold J. Gussman, D.D.S. She did the dentist's filing and stuffed envelopes for the "Come-In-We'll-Make-You-Smile" six-month checkup reminders he sent to his patients.

She'd been working here part-time for five years. Just yesterday, she'd walked the two blocks to Office Max on her lunch hour to buy one of those little plastic water bottles with the sponge tips so she could sponge the envelopes instead of having to lick them all.

Five years, and she'd finally made the switch from tongue to sponge.

It just showed how she felt about change. If she'd been in charge of the pilgrims, the citizenry of the United States would be huddled around Plymouth Rock to this day.

Pushing heavy brown bangs off her forehead, Elaine rubbed a spot of tension over her right eyebrow and sighed. It was difficult to respond to life's little challenges.

Take, for instance, right now.

She was covering for Sue, Dr. Gussman's receptionist, who had slipped out for a potty break. In looking at the appointment book a minute ago, Elaine had seen that Steph Lowry would be coming in at four-fifteen for a tooth bonding.

Steph Lowry.

Steph. Short for "Stephanie."

Lowry. Short for "the vacuous, bubble-headed, plastic-breasted bleached blonde who stole my husband."

Not that Elaine was holding a grudge. But surely the imminent arrival of her barely ex-husband's younger, blonder new bride called for *some* reaction. Something more than the "Oh, you're having your wisdom teeth pulled? Don't worry, it won't hurt a bit" dental receptionist's smile that felt as if someone had superglued her upper lip to her gums.

That's me, Elaine thought. *No point in making a scene.*

She had not been raised to respond in anger, or with any other less-than-gracious emotion.

So never mind that she wanted to write Root Canal in the appointment book next to Steph Lowry's name. Dignity was eternal.

"Thanks for manning the front, sweetie. I had to pee like a racehorse." Sue Kelsey, Dr. G's receptionist for the past nine years, elbowed Elaine away from the desk and ran a porcelain nail down the column of afternoon appointments.

"We're double-booked with two fillings at six," she groaned. "What a pisser. I won't get out until seven." The permed red curls she wore down to her shoulders bounced when she shook her head. "Rats. It's a total waste of daylight savings time. I crave at least a little sunlight when I go home, you know? Are you out of here soon? Are you?" Sue slapped Elaine's forearm with the back of her hand. "Hey."

"Hmm?"

"Are you leaving soon?"

"Leaving?"

"Yeah. Going home. *Sayonara. Hasta la vista.* Outta here, suckers." Squinting behind gold glitter-rimmed glasses, Sue studied her officemate. "What's the matter with you? You look like you shot yourself full of Novocaine."

Elaine struggled to focus. Novocaine sounded kind of nice right about now. A little afternoon respite. Like high tea, only numbing.

"I'm fine." Elaine forced some cheer into her voice even though her stomach felt like it wanted to climb out through her mouth. A glance at her Timex—the one Kevin had given her three years ago on their tenth anniversary—told her it was four-thirteen. Unless tardiness was one of the new-and-improved Mrs. Lowry's downfalls, she would be here any minute.

So typically sensitive of Kevin to recommend his first wife's dentist for his second wife's teeth.

Sue must have taken the appointment when Stephanie called. Had she noticed Steph's last name? Elaine dreaded the thought of questions. Sue didn't know about Stephanie. No one at the office knew that her husband had left her for a younger and depressingly firmer woman. All Elaine had told her co-workers was that she and Kevin had decided to split, they were both getting on with their lives and wished each other well…yadda, yadda.

Granted, diplomacy like that *could* be considered the coward's way out, and, no, she didn't expect Dr. Phil to ring her doorbell offering kudos on her outstanding coping skills. But it was easier this way. It *was.* She rarely saw her co-workers outside of work, anyway. And the truth was, it didn't matter how nice you were: When your husband left you for the Tae-Bo instructor at your coed gym, people talked.

Elaine's stomach gurgled, ulcerlike. If she could simply hide until this little quirk of fate had passed…

Grabbing her work, she retreated to the file cabinets against the far wall. She kept her head down and her back to Sue and the reception window, but she knew the moment Stephanie arrived. The hair on the nape of Elaine's neck stood up and her bare ring finger started to spasm.

"Hi, I have a four-fifteen with Dr. Gussman."

The high, nasal voice was unmistakable. Steph Lowry sounded like a canary with a sinus infection. It was her only unattractive attribute. Well, that and the fact that she stole other women's husbands, but why quibble?

"Do you have a key for the little girl's room?" Steph chirped after Sue asked her to sign in.

Elaine gritted her teeth hard enough to ruin all of Dr. Gussman's fine work. *Little girl's room.* Puh-lease! Like anyone needed a reminder that the bloom was still on Stephanie's rose.

Apparently Sue handed over the key, because Stephanie cooed, "Ooh, thank you," then giggled. "I have to go all the time now." She spoke confidentially, woman to woman. "I had no idea it was so much work being *pregnant!*"

Sue murmured something in reply, but Elaine didn't really hear. Her heart dropped and her stomach lurched. She was going to pass out....

No. She was going to vomit first and *then* pass out.

Locking her fingers around the cold metal drawer of the file cabinet, she sucked air in shallow breaths and wondered whether anyone would take her side if she remained upright by clasping her hands around the neck of a pregnant woman.

Elaine didn't have to see Stephanie to be able to picture her. The image of the sunny California blonde who had been her casual acquaintance and her husband's lover was printed indelibly on her mind.

Stephanie warbled another "thank you," then left the office in search of the bathroom, and Sue went in back to tell Dr. Gussman his next patient had arrived. Elaine stood very, very still and tried not to toss her cookies. All at once she started to shake. Hanging on to the file cabinet, her arms tingled and her heart began to race. She felt dizzy and hot and clammy.

"I've got to get out of here."

She didn't stop to think twice. Wanting only to leave before Sue returned to her desk, Elaine took the few remaining files and shoved them behind the *W*'s in the bottom drawer. Grabbing her purse and the blue cardigan she'd brought with her this morning, she scribbled, "Finished early. See you tomorrow.—E." on a yellow Post-It and stuck the paper to the appointment book. As calmly as she could, she moved through the waiting room then flew out the door and down the hall.

The elevators in the seventy-year-old building moved like sap down a maple tree. Unwilling to linger when Stephanie might emerge from the little mistress's room at any moment, Elaine opted for the stairs.

Pregnant. *Pregnant. Preg-Nant.* The word repeated with every click of her heels down the cold, concrete steps. Kevin and Steph Lowry were with child. Divorce had only been the legal end to her marriage. This news was coup de grâce.

A chill ran through her. Struggling into her sweater twice— the first time, it was inside out—Elaine hung her purse over her shoulder, stuffed her balled hands into the cardigan's deep pockets and continued down the stark stairwell.

All she had ever wanted was to be a wife and mother. She had loved her home, her yard and her neighborhood, her part-time job at Dr. Gussman's and her volunteer work for the garden club. Kevin had always wanted more and better, but not she. All she had needed to make their life together complete was a child. But Kevin had said, "Let's wait." So they'd waited.

And waited. And waited.

The timing had never been right. There had always been something else Kevin thought they should do first, someplace he had wanted to visit, a new career move to focus on. Something. And she'd let it go, trusting in the day her husband would want a baby as much as she did. She'd wanted everything to be perfect.

Now she was thirty-seven with a biological clock that

screamed "Cuckoo" every hour, and Kevin was off building a nest with Mrs. More and Better.

Elaine's mind and feet began moving like the chorus in *Riverdance* as she ran down three flights of stairs. She was moving downhill, but with each step her chest seemed to grow tighter and heavier, her breath becoming more labored. Her skin felt hot; her head swam. Finally at the stairwell to the second floor, she started to stumble, catching herself just before she fell by bracing her palms on the wall. Her rubbery legs would not carry her another step.

Turning around, her back against the cold, flat concrete, Elaine allowed her quivering body to slip slowly down until she was seated with her knees to her chest. Bunching her sweater in her hands, she pressed her face into its folds...

And screamed.

And screamed...and screamed...and screamed.

Elaine howled with the pain of long-broken dreams. She howled because, in the final analysis, it was she who had allowed them to break. The sound of her rage was muffled by an off-the-rack acrylic-wool blend but nothing could suppress her grief.

When she was finished, she wiped her eyes with her sleeve, smearing mascara on the cuff. For several minutes, she sat there not thinking of anything, really, until slowly it dawned on her: she felt better. Less stuffed, like a hall closet after spring cleaning, purged of last season's broken umbrellas and single mittens.

Rising, she tested her legs. Shaky, but not bad.

Walking more sedately down the remaining two flights, Elaine allowed images to waft through her mind, images she'd kept at bay for months. During the years she had wanted desperately to be a mom, she'd had a recurring dream about a female child with toffee-colored hair and light eyes. In the dream the little girl held a bouquet of wildflowers out to Elaine, but each time Elaine reached for the gift, the girl would slip farther away, as if she were being pulled back, and a high but lovely voice would whisper, "Whatever you decide is all right."

Elaine had never been able to decipher the meaning of those words, but she'd always known that in the dream the sweet girl was her daughter.

Today for the first time, the message made sense.

Whatever you decide is all right. "I can still choose." The simple but crucial realization nearly made her stumble again. Having a child was no longer anyone's decision but hers. Sitting on a concrete stairwell, crying into her sweater, she had cleared space in her heart, and she knew without having to think twice how she was going to fill it. Could there be any question?

Family was still her dream. She would not give it up. The head count at her breakfast table might be different than she'd originally planned, but one way or another, she was going to have her baby.

A converted Craftsman in the southeast section of Portland had been Elaine's home for the past nine months. With its pillared front porch and etched glass built-ins, the two-bedroom duplex suited her well—better, she sometimes thought, than the rambling five-bedroom contemporary she had shared with Kevin. And the rent was amazingly low.

Walking up the broad porch steps, Elaine stuck her key in the lock and let herself in.

Crying had left her with a dull ache behind her eyes and nervous hunger, so she went to the kitchen for aspirin and carbohydrates. Quickly she downed two Extra-Strength Bayers then opened the freezer and summoned a smile for her old pals Ben & Jerry, the only men she'd had in her apartment in the time she'd lived here. Grabbing a carton of Cherry Garcia and a soup spoon, she took the ice cream with her into the bedroom while she changed out of her work clothes. Outside the window, she could hear the rumble of a gas-powered motor.

At first the sound seemed out of context, and she couldn't

quite place it. Then her brain made the connection: power
motor…backyard…

Gardener!

Elaine hadn't seen a gardener in all the while she'd lived
here. Her absentee landlord offered outstanding rent and a
twelve-month lease, but little in the way of home improve-
ments. The only landscaping was a row of pansies Elaine herself had planted and a lone ornamental cabbage that listed
drunkenly to one side, courtesy of one of the neighbors.

Now the presence of a gardener seemed like kismet. If she
was going to raise a child here, she wanted the duplex to look
and feel like home.

Quickly Elaine stripped off a teal green T-shirt with a huge
smiling mouth silk-screened across the front and a pair of stark
white, how-wide-*can*-my-hips-look? nurse's pants. Reaching
down to a dresser drawer, she pulled out a simple cotton jumper
and slipped it over her bra and panties. Hopefully, her landlord
wouldn't mind if she had a little tête-à-tête with the gardener
regarding fall planting. This would be Step One of "The Baby
Preparation Plan." Granted, it wasn't as proactive as taking
extra folic acid or visiting a sperm bank, but home enhance-
ment felt like a good solid place to start. Very Earth Mother.

Grabbing her Ben & Jerry's, she hurried to the laundry room
and the door that led to the backyard. A lacey half curtain only
partially blocked her view.

With a spoon of ice cream stuck in her mouth, she peeked
out. The large rear yard still had enough life in it to look fairly
decent when it wasn't totally overgrown.

Hmm. The gardener had done a nice job so far. Most of the
weeds were gone, half the lawn was trimmed in neat even rows,
and he—

Whoa.

Craning her neck for a better look, Elaine blinked in surprise.

Oh…whoa.

Gardener Guy was half-naked. He had removed his shirt and
tied it around his hips. Pushing a power mower toward the far

fence, he afforded Elaine a clear view of broad, well-defined shoulders, a trim waist and a jeans-clad tush.

Oh, my. Elaine hadn't spent much time ogling males, so she was no expert, but as tushies went, this one seemed…darn-near perfect.

He reached the end of the yard, backed up and precisely aligned the machine with the row of lawn he'd just cut. There was something in his manner—in the way he marched across the lawn, the dedication in his bearing, that seemed comforting.

Swirling more ice cream onto her spoon, Elaine allowed her gaze to wander enjoyably up his body again, taking note of lightly tanned skin and a very pleasing amount of dark chest hair over an equally pleasing chest. She sensed she shouldn't be doing this—it was hardly polite—but what the heck? She'd earned a few ogling privileges! And it was curiously fun. Like live TV for divorcées. When the man paused, raising his hand to wipe his brow, Elaine felt her body flush with a tingly sense of familiarity as she saw his strong neck and clean jaw, a nose with handsome character and—

Oh, dear Lord. That was no ordinary afternoon fantasy trimming her grass, it was—

Mitchell Ryder, Esquire. Chocolate cherry ice cream splattered the window in a fine spray as she choked.

She could only stare, surprised to the point of confusion. *It couldn't be,* she thought as he lowered his hand, arched his back in a stretch and looked right at the door.

She didn't pause to think. With a sharp "Yipe!" Elaine ducked below the level of the smeary window, her back to the door, knees tucked up, Ben & Jerry's carton clutched against her.

"Calm down," she whispered to herself. "Calm down." Her heart was pounding a mile a minute. That was Mitch Ryder, all right, *über* divorce lawyer, the man known in legal circles—and to anyone he wasn't representing—as "The Eel." His reputation for calm, emotionless litigation made him a favorite among judges, a real lawyer's lawyer. The last time

Elaine had seen him he'd been about to make partner in the same firm her ex-husband belonged to.

No, wait a minute. That wasn't the last time she'd seen him.

Elaine shook her head. Silly her. She had seen Mitch Ryder again in divorce court when he had represented her husband, and managed to make her own hundred-and-fifty-dollar-an-hour attorney look like a very expensive *prelaw intern*!

It had been so humiliating to have her marriage dissected by someone with whom she'd once shared aperitifs.

Mitch had been to her house several times for cocktail parties and business dinners. What she remembered was that he'd arrived promptly, left early and always thanked her personally as he did so. The year she and Kevin hosted a madrigal-themed Christmas brunch, Mitch had come to the kitchen, where Elaine had been sponging spilled mead off her Italian tiled floor. Wordlessly he had grabbed a towel and bent down to help, literally waving away her protests. Crouched near him on the ceramic tile, their knees almost touching, she'd felt her face flame.

"You like this, don't you?" he asked when the floor was cleaned.

Elaine released a little puff of inappropriately breathy laughter as she reached for his wet towel. "Wh-what? Wiping spills?"

"Inviting people in." He held on to the dish towel, surprising her, until she looked up at him. "You have a gift for making people feel comfortable, Elaine."

Really? That was exactly what she liked to do. And *he* had a gift for making women feel like he truly saw them. His golden-brown eyes never wandered when he spoke.

Elaine knew she absolutely should not have felt that frisson of awareness when he said her name, and she certainly wished she could forget it now. Unfortunately the memory popped to mind to torment her at the most inopportune times. She'd remembered it vividly, for example, the day Ryder had informed the judge that her husband had fallen out of love years ago, but hadn't wanted to "hurt" her.

Bastard, Elaine had thought at the time, fairly certain she ought to have meant her husband, but actually referring to Mitch. There had been times during the divorce proceedings when he'd turned to her and she could have sworn she'd seen regret in his eyes. Or maybe it had been pity. The emotion had been little more than a flash, in any case. Most of the time, he'd seemed devoid of feeling, even toward his own client.

To Elaine, though, every word uttered in that courtroom had felt deeply, agonizingly personal. God, she'd hated everything about the divorce. She'd felt drained, pummeled every single day. And, finally, she'd felt that most frightening of feelings: dead indifference.

That's when she had given up, told her lawyer at the lunch break to ask for half the proceeds from the sale of her and Kevin's home and to let the rest go. No alimony. He could keep the expensive antiques and the vacation home, the bonds and the stock portfolio. Half of everything should have been hers, but she didn't care anymore. It cost too much to fight.

Her attorney had been violently opposed, of course, but Elaine hadn't budged. The day it was all over, she'd walked to a city park near the court building and perched stiffly on a wrought iron bench. Wrapped in a winter coat, numb to the wind chafing her skin, she'd sat and stared at a fountain for who knows how long, until a young couple claimed the bench opposite hers....

In their early twenties, dewy even in frigid December, their giggles were at once intimate yet somehow universal. With the sack lunches they'd brought discarded beside them, they snuggled and kissed, pausing now and again to stare at their own clasped hands as if they had never seen such a romantic sight.

Watching them, Elaine felt her chest squeeze and her throat start to close, and she realized it had been years since she'd known what it was like not merely to *be* young, but to *feel* that way. To feel fresh and ripe with plans and giddily, incautiously in love.

Swallowing the grief that surged to her throat, Elaine rose from the bench, turned to walk away and found herself locking gazes with Mitchell Ryder. He stood fifty feet ahead of her, carrying his briefcase. Wearing a wool trench coat, he looked like he belonged in a window seat at Higgins Restaurant, not standing in line at a two-dollar-a-piece Polish dog stand. He stared at her with the same steady intensity with which she'd gazed at the lovers, and Elaine knew instantly he'd been watching her the whole time. The expression in his eyes was different from any she had seen there before. Mitchell ''The Eel'' Ryder was looking at her with what could only be called compassion.

Embarrassment threatened to drown her. She walked away, moving quickly along the crowded city block, but her wobbly legs wanted to give out. When the Heathman Hotel appeared on her left, she darted in, heading immediately for the bar.

Normally a white wine spritzer gal with a one-drink limit, Elaine sat down and ordered a brandy. She didn't even bother to take off her coat. At this moment she thought she might never feel warm again.

Her drink hadn't even been served yet when Mitch Ryder slipped onto the bar stool next to her. He said nothing for several moments, didn't glance her way, merely called for an expensive scotch and waited for it to arrive. Then still without looking at her, he said in a hushed tone, ''Why did you give up? You could have held out for more than you got. A lot more. Your lawyer should have made you see it through.''

He sounded angry, which Elaine thought was a little ironic, considering.

Brandy snifter cupped between her cold palms, she drank quickly, too quickly, but the brandy burned a path to her stomach that at least served the purpose of making her feel warm. She sat, trying not to cough, focusing instead on the heat. After a moment, the drink gave her a pleasantly light-headed feeling, and fortified, she answered, ''I don't want to 'see the divorce through.' I wanted to see my *marriage* through. And I don't want more money. I just want it to be over.''

In the silence that ensued, Elaine finished her drink, but instead of getting up to leave, which had been her plan, she ordered another. She had a question for Mr. Ryder, too, and it burned like the brandy. ''Why did you represent Kevin?''

A muscle jumped in Mitch's jaw. Beneath the dulcet music and soft murmur in the Heathman's classic lounge, he answered, ''It wasn't personal. It was business.''

It was an awful answer, and she said so. Her husband had cheated on her. Either you were a person who cared about that kind of thing or you weren't.

For the first time since he'd sat down, Mitch turned toward her fully. ''I am,'' he said. The stern masculinity so characteristic of his face seemed even more sober today. ''Covington asked me to handle the case.''

Henry Covington was the founding partner of Mitch and Kevin's firm. Elaine remembered he was also a law professor and that the younger partners thought of him as their mentor.

''If it means anything at all, I regretted that decision every time I walked into the courtroom.'' His gaze remained focused and steady.

Elaine stared back a long while without answering. The brandy snifter was still in her hands. Taking a last, long swallow, she set the glass on the bar and opened her purse to pay for her drink.

Without warning, Mitch's hand covered hers. ''Don't leave....''

Huddled against the back door, out of sight, Elaine closed her eyes.

She now wished she had left. She *should* have left.

Mitch Ryder was officially her biggest, baddest mistake ever. Her only consolation from that night until present day had been her assumption that she would never see the man again.

Forcing herself to open her eyes, one at a time, she stood up slowly, peeking out the window.

He was gone. The mower stood alone in the middle of the yard. Smooshing her cheek against the glass, Elaine strained to see to her right and caught sight of him as he rounded the corner of the house. Leaving the ice cream on the counter, she ran to the living room. If she lifted the edge of the curtain just a little...

When the doorbell rang, she yelped. Traversing the space from window to door quickly on bare feet, she placed her palms on the door, leaned forward and looked through the peephole.

Feeling her heart flutter as she peered at Mitch Ryder's face, she thought, *Don't panic,* willing her heart to settle into an even rhythm so she could think clearly. There was no need to panic.

Except that six months ago, she had agreed to have another drink with Mitch Ryder and, for the first time in her life, gotten too toasted on brandy to drive home. The next day all she could remember was that they'd gotten into her car that night and she'd awakened in her big king-size bed the next morning...

Alone.

Nude.

And she almost never slept nude.

Lying under three-hundred-thread-count sheets in her thirty-seven-year-old birthday suit she had been hungover, yes, but curiously serene.

Since she had neither seen nor spoken to Mitch since that night, today she had no idea whether he was the second lover she had ever had in her life or merely...the divorce lawyer who had seen her naked. Either way—

That he had shown up today was positively too cruel. First Stephanie with her glad tidings and now this.

Resting her forehead on the door, Elaine barely resisted the urge to knock herself unconscious against the solid wood panel.

Please let this be a bad dream, God. If I wake up and he's gone, I promise I will give up simple carbohydrates forever.

Chapter Two

Mitch stood outside Elaine Lowry's rented front door and tried not to let his mounting anger get the best of him. The duplex she'd been living in for the past several months was the pits. According to his friend at Portland Property Management, the building was structurally sound. But cosmetically?

Mitch flicked a barklike wedge of peeling brown paint off the door frame and swore under his breath. This was not the type of place he'd pictured for Elaine when he'd asked his friend at the management firm to find her a ''good deal.''

Standing with his hands on his hips, head lowered, he waited for her to answer the bell. The work shirt that had been tied around his hips now covered his torso, albeit half buttoned and untucked. Perspiration trickled down the nape of his neck, and he swiped it away, grumbling as a wasp dive-bombed past his face. He looked up to see a nest under the eaves. Great. Another thing he'd have to take care of.

He did not want to be here. *Should* not be here. In life, as in work, Mitch preferred situations that were black-and-white. Cleanly opened, cleanly closed, like the best cases.

Elaine Lowry was not black-and-white. She was a problem for him in walking, talking Technicolor.

For the past decade and a half, Mitch had made quite a reputation for himself and his firm by representing high-profile divorce suits. He considered it his job to make people act responsibly and with integrity when feelings were hurt, egos were bruised and money was involved. Quite a challenge and one he enjoyed. Usually. Representing Kevin Lowry, however, had been as rewarding as sticking needles in his eye.

Raising a fist that was clenched too tightly, Mitch flexed his fingers, balled them again and knocked on the door.

He never got personally involved with one of his own clients; he certainly never got personally involved with the opposing attorney's client. Never. Capital *N,* capital *EVER.* He'd crossed the line. And he was about to cross it again.

It wasn't his business to make sure she was protected financially.

It wasn't his business to make sure she was well housed.

It wasn't his business to make amends for her marriage or her divorce or…anything else. Yet here he was.

"Just make it fast," he hissed to himself, knocking on the door one more time, harder than he needed to. He would stay briefly, speak his piece, make sure she was at least comfortable here and maybe give her the name of a good financial advisor. She could do what she wanted with the information. Or not. It was none of his business.

Elaine's nose, lips and chin were pressed against the door when Mitch knocked. Caught off guard, she jumped, nearly blinding herself on the old-fashioned peephole. She twisted the knob and opened the door.

"Wait a minute! Don't open—" Mitch started to say, but it was too late; a wasp so big it was probably in violation of the leash law, flew straight at her face.

Elaine yelped and flailed her hands.

"Don't move!" Mitch ordered with the same deep authority she remembered from the courtroom.

Unfortunately the wasp kept buzzing, so she kept flailing. Then the buzzing stopped, and her nose felt like an entire pincushion had launched itself at her.

"Ow!"

"Damn it." Mitch pushed the door open in an effort to reach for her. It banged into her bare shin.

"OWWW!!!"

He swore more colorfully. "Sorry. Are you all right?"

"No, I'm not all right!" Elaine shook as she pointed to her nose. She could see the wasp if she crossed her eyes. "Get it off, get it off!"

"Stop hopping." He grasped her elbow with a strong hand and pushed her a step back, following her into the room. Holding her steady, he examined her face from a distance of less than a foot. "It's got you."

She stared back at him; pain and exhaustion that was about a lot more than a wasp sting filled her to overflowing. "This newsflash just in," she snapped, "I Already Know That."

Mitch's brows rose ever so slightly at her tone, but he didn't seem offended. "Hold still." Reaching up, he slapped the wasp and—inadvertently, she assumed—her nose.

"Hey!" she protested.

The wasp buzzed away, still alive and only a little worse for the wear.

"Duck," Mitch ordered, using his hand like a racket to swat the insect out of the house. He slammed the door shut.

Turning back to her, he ignored the glare she attempted to give him. Her poor nose was starting to throb already. She cupped her hands around it.

"Where's your bathroom?" he asked. Elaine pointed, and Mitch took her elbow, overriding her little tug of resistance.

He found the light switch and flicked it on, then pulled her in front of the sink to the medicine cabinet. "Are you going to put your hands down so I can see your nose?"

"No." Her voice emerged muffled. Call her vain, but if sensation was anything to go by, her nose was swelling already, and she didn't have the smallest shnoz to begin with. "It's fine."

Reaching up, Mitch drew her hands away from her face, gently but insistently. He had large hands; one easily wrapped around both her wrists and with the other he tilted her face and gazed at it, taking his time. "Not too bad," he said finally.

Elaine licked her lips. "It isn't?"

When he shook his head, she expected him to let her go, but he didn't. He continued to hold her. His touch, however, was light. It was impersonal.

It was driving her crazy.

Elaine's heart pounded far more than it should have under the circumstances, unless, of course, wasp venom was making her delirious. She knew she was staring at Mitch's mouth, but felt helpless to look away.

And then the hand cupping her chin moved. He ran his knuckles lightly across her cheek. When he reached her jaw, his fingers unfurled to wander into the hair at her nape.

Oh, Lord, they had *slept together.* Elaine knew it the moment he touched the back of her neck. She couldn't remember the last time a man other than Kevin had touched her there, except for Dr. Larson when she'd had swollen glands last winter, and he was seventy. Yet Mitch's hand did not feel new or strange or even unfamiliar. She *remembered* it. Her body remembered it.

A shower of tingles raced down her back, along her arms and, incredibly, over her thighs. During the last few years of her marriage to Kevin, she'd forgotten she even had thighs. Mitch was barely touching her and suddenly she felt every pore.

"Where's your antiseptic?"

Elaine licked her lips. "Where's my—" She blinked, blurry

with desire, but not too blurry to realize what he'd just asked. Her lips formed a confounded *O*. "What?"

"Antiseptic," he repeated. "That sting is…pretty nasty."

"Is it?" Her racing heart skidded to a dull, heavy thud. Embarrassment washed up her neck and face. What she remembered clearly from that night in the bar was the incomparable comfort of Mitch's presence. The case had ended. Her marriage was over. Sitting in a bar, in her winter coat, in the middle of the afternoon, she'd felt more alone than ever before in her life. She'd tried hard not to show despair, humiliation, or any of the myriad emotions she'd felt. She'd tried not to look at Mitch's face, so often shuttered and unreadable, but on that day almost…compassionate.

Then over the sound of waves crashing in her ears, she'd heard him say, "He's not worth it, Elaine."

He'd sounded so sure and so angry and so *on her side*.

That had to be the reason she'd agreed to stay. And why she had found herself, over an hour later, still sipping brandy and actually laughing at the awful jokes Mitch told her and which she was surprised he even knew. And why, when he'd said finally, "I'll take you home," she'd unresistingly handed him her car keys, bundled into the passenger side and had felt—for the first time since she'd realized her life was falling apart— safe.

But a moment ago, standing in the confines of her small bathroom, with Mitch touching her, she hadn't felt safe at all. For an instant, with his brown eyes fixed on her, she had felt the thrill that something wild and unknown was about to happen.

Men!

Anger kindled in Elaine's stomach. Tightly she said, "Your hand is on the back of my neck."

Mitch frowned quizzically.

"Your hand," she bit out again. "It is on the back of my neck." *And clearly that was an erogenous zone.* "I can't get to the medicine cabinet."

"Oh."

He let her go. Elaine's neck felt cold and bare.

They did an awkward dance as she moved around him. Catching sight of her own face in the mirror, Elaine longed to sit down right where she was and weep. Her nose where the wasp had stung her was red and inflamed and now that her adrenaline was calming, she could feel the throb again. Every part of her felt like it had been stung. Glancing above her own head, she saw Mitch's reflection as he watched her.

She shoved the sliding glass of the medicine cabinet harder than she needed to, but could barely see the contents through the tears filling her eyes. *Not the damned tears again,* she groaned silently, pressing her lips together to refuse the emotion. No, she was not going to cry over this...this...whatever it was. Stupid...hormonal...*mistake*.

"Excuse me," she said tightly, without turning around. "Would you please... This bathroom is just not that large." Nothing happened. He didn't move. "Would you leave?"

Mitch frowned heavily.

Elaine waited with forced calm, hand on the Neosporin, until she heard him walk quietly across the tile floor and through the hall. Without looking, she reached out, grasped the bathroom door and slammed it as hard as she could. She had no intention of crying in front of Mitch Ryder, and she certainly wasn't going to cry *over* him.

She had plans, born of her heart only. If she intended to get on with them, she had better get used to feeling alone. No doubt she was going to feel alone a lot in the coming months as she embarked on a journey usually traveled by two.

As for discovering what had happened the night she left the bar with Mitch, that was a mystery that would have to remain unsolved. What difference did it make? She didn't need an affair; she didn't want the headache.

What she wanted was a pint-sized headache who needed all the love she had to give.

Splashing cold water on her face, Elaine dabbed her nose

WENDY WARREN 27

with antiseptic, replaced the tube and closed the medicine cabinet. Time to get down to business. She had a pregnancy to get under way. And a possible ex-lover to get rid of. She didn't want Mitch Ryder here one moment longer than necessary.

Mitch looked down at the oak floor, grateful for the dimness of the living room with the curtains closed. As if the dimness would keep him from having to see himself too clearly.

What the hell was going on with him?

He had come here to relieve himself of the gnawing, uncomfortable sense of personal responsibility Elaine's case had engendered. He had come here so he could feel less involved after he left. So far, his plan could be considered a failure.

Mitch wasn't stupid. He knew what people—co-workers, most clients, his ex-wife—thought of him: that he was cold, impenetrable, virtually emotionless. That was fine. Experience told him their estimations were accurate. He'd long since stopped feeling guilty for his own inadequacies. That which had made his personal life a failure had lent strength to his professional life once he'd learned to use rather than deny his personality traits.

He shook his head. Every time he tried to make amends to Elaine—so he could walk away with a clear conscience—he got sucked in further. And yet he felt compelled to go on trying. Why?

Mitch's sister, the youngest partner on record at the respected law firm of Cowden, Hardy, Hardy, Nash & Ryder, would tell him to snap out of it. "Do what you're good at— pay someone else to do the other stuff" was M. D. Ryder's credo. By "other stuff," M.D. meant anything having to do with emotion. Mitch had lived by the same philosophy and on those rare occasions he hadn't—his brief marriage, for example—the results had been suitably disastrous.

His sister was the only person he knew who could separate emotion from…well, everything better than he could. Family quirk.

"Do what you're good at, forget the other stuff," Mitch muttered, reminding himself that he had a reason for being here, a reason he could handle quickly and then leave.

He was staring at the closed curtains, at nothing, really, when Elaine emerged from the bathroom.

Her bare feet stepped quietly across the wood floor. She continued on to the kitchen without glancing at him. "I'm getting water. Do you want anything?"

Mitch frowned. From the start, he had admired Kevin Lowry's wife for her innate warmth, for the gentle grace that came as a surprise every time he saw her. Now her tone was formal, brusque and businesslike.

"Water's fine," he said, following her into the kitchen.

As she pulled glasses out of a cabinet and a jug of ice water from the refrigerator, Mitch filled the yawning silence by taking his first really good look at the interior of the duplex.

Like the exterior, the interior had aged and was not as well maintained as it should have been, but the big, raw bones of the divided house were good. What he appreciated most, though, was the simple way Elaine had decorated, with dish towels in a bright sunflower pattern, yellow checked curtains on the windows, and several teapots—one that was covered in ridiculous red cherries—on wooden shelves above the cabinets. Late afternoon sun reached soothing streamers of light through the well-placed windows, enhancing the soft glow of butter-yellow walls.

The kitchen in his Mountain Park condominium was white and stainless steel. A twice-weekly housekeeper kept everything sparkling, though he rarely gave her anything to clean. He didn't cook. Take-out was infrequent. Occasionally he nuked a frozen meal, but by and large he ate in restaurants and used the kitchen primarily as a wine cellar for occasional entertaining. Elaine *lived* in her kitchen. It was oddly appealing.

Filling both glasses with water, she set one on the counter in front of him and sipped from the other, eyeing him over the top of the rim. Mitch started to drink then noticed his glass was only half-full. *Here's your hat, what's your hurry?*

Draining the glass, he set it down. She made no move to refill it, and Mitch smiled. Had to. He'd met few people as unintentionally candid as Elaine Lowry. Clearing his throat, he got down to business, presenting his opening gambit as if addressing a court. "You're wondering why I'm here."

She crossed her arms. "I'm wondering how you knew my address."

Right. He'd forgotten that would be a question.

"I assume Maggie gave it to you," she continued before he could respond. "Which is profoundly unprofessional, but I will take that up with her next time the rent is due."

Maggie Lewis owned Portland Property, the company that managed this rental. Mitch had handed Elaine his friend's business card the afternoon he'd followed her into the Heathman. Later he'd phoned Maggie personally and told her to find Elaine someplace clean and safe where the rent was cheap and likely to stay so. This duplex had been absentee-owned for over a decade. The rent had been raised only twice in that time. Unfortunately the owners had decided to sell one month ago, taking advantage of the spike in area home prices. New owners were sure to increase the rent. Maggie had mentioned the fact to Mitch in passing.

"So other than a love of lawn mowing, what brings you here, Mitch?"

He scowled. He could overlook her patent hostility because she hadn't realized yet that he was on her side. But she would soon. He decided to warm things up a bit before he answered her question. "How's your nose?"

"It hurts. I think I'll go to bed early."

Mitch plowed a hand through his hair and surrendered. *Okay. Get to the point.* Once he clarified the situation, she would realize he was here to make amends. No doubt she would be surprised by the news, so he'd give her a moment to process it. Because he tended to feel uncomfortable with profuse expressions of gratitude, he would take his cue to leave when the *thank-yous* began.

"If you recall, Maggie is a former client. I represented her in her second and third divorces."

Elaine raised a brow. "I hope she got the frequent flyer discount."

"I beg your pardon?"

"It's a joke."

"Oh." She was being wry. Unfortunately, humor was not his forte. He'd been told that on a number of occasions as well. Clearing his throat, he attempted to get back on course. "As I was saying, I know Maggie, and because I referred you to her originally, she thought I would be interested in any changes that occurred in your current living situation."

"There aren't any changes occurring in my living situation." Elaine frowned then stared at him hard. "Are there?"

Mitch hesitated, his assurance beginning to waver. Something told him his news was not going to be quite as graciously received as he'd originally thought.

The furrow between Elaine's brows—the one she was going to Botox come Monday—deepened. Mitch had tucked Maggie's card in her hand, and she'd used the referral because she knew she needed the good deal he had said Maggie would provide. She had a nest egg—half the proceeds from the sale of the house she'd owned with Kevin—but that was in savings, and her thirty hours a week at Dr. Gussman's didn't stretch very far. She'd been looking for a new job, but the market was slim in Portland. The cheap rent here had turned out to be her saving grace, so— *Oh, no.*

"The new owner wants to raise the rent," she deduced. "Maggie told me she was certain he wouldn't raise it for at least a year." She made no attempt to check the panic coursing through her. Welcome to the perfect end to her perfect day: special delivery notice of a raise in rent. There wasn't enough ice cream in all of Portland to make this news go down sweetly.

With her lower lip pushing hard against her upper, she went ahead and glared at Mitch even though it wasn't his fault and she'd been darned grateful to him for turning her on to Maggie in the first place. Stubbornly, she crossed her arms over her chest. *Screw logic.* She wasn't in the mood. And then suddenly it occurred to her.

"So that's why you came out here." Her eyes widened. She put a hand on her forehead. "And that's why you were mowing my lawn. It was a pity mow!"

"Your rent is not being raised. I came out here—" Mitch paused for a moment and stared. "A pity mow?" He shook his head. "I came out here to tell you the duplex has been sold."

"Sold." It took a protracted moment to process that information. Mitch wore a small smile, as if he considered this good news. "Sold? Sold is worse than the rent being raised," she told him as if she were explaining why we don't bite to a stubborn five-year-old. Lord, she was exhausted. She had lost too much; she was not losing her run-down duplex with the tilting ornamental cabbage. "They can't do this. No way! *I...am not...going...anywhere.*"

She grabbed a dish towel—anything she could harmlessly wring to within an inch of its life—and used it to point around the kitchen. "Do you see those walls? I painted those walls. *I* did it. I went to classes at Home Depot for a month to learn how to glaze. I've invested something here. Time, energy, *expectation.*" She flung out an arm. "I gave my youth to those walls! One person cannot just waltz in and stomp all over another person's dreams."

"That wall is your dream?"

"*Yes,*" she said, but that sounded pathetic, so she backpedaled. "No. That's not the point."

"What's the point?"

He asked gently, like he'd asked her a lot of things during the divorce, and those damn ready-to-roll tears threatened again. She took a breath. "The point is I have a lease. I'm not going anywhere. I'll get a lawyer."

"You're one tough cookie, Elaine." Amusement shone in his eyes, but not only humor. There was appreciation, too. He wagged his head. "Stop glaring at me a minute. I think you're right. You shouldn't let anyone get in the way of what you want. And you do have rights. If you're not satisfied with your current lease—for any reason—we can draw up a new one to keep on file with the rental agency."

Elaine's confusion showed plainly in the furrow of her brow. "'We'? You're a divorce lawyer."

"Yes." Mitch cleared his throat. Now was a good time to tell her the rest of his news. She'd worked herself into a pretty good froth over a misconception. He was about to bring comfort and relief. Though most people didn't think of divorce lawyers in this way, bringing comfort and relief was part of the job description. He was tying up loose ends so Elaine could feel safe and secure in her home, and he could put an end to the guilt that had been gnawing at him. Then he could stop thinking about Lowry vs. Lowry and get on with life the way he knew it.

Holding out his hand, he introduced himself as if for the first time. "How do you do? I'm your new landlord."

The door on Mitch's newly purchased Toyota Tacoma slammed with a satisfying crunch.

He attempted to start the vehicle, realized the key wasn't in his hand, dug it out of his pocket and shoved it into the ignition. Grinding the gears, he backed out of the driveway.

Elaine had been slightly less appreciative for this turn of events than he'd anticipated. Her exact response, in fact, when informed that he had purchased the duplex and intended to give her a five-year lease guaranteeing her current below-market rent had been, "No, thank you. I'm moving."

Moving. Two seconds after she'd just insisted she'd fight tooth and nail to stay!

Punching the steering wheel, he expelled a slow hiss of air. Who the hell could figure out people? Did she have any idea that he'd lain awake nights wondering if she could swing more rent right now in the event a new owner raised it, not to mention wondering how long her money would last and whether she was investing wisely? Then he'd got the idea to buy the duplex. According to the real estate agent he'd consulted, it was a sound investment—well-priced property in an up-and-coming area. Mitch figured he'd work a little less than he normally did on the weekends and become a handyman for a couple of months, getting his exercise here instead of at the gym. It was supposed to be simple.

He'd anticipated Elaine's relief, her pleasure and, dammit, yes, her gratitude. He had not imagined she would look at him like he'd come to tell her he was putting a freeway through the family farm. He was offering her an updated, rent-controlled duplex, for crying out loud, in a city that had no rent control. And with him as her landlord, she could trust him to keep an eye on things. But following her initial shock had come a look of profound resentment.

The hell with it. He'd tried to make amends. The lady wasn't interested? Fine.

"Stick to what you're good at."

The new-car smell in the cab of this pickup reminded him that he'd bought a truck and gardening tools with the expectation that he was going to be a landlord for a long time...but the hell with that, too. Abusing the stick shift as he came to a stop sign, Mitch realized he had no desire to go home to an empty apartment. He did, however, have to find someplace in his complex to stow the gardening tools, then shower and change. A glance at the digital clock in the dashboard and a quick calculation told him it would be approximately seven-thirty by the time he was done. Seven-thirty on a Friday evening. Between now and then he had plenty of time to find a dinner companion. A rare-steak dinner at Jake's, a scotch and some logical conversation was just what he needed to forget Elaine Lowry.

Chapter Three

"So let me get this straight." Gordon Shapiro, Elaine's best friend since they'd studied for their bar and bat mitzvahs together over two decades ago, gazed curiously across a green Formica-topped table. "Your new landlord is your ex-husband's divorce lawyer, and you *may* have slept with him—the lawyer, not the ex—but you're not sure."

Elaine nodded. "Right."

"Hmm." Gordon shook his head. "I feel terrible then."

"*You* do. Why?"

"In high school I voted you 'Most dull.'"

Elaine plucked a Splenda packet out of a ceramic dish on the kitchen table and threw it at her old friend. "I always suspected you were the one who put me over the top." At six feet one inch and two hundred pounds, Gordon looked like a handsome linebacker, but he commiserated like a big, cuddly teddy bear.

Laying her head on the table, Elaine groaned. "What am I going to do? I can't stay there if *he* owns it. And I'll never find a two-bedroom in a great area with that kind of rent.'' She thumped the table with her fist. ''Damn him.''

Reaching for the latte he'd made Elaine and which she hadn't yet touched, Gordon carried it to the kitchen counter.

''So tell me,'' he said, fiddling with the controls of his new cappuccino machine, ''if you're not even sure you slept together, why are you so angry with him?''

''Because he offered me five years of guaranteed rent control!''

''Ah, right.'' He nodded. ''That bastard.''

Elaine sat up and shook her head. Gordon Shapiro had loved her through braces and Retinol A, through bad hair and bad jobs and through Kevin. He knew her as well as anyone, better than most. She leaned far over the table to explain. ''Mitch Ryder thinks I'm going to be alone for five years. He slept with me, and he thinks I'm going to be alone that long.''

''You don't know for sure that he slept with you.''

''Well, according to the evidence we know he saw me naked.''

''Right.'' Gordon frowned. ''That's not good then.''

Elaine slumped over the table again. While Gordon made fresh lattes, she rose, crossed to the kitchen window and stared out.

She'd always loved visiting Gordon on Friday evenings. He lived three blocks from a large synagogue in the northwest section of Portland. Come twilight, families would pass by Gordon's window, walking to shul together—mothers, fathers and children attractively dressed yet relaxed and happy as they started the Jewish Sabbath by strolling together.

''We used to do that,'' Elaine murmured, leaning her shoulder against the window frame and her forehead against the glass. ''When I was in grammar school, my parents would take Sam and me to temple every Friday night, and the rabbi would say a prayer for families. All the parents would put their hands on top of their kids' heads and bless them. My dad's hands were so big he could reach down and tickle my cheek with his pinkie. It was the best feeling in the whole world.''

Watching her, Gordon smiled back. "Better than Wavy Gravy?" He named their very favorite Ben & Jerry's flavor. "I stocked up."

She shrugged apologetically. "Yeah. Better than that." She looked out again. "Even as a kid, I couldn't wait to be the parent someday." In an instant she was assailed by the real reason for the ache inside her, and her eyes began to well. "I'm so scared to have a baby on my own, Gordon. I don't want to be scared, but I am. I'm even more afraid that I'll chicken out."

Gordon sympathized, but had little idea how to soothe such a pain. "Maybe you should start dating," he said.

"What?" It was freakish how quickly her heart started to pound. The memory of falling asleep on Mitch's shoulder rose instantly to mind. "I don't want to date."

"Nobody *wants* to date. It's what you do so you can get to the good stuff."

"Pass. The 'good stuff' is highly overrated, anyway."

Gordon returned to the table with a fresh latte and a bowl of popcorn and sat. "I consider it my personal duty as your best friend to tell you 'Nuh-uh.' Honey, you were with Kevin way too long."

"Yeah, well not so long that I don't remember dating. It's not worth the anxiety. All you do between dates is exfoliate and worry. Does he like me? Will he call again? Should I call him?"

"I love wondering that."

Elaine shuddered. "Not me. Anyway, I've got more important things to think about. I've got to find a birth partner. I've always wanted to try natural childbirth, so I'll need someone who can go to classes with me and help me breathe and—" Gordon was cringing already. Elaine's heart plummeted. "Not your cup of tea, hmm?"

Looking up at her, his eyes full of affection and regret, Gordon said, "Sorry, pumpkin. You know how I am with blood."

"But the miracle of birth—"

Gordon shook his head.

Elaine sighed. She'd known it was too much to hope for, but figured it was worth a shot. Gordon had been surprised but supportive when she'd first related her decision to have a family, but he'd never been that nuts about kids, even when he was one. This wasn't going to be like the movies, where two single friends raised a child together.

Elaine could feel depression threaten as the dreaded "if onlys" floated through her mind. If only she'd married more wisely. If only she were married now to someone who would rub cocoa butter on her stomach and bring home books on attachment parenting and read aloud from them in bed. If only...

She turned again to gaze out the window. The one thing she had promised herself she would not do after her divorce was stay angry or get stuck in some postdivorce time warp. She'd spent twelve years of her marriage acting like Doris Day on Valium. Happy, happy, happy. The only thing worse would be to turn into Divorced Doris in need of Prozac.

"I'm not ruining this for you, am I?" Gordon asked, concern filling his voice.

She turned toward her friend and had to smile. He looked so guilty. "Nope. Not even close," she assured him and knew suddenly it was true. The fact was that every stumbling block she thought of only made her want to have a baby more. "I'm going to do it, Gordy. I'll just take the next logical step and worry about the rest later. I'm through with the picket fence fantasy." She gave him a huge brave smile. "Come Monday morning, Gordo, I'm visiting a sperm bank."

After an initial blink of surprise, Gordon nodded. "Now that I can get on board with. I'll go with you."

Elaine laughed. "We'll see, Gordon."

At 5:00 a.m. Saturday morning, Elaine's eyes snapped open. She rolled over, burying her face in a pile of cool, soft pillows, but awakened again at five-thirty, six-fifteen and a quarter to seven.

Birds sang outside her bedroom window, the morning light poked around the lowered shade, teasing her, and she was helpless to resist its lure. For the first time in ages she had something more exciting than breakfast to get up for.

Showering quickly, she dressed for a day of running around in weather that was supposed to inch toward seventy. Indian summer. It was amazing, really, what a change in perspective could do. Yesterday, she'd been exhausted, older than her years. Today she felt fit and alive.

Ready and able to make a baby.

The conviction that she could pursue her dream on her own had not waned overnight. Today and tomorrow she planned to do as much research as she could. By Monday morning she'd be ready to get the ball rolling.

Inspired by the idea that she was finally in charge of her dreams, Elaine was too hyped to sit still. She took a brisk walk through the neighborhood then drove to Pappaccino's for a toasted bagel and a hazelnut latte while she waited for the stores to open.

Come 10:00 a.m., her first stop was Barnes & Noble, followed by the library, where she checked out several books and researched alternative insemination on the Internet until an assistant librarian kicked her off the computer.

After the library, Elaine hit the craft store, Babies R Us, and PetCo to look—*only* look for now—at the puppies. Eventually she wanted her child to be raised around animals. Thoughts of country homes with space to roam flitted through her head as she laughed at the gymnastics of an exuberant Lab puppy before she made her seventh and last stop before home—the health food store.

Grabbing a basket, she wandered the aisles, acquainting herself with sprouted grains, fermented soybeans and "natural" chickens that, according to the literature they came with, had been raised at a veritable Club Med for poultry. Unfortunately she couldn't bear the thought of eating something so happy, so she pressed on to the organic dairy case. If she was going to make a baby, she had to prepare her body. Good nutrition was a cornerstone of fertility.

By the time Elaine arrived home, laden with shopping bags and information, perspiration trickled beneath her T-shirt, her limbs felt rubbery and her stomach howled for food. She could have killed for a burger—the kind someone else made and which took three minutes, max, to serve up—but fast food was strictly off-limits from now on. She consoled her tummy by promising to feed it a yummy tempeh Reuben sandwich as soon as she got all the perishables put away.

Low blood sugar was probably the reason she didn't react strongly when she saw the Toyota truck parked outside the duplex. Mitch was back. Not that she was surprised. He owned the building, after all, and he had said he was going to work weekends fixing it up. What he did with his duplex was his business; all she had to figure out was whether she intended to stay here or not.

Or not would have been ahead by a mile except that Elaine couldn't imagine being able to afford anything more appropriate given her current job, her savings…and her plans. Which meant, of course, that she was going to have to call a truce with her landlord. She didn't want his rock-bottom rent; she refused to accept it. Why he considered her his personal charity case, she didn't know and refused to ponder. Stress interfered with ovulation.

Business, pure and simple—that's all she wanted to think about where Mitch Ryder was concerned. Decent housing at a fair-to-both-of-them price was the deal she was determined to strike. When she found a better job, she would find better housing. Or, at least, comparable housing with a different landlord.

Hefting two of the grocery bags into her arms, Elaine lugged them up the porch steps, setting them by the front door while she fiddled with her house keys.

The apartment unit next to hers had been vacant since she'd

moved in. Today the windows were open for the first time and she heard someone, Mitch evidently, working inside. Rhythmic hammering filled the air.

Elaine quickly decided to unload her purchases and feed herself before she faced him.

He had other ideas.

On her second trip from the car to her front door, she turned with three shopping bags in her arms to find him striding toward her, a scowl of displeasure directed her way. "What do you think you're doing?"

Surprised, Elaine had to think about it a minute. "I'm carrying my packages to the house," she said mildly, deliberately meeting his scowl with a frown of concern. "That's not a violation of my rental agreement, is it?"

Mitch scowled harder. "Funny." He reached for the bundles, all the bundles, in her arms without asking. "I mean, what are you doing carrying so much at one time?"

After a futile protest, Elaine plunked her hands on her hips and eyed her purloined bags. "What are *you* doing carrying so much at one time?"

The scowl cleared briefly to make room for surprise. Then his eyes narrowed. "Are you one of *those* women?" He hitched his chin at her, indicating she should continue moving toward the door. "The kind who wants to believe she can do everything without a man?"

You have no idea. She nearly laughed out loud, but he didn't appear to be in a laughing mood and the packages were heavy, so she let them in the door without further ado. Mitch followed her to the kitchen.

"Just set it all on the counter, thanks."

He elbowed the first bags she'd brought in farther back and placed his in front of them. "You were busy today."

As she nodded, her stomach growled loudly, reminding her just how busy she'd been.

Mitch cocked a brow. "Do you have anything else in your car?"

"Yes."

"I'll get it. You start unpacking and make yourself something to eat."

Elaine was inclined to be grateful. Kevin had stopped helping with groceries so long ago, he'd completely missed the "Paper or plastic?" revolution. On the other hand, she figured Mitch's authoritative tone and her newly avowed status as one of *those* women made her honor-bound to decline.

"That's okay," she said. "I'll get the rest of my things and then—"

Grrrrrr. Her stomach protested decisively.

Mitch shook his head at her. "Eat something, Elaine. You have a great body, but your legs are skinny." Without waiting for or inviting a reply, he turned and strode out of the duplex.

Elaine stared after him speechlessly. For a recently divorced woman with Ben & Jerry's running through her veins, those words were music to her ears.

Mitch headed for Elaine's red Volvo to bring in the rest of her purchases.

He'd been hard at work since quarter to nine this morning, surprised to find Elaine gone so early, but deciding it was better that way. No arguing, no verbal sparring. He'd get more work done.

Except that his peaceful morning hadn't been nearly as enjoyable as his contentious evening the night before with Elaine.

After he'd left her, he'd ended up having dinner with his sister, who had been useless in decoding Elaine's behavior. To his question, "Why would a woman get so damned riled about a rent discount?" M.D. had replied, "No idea." Then she'd ordered steak, rare, and a scotch and water from the waiter at Jake's. Mitch had gotten the picture: If he wanted to know how a woman's mind worked, he would have to ask someone who thought like a woman, which pretty much ruled out M.D.

In lieu of ruminating about Elaine, he'd decided simply to distract himself. The physical work today had felt good, and he'd been congratulating himself on not wussing out by hiring someone to handle the minor repairs in the vacant unit when Elaine wobbled by the window, lugging the first group of grocery bags. Once again he'd had a nearly instantaneous protective response. *Carrying all those heavy bags,* he'd thought, *can't be good for her.*

Jeez! Was part of his brain misfiring? Had a crucial synapse died? *As of last night, Elaine Lowry is only a tenant,* he reminded himself.

Reaching into the open rear door of her car, Mitch saw that the remaining bags held books. There were two plastic bags with a bookstore logo and a large canvas bag that had Multnomah County Library printed on the side. Some of the library books had spilled out onto the seat.

Leaning farther into the car to scoop them up, Mitch realized he was curious about what Elaine read and about the sheer quantity of reading material. Come to think of it, though, having a plethora of books seemed to fit her image. Underneath the quirky outspoken feminist lurked a shy, bookish heart. Definitely the quiet evening at home with a cup of tea and fuzzy slippers type. Though the women Mitch dated were happier in sophisticated restaurants and clubs than they were ensconced on their own sofas, Mitch liked that about Elaine. He liked—

What the hell?

He looked more closely at the books on the back seat.

Fertility Nutrition.

Soy Drinks for Hormonal Health.

Dragging the canvas bag closer, he pulled out more books.

Yoga and Your Pregnant Body.

Baby's First Year.

When he dug into the Barnes & Noble bag, the first book he withdrew was *Forty Thousand Names for Baby.*

He felt as if steam were shooting from his ears, like a character in one of the Saturday morning cartoons he and M.D. used to sneak into the TV room to watch. *What the bloody hell…*

Pregnant? Was Elaine pregnant? The image of her womanly body entered his mind and lodged there as he slammed the door and strode back to the apartment with her books.

She was in front of the refrigerator, bending over as she squeezed vegetables into the crisper, her shorts inching up to expose a generous amount of smooth, lightly tanned skin. Had he actually called those shapely legs skinny?

Mitch dropped the book bags to the floor. Elaine glanced over her shoulder and smiled, the first genuine smile she'd given him since he'd shown up yesterday. The curve of her lips was as sweet and sexy as…as her other curves.

Feeling his mouth go dry, Mitch stood uselessly and stared until Elaine requested, "Would you hand me the rutabaga?"

He stared dumbly, making no response at all. She pointed. "The rutabaga. It's right there by your—"

Mitch took the pointing hand and abruptly hauled Elaine to her feet, ignoring her surprise while his gaze fell immediately to her breasts, her stomach, looking, he supposed, for evidence and trying hard to dismiss the churning sense of…what? Of something acutely uncomfortable in the center of his gut.

How far along was she? When had she decided to get pregnant? Had she *decided* to?

And then it hit him. She was living here alone. No sign of anyone residing here with her and no mention—so far—of anyone moving in. No ring on her finger.

"Who is he?" The question sounded like Mitch had forgotten to move his jaws when he asked it.

Elaine reclaimed her wrist from his grasp with effort. "What is the matter with you?"

"Sorry," Mitch bit out, referring to her wrist only. He still wanted information. "Who," he said, controlling his temper with an effort he could only characterize as monumental, "is the sonovabitch who got you pregnant?"

For just a second, Elaine thought she might have blacked out and missed something. She eyed Mitch suspiciously. "Are you deranged?"

With one swift move, he grabbed her library bag, spilled its contents onto the partly cleared counter and waved his hand accusingly.

Oh, the books. She looked from them to Mitchell, who, at the moment, appeared as darkly forbidding as a character from *The Scarlet Letter*. Amusement tugged at her. He looked like he wanted to avenge her honor.

Biting the inside of her lip, she shrugged. "Just a boy I know."

Mitch stepped forward with awful menace. "A *boy* you know?" he repeated as if he wanted to give her a chance to amend that.

"Well…" She reconsidered. "Knew."

Watching him, Elaine almost wished she could pull a little plug to release some of the pressure she could practically see building in his head. "Don't get so upset. I'm raising the baby on my own."

"You had unprotected sex!"

"I suppose that would be true. Yes."

"With a minor!" Mitch practically roared.

"Oh, for heaven's sake!" Elaine laughed. Taking her first stab ever at playing absolutely fluff-headed, she rolled her eyes. "He wasn't a miner. There aren't even any mines around here. He worked for Lou's Hardware. On school breaks."

Mitch appeared to be in serious danger of becoming a cardiac statistic.

Elaine had no idea what had got into her. She was normally such an agreeable person. Yesterday afternoon after Stephanie's unpleasant arrival, something in her had broken loose. She'd lost her final grip on the calm, circumspect, unchallenging woman she had become. She was going wild, and she rather liked it.

She did not, however, want to be responsible for Mitch having to start on blood pressure medication.

With her bottom still backed against the fridge, she leaned her upper body toward him. "I'm kidding," she said, noticing for the first time that his scowl turned positively boyish when he became confused. ''I'm not pregnant,'' she clarified. ''It was just a joke.''

''A joke.''

''Yes.''

''You're not pregnant?''

''No.''

Mitch glanced at the bags near his feet and pointed. ''What about the books?''

''You must not have looked at all of them.'' Reaching into the Barnes & Noble bag, she handed him two thin volumes. *Alternatives in Conception* and *Daddy Invisible—Everything You Wanted to Know About Artificial Insemination But Were Afraid to Ask.*

''I am planning to have a baby,'' she elaborated. ''On my own.''

Mitch studied the titles, flipped the *Daddy Invisible* book over and scanned the back cover.

Crossing her arms again, Elaine leaned back against the refrigerator and waited patiently for the light to dawn.

It did. Mitch tapped the word *Artificial.* ''You're going to use…''

''A sperm donor. Yes.''

''Ooo-kay.'' He tossed the books onto the counter and released some of the tension with a breath. ''Whew. You know, I thought maybe you were getting reckless since your divorce. Some women do. They go temporarily…'' He made a circling motion near his temple and whistled.

''Insane?'' Elaine laughed. ''No.''

''No.'' Smiling, pressing his thumb and two fingers against his eyelids, Mitch chuckled with her. In a move so unexpected, Elaine never saw it coming, Mitch put both hands on the freezer unit above her head, bracketing her with his arms and growling into her stunned, upturned face. ''You're Just Out Of Your Ever-Lovin' Mind!''

Chapter Four

Autumn sunlight streamed through the window, causing tiny dust particles to sparkle like diamonds in the air, while a very tall, very outraged Mitch Ryder stood over Elaine, trying to intimidate her with his superior reasoning skills. She felt perfectly unintimidated.

He did have her backed up against an open refrigerator, however, and her tush was beginning to freeze, so she sidestepped to the left, slipping around him to dig through another bag on the counter.

"Put this in the freezer, would you?" she requested, handing him a carton of frozen tofu lasagna.

His outrage unflagging, Mitch grabbed the carton and tossed it into the freezer.

"And this." She passed him a pint of soy ice cream.

He took it and placed it atop the lasagna. "Why didn't you have children with Lowry if you're so keen on becoming a parent?"

Elaine glanced at him. "So I wouldn't be a *single* parent, you mean?"

He caught the irony the first time. "All right, nothing's forever. At least you'd know who the father is."

"Yeah, that'd be a real bonus. I'd get to see him and his new wife every weekend." She removed a package of frozen organic Tater Tots from the grocery bag and held it out. "Maybe I don't want to know who the father is. If I'm going to be a single mother, anyway, this is simpler. You can't argue over visitation rights with a sperm donor."

Mitch turned to throw the Tater Tots into the freezer and slammed the door. "Yeah, let's talk about that. You're going to have a baby with someone you know nothing about. Great concept."

Elaine smiled as if she'd taken his words at face value. "I know! So much better than marrying someone and *then* finding out you know nothing about him. As a divorce lawyer, I'm sure you know what I mean."

After a brief, unfruitful pause during which he tried to come up with a rebuttal, Mitch angled his head. "Touché. I'm sure every one of my clients and my ex-wife would agree, but—"

"Ex-wife?" Elaine gaped. "You were married?"

He actually winced. "A long time ago."

"*You?* I thought you were a serial bachelor."

"I am now."

"Any kids?"

"No. Now, about your buying sperm—"

"Did you want any? When you were married?"

If ever a man wanted to kick himself for opening his big fat mouth, it was Mitch at this moment. He rubbed his brow with the heel of his hand. "It's all ancient history, Elaine. I wanted a lot of things before I realized the ramifications. It's a common mistake. Like wanting a child while ignoring the ramification of not knowing *who in the hell fathered it!*"

The waterfall of questions Elaine had about his marriage

dried up in the face of having to defend herself. Just as, Elaine suspected, he'd intended.

"I will know as much or as little about the donor as I care to," she refuted. "It's up to me. I can request an information sheet so detailed I'll know what he eats for breakfast." She picked up the library book about artificial insemination and tapped it. "It's all right here. Plus, at some sperm banks the majority of donors are graduate students, so I can expect the father of my child to be motivated and intelligent."

Mitch took the book from her and began paging through it. "Yup. Takes a real brain trust to masturbate into a paper cup."

Elaine grabbed the book. "I was referring to my donor's commitment to higher education. Also, I'll know his area of interest," she shot back, "so I can avoid the law students."

Mitch nodded, acknowledging the gibe before he pointed out, "And for this information, you are trusting the people you are *paying* to provide you with the sperm. Is that correct?" He folded his arms over his chest, and Elaine thought the posture made him look so smug, she shoved a bag of frozen peas at him so he'd have to uncross his arms.

Without being told, Mitch turned to put the peas away, but when he saw the jumbled contents of her freezer, he began rearranging items as he spoke. "You're not going to have any idea who this guy really is."

"Yes, I—"

"Proof, Elaine. You're not going to have any proof. They can tell you he's a Stanford medical student, and for all you know, you'll be giving birth to Joe the three-legged harmonica player's baby."

Elaine stared at Mitch's back while he reorganized her small freezer. She had a sudden stinging urge to pitch beets at his head. She was planning to do what thousands of women before her had done, and she needed a shot of courage, dammit, not ten reasons why this disaster could outstrip the *Titanic*.

"What concerns me most, though, is your idea that you'll be better off if the father isn't involved."

Elaine pulled a beet out of the bag and raised her arm.

"You may avoid the issue of visitation rights," he continued, moving frozen foods, "but you're also going to be on your own financially while Mr. Genetically Gifted is running around, avoiding responsibility for you and the child he fathered, which, I think you'll have to agree, says something about a man's character."

"Is that why you haven't had children? Because you don't want to take responsibility for them?"

"That's right." He surprised her by agreeing. "You know what that's called?"

"The Peter Pan Syndrome?"

"No! Integrity. It is called integrity." Perfecting the alignment on a stack of frozen dinners, he stepped back. "There." He moved aside so Elaine could view his handiwork.

Lowering the beet, she peeked in. Her freezer looked like a well-packed suitcase. Frozen dinners occupied the left side. Boxed vegetables were stacked in the middle, bagged items in the door. Her ice-cream containers formed a happy pyramid on the right. He had organized her freezer in one minute flat.

Chewing the inside of her lip, Elaine nodded. "Hmm. That's beautiful. Logical and neat." She glanced at Mitch, who was, she noted, mighty pleased with himself. "You know, a year ago I would have taken a picture of this so I could duplicate it myself. Back then, 'Order' was my middle name." Reaching in, she put a hand on a frozen dinner in the middle of the stack.

"Hey, careful, you'll—" She pulled the dinner, and the top portion of the stack slid to the right. "—make them fall," Mitch finished.

"But I don't appreciate logic much anymore," she told him matter-of-factly, tossing frozen lasagna and kung pao chicken on top of the vegetable boxes. "I don't care about neatness." Grabbing a container of ice cream on the bottom of the pyramid, she sent the entire structure tumbling. "I had a neat and organized life, and you know where that got me? I come home every day to a neat, organized *empty* house." She began shuffling the contents of the freezer as she spoke. "Now I want messes." A bag of peas landed on the ice cube tray. "I don't want everything divided and in its proper place." Frozen blueberries hit the back of the freezer. "I want it all mixed up. I want what I want, and I don't care what it looks like." Slamming the door before the contents could spill out onto the floor, she whirled on Mitch. "So don't touch my frozen foods!"

There followed a protracted pause that Mitch broke by asking mildly, "This isn't about the freezer, is it?"

Elaine answered by stating emphatically, "I don't need someone to take responsibility for me. *If* I ever get involved with a man again, it won't be so he can 'assume responsibility' for me and my child."

Mitch scowled. "That's a bad thing? I'm the enemy for suggesting someone should look out for you?"

"That's not what I said—"

"Good. Because I'm a lawyer. I make my living by injecting a note of reason into what might otherwise be a situation driven by emotion."

"Oh, brother."

"You may perceive my advice as unwelcome at this moment, but when you calm down, you'll see—"

"When I calm down?"

"—how important it is to view a situation from all—"

"Out."

"—sides."

Elaine started shoving him toward the back door. "Go away."

"You see? Right now, this is highly emotional."

She opened the door, placed both hands on Mitch's chest and shoved as hard as she could. Five feet four inches, one hundred and fifteen pounds of underexercised female wasn't much of a force against one hundred and eighty pounds of well-muscled male, but Elaine had the element of surprise on her side.

Mitch stumbled back, tripping over the doorstep. By the time he caught and righted himself, she had closed the door in his face.

Two hours later, with a half-eaten sandwich on a table by her side, Elaine lay on her couch, reading. The tempeh Reuben turned out to be a seasoned soybean patty with Russian dressing and sauerkraut. It tasted okay and was guaranteed to be healthful, but Elaine had indigestion nonetheless. She wasn't sure whether it came from the food or from rereading chapter six of *Alternative Insemination, Every Woman's Guide.*

According to the book, which promised to walk the reader through the "joys and perils" of alternative insemination, the procedure wasn't all that simple. Elaine would have to keep close track of her own fertility and because she wasn't going to have sex to conceive, she wasn't going to get more than one shot a month at this. Also, since she was thirty-seven and fertility tended to "nosedive" after thirty-five, there was no telling how many times she might have to repeat the expensive procedure. She might even have to consider treatments like Clomid. Also, the book strongly suggested having emotional support present because some women found the procedures stressful and mentally exhausting.

Tossing the book onto the coffee table, Elaine pressed a pillow against her stomach, rolled onto her side and thought. So far she'd told two people—Gordon and Mitch Ryder—about her plans. Their enthusiasm had been less than overwhelming.

She'd spent half her life supporting other people's dreams and ideals. For once she expected no less for herself. But from what corner would the support come?

Her brother, Sam, had already given their parents grandchildren. Elaine suspected her mother and father had given up on her a few years ago. She truly didn't know how they would react to her decision to pursue A.I.

Hugging the pillow tighter, she pondered. According to *Every Woman's Guide,* she didn't have a lot of time to futz around. At thirty-seven her ovaries were shrinking by the minute. For the first time, Elaine began to wonder whether she was fertile at all and what she would do if she wasn't.

Would she be willing to undergo the invasive medical interventions mentioned in the book? Would she be willing to do it all alone?

The closer she inched—no, jogged, really—toward forty, the more aware she became that everything was changing, both in her body and in the way others perceived her. Younger women no longer gave her that telltale once-over to see if she was competition. At the supermarket when young men offered to help carry her groceries to the car, they really meant, *Can I help carry your groceries to the car?*

It didn't matter how progressive or self-actualized she was: a thirty-seven-year-old divorcée was forced to find a new way to define herself.

Rising, pillow in hand, Elaine padded to the mirror above the sideboard in her dining room and looked at herself, searching for the balance between kindness and objectivity. At five-four, she was petite and still thin enough—despite Ben & Jerry's best full-fat efforts—to buy size eight jeans. Thick reddish-brown hair that swung gently between her jaw and shoulders further contributed to her youthful appearance…until she looked into the mirror straight-on, and then…

Oy vey. When she examined herself head-on, her fair, translucent skin—a plus at age twenty—became a potential liability. Lines had formed.

Pursing her lips, Elaine pulled her shirt out from her waistband, unbuttoned the top button and tucked the pillow into her shorts. She felt only a little foolish, and once the pillow was in place, the effect it had on her was almost electric.

As if by magic, suddenly she had more than a worn sofa pillow under her shirt; she had an internal sense of purpose. Smoothing her T-shirt over her now expanded belly, she turned to view herself from the side, and of course it was silly, but for the first time in ages, she felt like she had an identity again.

Like trying on a uniform before starting a new job and discovering the fit is just right.

And then for the teeniest, tiniest second she allowed herself to picture more than the belly; she pictured the whole kit 'n caboodle—one child by the hand, one on the way *and* the man, smiling that private, sexy, me-man you-woman smile that said, "Look what we did."

The image was so darned appealing that the tiny second she'd meant to spend on it extended into another and another and then just one more, until finally Elaine sank into the fantasy like it was a tub of hot water, letting the image grow clearer and more detailed until it became obvious the man smiling at her was Mitch Ryder.

Damn it.

Reaching under her shirt, she yanked out the pillow.

A woman could get pretty disgusted with herself over this sort of thing.

Granted, he was the only eligible male she'd spent any time with in ages, and granted, he was attractive…in a straight-backed, bordering-on-pompous way.

But he listened. And he seemed to care, for some reason, what happened to her. And that was hard to ignore.

Elaine scrunched the pillow between her hands. In the end, she knew exactly why she'd pictured him. It was *that night*. The memory—or lack thereof—of that night hung over her like a rain cloud ready to burst, and the worst thing was Mitch's silence. He knew what had happened, and yet he never mentioned it, never even alluded to it. He was an overprotective, overbearing, buttinsky, and yet every time she saw him there were a few seconds—usually right before he opened his mouth and ticked her off—when she felt…dare she admit it?…a surge of desire. A fleeting—and, really, it *was* fleeting—sense of the absolute rightness of being with him.

"Rrrrrggghhhh!" She smooshed the pillow as hard as she could to release some of her aggravation, then sent it sailing like a Frisbee back into the living room. She checked her watch—four-fifteen. A run along the river—that's what she needed. When she set her feet to the pavement, her mind cleared. Seratonin rose; sanity returned. She hadn't run in ages, but knew where her shoes and running shorts were without having to think about it and was ready to go fifteen minutes later.

Wrapping a scrunchie around her ponytail, she grabbed the remainder of a bag of French bread to feed to the ducks (according to *Fertility Nutrition,* white flour upset insulin balance and wreaked havoc on the hormones) and took an organic apple for herself. She felt virtuous before she was halfway out the door. She was being proactive. Not a whiner. She wasn't staying home to worry or to obsess about a man; she was doing something good for herself and her baby-to-be.

Locking the front door, Elaine dropped her keys in her pocket and prepared to head out. As she turned toward the porch steps, however, she stopped short. A tall, slim woman dressed in pleated, straight-leg trousers and a man-tailored shirt that looked like it was pressed to within an inch of its life peered in the window of the apartment next door. She had thick dark hair cut in one of those choppy, supershort cuts Elaine so admired, but which made her look like a little girl whose brother had played "barber" on her head.

The other woman, however, looked just right in the charming cap of hair. Her bone structure was strong and classic. Her entire appearance telegraphed confidence, a woman who could be counted on to lead the crowd rather than follow. With a tanned, ringless hand, she rapped on the window, obviously frustrated when there was no immediate response.

Elaine stepped forward. "May I help you?" The stranger turned toward her with penetrating brown eyes. "I live next door," Elaine explained, hoping to appear helpful rather than nosy. She gestured. "The apartment you're looking at is vacant. Are you hunting?"

Taller than Elaine had first thought, the woman looked first at her then at the duplex as if the question didn't quite compute.

"Hunting?" Then she burst out, "You mean apartment hunting? Here? God, no!" She surveyed the old wooden eaves, the broad concrete porch with its hairline fractures and actually shuddered. "I'm looking for Mitch Ryder. He left this address on my answering machine."

Elaine took another, longer look at the brunette, who appeared to be in her early thirties, and glanced at her watch. "Ah, he was here, about…hmm…an hour ago? Maybe?"

The other woman frowned, and Elaine knew she should wash her own mouth out with soap. Could she be a bigger fake? She knew darn well Mitch had been in the apartment as recently as fifty-two minutes, forty-five seconds ago, because her watch had a sweep second hand and that was when the hammering had stopped. But she wasn't going to parade her interest in front of a woman whose long neck and lithe body could make Audrey Hepburn look stumpy.

"Do you know when he's coming back?"

"No." At least that was the truth. "No idea. Sorry."

"Thirty-six years of impeccable reliability, and he has to screw it up now—" peeking through the window again, Mitch's visitor appeared to be speaking mostly to herself "—when I am absolutely, freakishly starving."

"Would you like an apple?" Elaine held it up, feeling a bit like the wicked stepmother in *Snow White*. Was this woman Mitch's girlfriend? Come to think of it, she couldn't remember his ever bringing a date to the office get-togethers.

The brunette looked at the apple, but shook her head. "Nah. I don't want to kill my appetite. I want beef. I hope he brought clothes to change into." Still mumbling, she tried the front doorknob, surprising both of them when it turned easily and she was able to wait inside. As she crossed the threshold, Elaine heard her say, "Jeez, what was he thinking? He could have had two condos in Lakewood for the price of this place."

Elaine fought a terrible desire to go back into her apartment, station herself behind the curtains and wait for Mitch to return, but that nosy image was just too awful, so she directed herself down the porch steps. She was halfway to the sidewalk when she heard, "Oh, hey!" She turned. "Thanks, uh…"

"Elaine."

"Elaine. Right." And with that the brunette disappeared inside the apartment again and shut the door.

Elaine stared at the closed door for a time. Well, obviously he did see women and obviously he liked them slender as grass, tall as elms and surprisingly offbeat. Fine. Wasn't any of her business.

Setting off down the steps, Elaine prepared to outrun the emotions she wanted no part of. By the time she reached the corner, she was practically sprinting.

When she returned an hour later, the porch steps looked like the side of Mount Hood. Her pronounced limp was the result of a rather painful attempt to jump over a Chihuahua that had crossed her path at the park. Elaine's knees were not what they used to be, apparently; she'd successfully avoided crushing the tiny canine, but her knees had buckled upon landing. Neglecting to warm up hadn't helped.

Before she'd jogged ten minutes, her chest had felt like thick rubber bands were holding her ribs together. Lord, how would she work and care for a baby on her own when she was this out of shape? Plus, now she was starving. Her stomach growled, her legs groaned. She was too tired to go out for food and too hungry to think that tofu anything would satisfy her tonight.

Trudging to her door, she saw that the light was on in the vacant apartment. Vacant, but not empty. Mitch and the woman were seated on the floor, smiling and laughing as they helped themselves to bags of food laid out between them on the carpet.

She watched the woman take Mitch's burger and help herself to a big bite. The gesture was natural, as if they'd done this many times in the past.

Apparently preferring his burger to her own, she handed Mitch her sandwich and kept his. He pulled a comically woeful expression then reached out when she wasn't looking to pull a piece of bacon from the sandwich she'd appropriated, popping the strip into his mouth before she could snatch it back.

Then they both laughed, and it all looked so cozy, Elaine had the most awful impulse to bang on the window and shout, "Knock it off in there!"

Getting a second wind, she gave in to her next awful impulse: hobbling back down the porch steps and around the house to peep through the side window. Since it was still fairly light out, this seemed like a good plan for a budding voyeur. The shrubbery on this side of the house was tall, terribly overgrown and made good camouflage.

It was also scratchy. Branches poked and scraped at Elaine's arms and legs while she wedged herself into position.

These old-Portland-style homes had windows that were relatively high off the ground to accommodate daylight basements and tall front porches, so Elaine had to stand on tiptoe and jump a little to get a good view. Mostly what she could see was the back of Mitch's head and the woman's profile as she reached into a bag, pulled out several long, skinny fries and ate with unabashed enthusiasm. They spoke the entire time they ate, and though Elaine couldn't make out words through the closed window, she could see that the conversation flowed easily. They laughed frequently.

At one point, Mitch's shoulders shook. The man she regarded as rigid, self-righteous and a stick-in-the-mud was sitting on the floor with an idiosyncratic but lovely woman, scarfing burgers and fries and, unless Elaine missed her guess, fresh marionberry milkshakes from Burgerville.

A wave of sadness washed over her, and she began to wonder whether, in fact, *she* was the stick-in-the-mud? Because, criminy, she was legally single, as footloose and fancy-free as she was ever going to get, and she hadn't even flirted with anyone since her divorce. Here it was, Saturday night, and the only thing waiting for her at home was a little light reading about artificial insemination and half of a cold soybean sandwich, hold the canola mayo.

She was about to detangle herself from the shrubbery, if not the humiliation of being a Peeping Tom, when she saw Mitch's friend look at her watch, scoop up a bag of food and stand. Mitch rose, too. Elaine's heart pounded, as anyone's heart might when she realized she was about half a minute away from looking like a complete idiot. A complete idiot with questionable morals.

She had mere seconds to make a decision: attempt a run to her front door and risk running smack into the happy couple and, worse, being seen coming from around the corner, or stay where she was until Mitch returned to the apartment. Mitch decided for her when he opened the door and stepped onto the porch.

Elaine froze, hoping the scratchy bush would freeze, too.

"So I'll see you tomorrow, right?" The woman's distinctively deep voice carried easily.

"Is there any way I can avoid it?"

"No. If you don't show up, I'll hunt you down."

Mitch laughed. "I'll be there. In fact, I'll pick you up, and we'll go to the airport together."

There was a moment of quiet. What was going on? A hug, a kiss? Elaine strained to hear.

"Love you," the woman said.

"I love you, too." The affection in Mitch's voice was evident.

Love? He loved her?

Footsteps led away from the porch and over the walkway.

When Elaine heard a car door slam, she got ready to make her move. As soon as Mitch reentered the apartment, she would extricate herself from this bush, sneak across the yard and pretend she'd just returned from a five-mile run.

She waited. Mitch must be headed back to the house, but the front door didn't open. Footfalls sounded, however, leading up to the house, closer and closer to where Elaine was standing.

She held her breath through several tense moments then heard a strange plumbing-type squeak. Poking her head between branches and leaves, she glanced around.

Geysers of water sprang up over the lawn as oscillating sprinklers burst to life. The first blast of cold water made her yelp in surprise. She fought her way out of the foliage only to get soaked to the skin by another wet blast. Because she couldn't see exactly where the water was coming from, she wasn't sure which way to run. She was aware, however, of some very girly squealing sounds that seemed to be coming from her own mouth, and she heard Mitch say, "What the—"

A moment later, the water stopped, and she was standing on the lawn in a sopping wet T-shirt and shorts. Mitch stepped around the side of the house. "Elaine?"

She wiped her face, opening her eyes one lid at a time. Clearing her throat, she prepared to do some quick talking, but Mitch wasn't interested in an explanation. Yet, anyway. He took her arm and hustled her into the open apartment.

Leaving her briefly to drip in the entryway, he returned with a soft dry bath sheet. "I brought towels in case I had to shower here," he said by way of explanation. "Let's get you out of that T-shirt."

"I don't think so!" Elaine grabbed the wet hem.

"The towel isn't going to do much good if you keep those wet clothes on."

"I'm not getting undressed in here."

Mitch lowered the towel. "Right. Because you'd rather be the only participant in a wet T-shirt contest."

Elaine looked down, gasped and crossed her arms across her chest.

"Do you want to change in another room?" He waved the towel toward the rear of the apartment.

"No. I'm going to go home. To *my* apartment. But I'll take the towel." She held out her hand.

After brief consideration, Mitch handed over the bath sheet.

Elaine wrapped it around her nearly transparent shirt and turned to leave. He almost let her before he said, "I'll be over in fifteen minutes to find out why you were peering through my window."

Elaine halted momentarily, but didn't turn around. "Make it twenty."

He arrived on her doorstep precisely twenty minutes later. The bag he carried smelled like a grilled onion burger and hot fries and had Burgerville written across the side.

"Come in."

Mitch crossed the threshold, appraising her freshly showered self. She'd dressed in white jeans, a sleeveless cotton turtleneck in pale peach, and gold Winnie-the-Pooh earrings. It was a classic butter-wouldn't-melt-in-my-mouth-so-I'm-sure-you'll-believe-me-when-I-say-I-most-certainly-was-*not*-peering-through-your-window ensemble.

She pointed. "What's in the bag?" As if she didn't know.

"Dinner." He raised the sack, redolent with the aroma of hot grease. "Freshly reheated. Have you eaten?"

Her stomach, a shameless opportunist, growled loudly.

"Not yet." Elaine prevaricated. "But I am on a kind of whole foods regimen. And I've been jogging quite a bit." Okay, so that was an exaggeration unless three ounces of soy-beans constituted a "regimen" and limping home from a mile-long jog equaled "quite a bit," but Elaine was willing to cut herself some slack. Especially since he'd just had dinner with a human willow. "I suppose I could cheat a little."

Mitch handed her the bag. She carried it to the dining table, barely restraining herself long enough to set out napkins. Reaching into the bag, she pulled out a warm, fat burger wrapped in paper that was barely able to contain drippy grilled onions and dressing. Mmmm. "You eat this way often?" she asked, remembering all the times Kevin had insisted they order pizza without cheese because he was watching his waistline.

"I rarely think about fast food unless I'm with M.D. Burgers are her favorite, but she'll eat anything that can clog an artery in five bites or less.''

Elaine's stomach stopped growling. ''M.D.?''

''The woman you saw in my living room.''

Nausea supplanted hunger. Wiping her hands on a napkin, she pulled a chair away from the table and sat. She'd had time to think this through while she'd showered. Honesty was always the best policy.

Unless you were about to admit to a tall, dark and handsome man that you'd spied on him and his girlfriend through a window you'd had to crawl around branches to get to. Then it was okay to lie.

''Not hungry?'' Mitch asked as she sat without raising the burger to her lips.

''Yes, I just…like to limit my fat intake.'' Ben & Jerry were probably laughing it up in the freezer.

''Fix yourself something else if you want,'' Mitch told her. ''You won't offend me.''

''Thanks.''

He grabbed a couple of her fries. ''So what was with the I Spy impression?''

Blood wooshed in Elaine's ears. ''I wasn't spying.'' She busied her fingers trying to open a packet of mustard. ''I thought I lost an earring. Near the bush by the window.''

Yes, twenty minutes to think of an alibi, and that was the best she could do.

''I'd been gardening around that area,'' she explained, canceling out years of impeccable integrity by lying through her teeth now. ''And then today I noticed I was missing an earring, so after my run I went over to look, and that's why I was in the bushes when you turned on the hose.'' Good Lord, she was serial.

Mitch watched her squeeze mustard onto the fries. ''That doesn't make sense,'' he said.

She looked up. ''It doesn't?''

He plucked a yellow-coated fry from the pile and grimaced. "Why would you do this to a French fry?"

Elaine closed her eyes briefly with relief. Food. He thought her *food* didn't make sense. She latched happily onto the new topic. "I love mustard on French fries. On pizza, too, but then it has to be brown mustard."

Mitch shook his head. "Criminal." He dug in the bag for a packet of ketchup, opened it and squirted red zigzags on the fries she hadn't desecrated. "M.D. saw you looking through the window."

Damn. Picking up the burger, Elaine surrendered. "I may have glanced." She concentrated on eating to avoid looking at Mitch's grin. She chewed for several moments, swallowed, and said, "All right, I was curious. No one at the office ever saw you date. It was a topic of conversation among some of the wives. And secretaries." To his arched brow, she responded, "And interns. It's understandable. You're single, attractive—"

The brow arched higher.

"—in a meticulous Atticus Finch sort of way."

"Atticus Finch?"

"The character in *To Kill a Mockingbird.*"

Mitch scowled. "I know who he is. I remind you of Atticus Finch?"

He reminded her of Gregory Peck. Tall, dignified, equal parts mystery and sincerity.

She shrugged. "You're both lawyers."

"Hmm." He regarded her a moment. "I didn't realize my love life was a topic of conversation."

"All enigmas become topics of conversation. Women love enigmas. And men know that."

"Do you love an enigma?"

Mitch had his elbows on the table; he was gazing at her steadily, the way Gregory Peck looked at Ingrid Bergman in *Spellbound,* like he knew something about her she didn't know about herself.

Elaine licked her lips. She opened another packet of mustard, squirted it in a little puddle and dunked the burger in, even though her stomach was beginning to feel too knotted to eat. "Yes," she admitted, "I like a good mystery. Mostly I like to solve them."

She cleared her throat, feeling her heartbeat increase. "Mysteries are like big question marks, and I've never liked question marks, even as a kid. Something about the way they hook over seems ominous to me." With the hand holding the burger, she formed an arch.

Mustard plopped onto the table. Mitch smiled.

"Oops." Elaine wiped the mustard away. "Anyway, I always want to erase question marks and put a period there instead. Know what I mean?"

He shook his head. "Not hardly. But go on, I'm riveted."

"Oh. Well, there's one question particularly that's been bugging me lately. I guess you could call it a mystery. Or at least it's a mystery to me." *Don't babble, Elaine. Just get there.* "And I would like to solve it so I can let it go."

Mitch dug for another fry with ketchup, no mustard. "Go on. You're telling me this because…"

"Because you know the answer to the question. And I want you to tell me."

He nodded slowly, contemplating her words. A frown settled over his brow. "If this is about Kevin, he was my client, Elaine—"

"Kevin? It's not about Kevin. I know you can't tell me anything about him, and I wouldn't ask, anyway. It's about you. Actually, I suppose it's about me. Well, us. Not that there's an *us.* Not in a couple sense." *Babbling again. Babbling.* She took a bite of the burger to induce silence for a moment. All she wanted was clarity. But Mitch was looking at her with that distracting blend of amusement and interest.

"What do you want to know?"

Elaine dabbed her mouth with a napkin. "Nothing earth-shattering. I was just wondering. You know that afternoon we had drinks at the Heathman?''

He nodded.

''And I drank a little too much.''

She waited for confirmation, and he nodded again.

''And then you drove me home.''

Mitch ate another fry. ''Yes.''

Elaine pushed the pile of potatoes closer to him. ''And then you walked me to the door. Right?''

''Right.'' He angled his head. ''Are you having a little trouble remembering that night, Elaine?''

''What? No, I'm not having trouble.''

''Because you mentioned a mystery—''

''I can clearly recall your walking me to my front door.''

''—and you said you're wondering about something.''

''I am.'' Elaine's mouth went very dry. Where was a marionberry shake when you needed it? ''I remember everything about the Heathman and driving home and…'' She hesitated. Mitch tilted his head, waiting. ''And I clearly remember waking up the next morning. Alone.'' She watched him pick up a fry, dunk it in ketchup and take a bite. ''And I was sort of, you know—'' She cleared her throat. ''Sort of naked. So I was wondering. Do you know how I got that way?''

Mitch choked on the fry.

Chapter Five

"You're supposed to wait for the international choking sign."

"I'm sorry. I thought I was saving your life."

"How? By breaking off a rib and shoving it through my heart?"

Elaine clutched the steering wheel of her Volvo and gritted her teeth. They'd left the emergency room twenty minutes ago—twenty minutes—and Mitch was still harping on her Heimlich technique. All right, so she'd forgotten to *ask* whether he was choking before she tried to dislodge the French fry he'd eaten. So sue her. She was trying to be proactive.

The doctor in the E.R. had explained that bones were a lot like, say, glass jars: Catch one at just the right angle, and you could shatter it. Not that she'd shattered Mitch's rib. Not even.

A low moan begged her attention from the passenger seat. Trying not to turn her head, she glanced right out the corner of her eye and saw Mitch holding his left side. He was leaning against the door, eyes closed.

Oh, brother. Six feet, two inches of broad-shouldered, gorgeously jean-clad wuss.

In the waiting room of Providence Hospital's bustling E.R., Elaine had noticed other women giving Mitch the once-over. One young woman, who'd appeared to be hanging on to her appendix by a shoestring and should have had better things to think about, had practically drooled with desire when she'd looked at him. And the nurse who had taken his blood pressure—shameless! Absolutely shameless. The moment she'd heard Elaine was a friend and not a "relative," she'd told Mitch with lilting southern charm that his blood pressure was as perfect as the rest of him, and would he like her to bring him up a "little nibble from the cafeteria," because her shift ended in fifteen minutes and she couldn't think of anything more important to do.

Oy! This, Elaine had thought, standing at the foot of the bed, rolling her eyes while Mitch had grinned at Florence Nightingale, was why Jewish women were typically first wives. Their mothers never taught them how to seduce invalids. A nice pot of chicken soup was not a "come-on." Elaine wondered if she even knew how to flirt.

She looked at Mitch again now. He appeared a lot less happy in the car than he had in the E.R. Elaine had to admit that she had never broken anything. Maybe it was agony. According to the attending physician, she'd given Mitch a hairline fracture due to improper placement of the arms during the aforementioned lifesaving procedure.

Spotting a Walgreen's sign, Elaine pulled into the lot, parked and grabbed her purse from the back seat. She asked whether Mitch wanted anything besides codeine. He wagged his head—just once, barely—without opening his eyes.

Shutting the door carefully to avoid jostling him, Elaine headed toward the discount store. She began to feel guilty. The doctor had, after all, written out a prescription for pain medication, so perhaps Mitch wasn't exaggerating. Maybe he really was in terrible pain. She would have to find some way to make it up to him.

Mitch opened his eyes one at a time to watch Elaine swish into the drugstore.

And, damn, she really did swish, he realized, unmindful of any sexist connotation as he watched the most luscious tush in his acquaintance wriggle through the glass doors.

Sitting up, he stared at Walgreen's windows, painted with their latest specials, and thought. He had just spent his most enjoyable two hours in recent memory, and it had all started with a simple confession.

He shook his head. He had never dreamed, not for a minute, that Elaine's tipsiness the evening he'd taken her home might result in her blanking out the entire night. He certainly remembered what had happened. A smile rose to his face. The fact that Elaine could not remember what had transpired between them meant he had a choice. He could give her the details she wanted—which was the moral, upright, honest response—or...

He could play with her a bit, the way he had been the past couple of hours.

Mitch chuckled, making his side twinge. When she'd grabbed him to perform the Heimlich, he'd been surprised by her strength, not to mention her vehemence. True, the fact that he hadn't been choking seemed to have slipped by her, but he was impressed with her determination.

Besides, no one had ever "saved" him before. It was heart-warming. Nope, he wasn't ready for the evening to end.

At least not until she told him exactly why she'd been staring through his window.

Slumping against the door again, he arranged himself to cause the least amount of self-inflicted pain. Then he put a hand on his side, closed his eyes and practiced his moaning.

"Are you sure this is the key?" Elaine felt a flood of internal heat as she tried vainly to jiggle Mitch's house key into his

front door lock. Aside from the frustration and obvious embarrassment of not being able to stick a stupid key into a stupid
lock, she was acutely aware of Mitch's presence as he hovered
over her, close enough for her to smell his pheromones.

They smelled really good. Damn it.

According to *Preconceptions, The Truth About Making
Babies For Women Over Thirty-Five,* when a woman liked a
man's pheromones, it was often an indication that they were a
good fertility match. This was an important consideration. A
woman's fertility took a nosedive every year past thirty-five.
Given that a couple only had a fifteen to twenty-five percent
chance of getting pregnant each month under the best of circumstances, those age-related dips could be a real pisser. Then,
when you factored in the possibility that a woman could actually develop antibodies that killed off her partner's sperm, a
little-known but well-documented cause of infertility, well, you
truly couldn't afford to underestimate the power of compatible
pheromones.

"Try again. I'm in no hurry." Mitch placed his right hand
on the door, above Elaine's head.

She could feel him watching her. Perspiration broke out on
the back of her neck. Geez Louise, didn't he know that particular posture, when executed by a tall man standing next to a
smallish woman, tended to envelop the woman, thereby making
her feel sort of, well, *hugged*?

Elaine struggled some more with the key. "I can't get it in."

Lowering his arm, Mitch leaned in, way in, took the key and
examined it. "Hmm." With a casualness that bordered on indifference, he tucked the first set of keys in his pants pocket.
"That's not the key."

Instead of handing her the set this time, he opened the door
for them. "After you."

"After me, what?"

"After you go in, I will."

"I'm not going in." Elaine shook her head. No. No way.
"I've got to go home." She was *not* going into that house with

Mitch and his screaming pheromones. "I have to leave right now, in fact. Bye." She frowned as Mitch's condition seemed to take a sudden turn for the worse. "What's the matter?"

Mitch clutched his side. Bracing his other hand against the door frame, he winced. "Nothing. Just a few—ow. Twinges. They're not bad." Which didn't account for the fact that he was speaking through gritted teeth. "No problem. Hey, listen." He touched her elbow. "Thanks for everything. I understand that you've got stuff to do. No problem. I'll run a bath as soon as I can bend over, and then get some rest." He turned, heading into the apartment. Slowly. "I think the bed's made. If not, I'll sack out on the couch. 'Night." He raised a hand to wave, but cringed and had to lower it. "Must've overexerted when I opened the door."

Elaine stared after him in sheer amazement. He was good. Better at guilt than her grandmother, and Bubbie had perfected the Never-Mind-About-Me-I'm-Happy-To-Die-Alone technique.

Reluctantly, Elaine followed Mitch into the town house. "You want me to call someone for you? A family member? A friend?" And then something occurred to her. "How about that woman who was with you tonight?"

"M.D.?"

"Mmm-hmm. Maybe she should come back and help you with your bath." Ooh, was that insinuating tone really hers?

While Elaine hung back around the door, Mitch continued into the living room, limping now. "She had to go back to work."

"On a Saturday night?"

"Yeah. Too bad. Would you mind closing that door? It's a little cold in here."

"It's got to be seventy degrees."

"No kidding? I must be having chills."

Elaine shut the door. She dropped her purse on the floor. "All right. You sit down. I'll start a warm bath for you and make sure your bed is made."

"Hey, you sure? It's Saturday night. I bet you have plans."

"I won't be here long," she said noncommittally. She glanced around, wondering if the only tub was in the master bathroom. The town house looked nothing like her duplex. No one could possibly imagine a cadre of little kids playing dump truck on the black-and-white silk rugs.

The sofa was upholstered in petal soft, dove-gray leather; the coffee table provided a cool contrast with a sharp-edged glass-topped design. Large modern canvases adorned the walls. Elaine had no idea if the art was brilliant or hideous. Kevin had always said that given her druthers, she'd decorate in greeting card art.

"Which way is the bathtub?"

She would do this as quickly and efficiently as possible and then scat. The heck with good pheromones. This was obviously a man without children on his agenda.

Actually, coming here was a good reminder. It was so easy to get sidetracked from one's primary goal, and her primary goal was to have a family. To come home to hollers of "Mommy! Mommy!" To find jam handprints on every surface only moments after she'd Formula 409ed the walls, and to wonder if she would ever, ever again dine somewhere that *didn't* offer a cup of crayons along with the menu.

She wanted nights filled with soft-as-powder baby skin and kisses as sweet as those jam handprints. If she had to disregard broad shoulders and rumbly voices and delicious pheromones to get what she *really* wanted, so be it. Marriage had not given her what she needed, and sex had never been that fascinating, anyway.

"I'd give my unbroken ribs to know what you're thinking right now." From his perch near the sofa, Mitch watched her like a cat waiting for a bird to make its next move.

"Where did you say your bathroom is?"

A resigned smile curled his lip as he walked past her. "I think you're what we refer to in the trade as a hostile witness."

He walked down a hall, decorated like the living room with

bamboo floors, white walls and ugly paintings. Elaine followed, trying not to look into the rooms they passed. It was none of her business how many bedrooms the place had, or whether there were photographs rather than paintings in any of them. Or whether those photographs might tell her anything at all about Mitch's private life. Because referring to her as a "hostile witness" was definitely the pot calling the kettle black. You couldn't part this man from his personal information with a cleaver.

When they reached the master bedroom, Elaine hesitated for just a fraction. It was decorated in shades of beige so as not to upset the flow of the rest of the house, but there was a difference here. Whereas the other rooms were rather off-putting, the bedroom said, *"Come in. Sit down."* Or on second thought, *"Lie down."* An armless chair and ottoman near the window provided a cozy place to read, but the king-size bed with tufted headboard was the true draw in the large room. Well, the bed *and* the man Elaine pictured in it.

Damn, there she went again!

"Like it?" Mitch asked as she hovered near the door. "I gave the decorator carte blanche in every room but this one."

"You decorated this?"

"I chose the furniture and the colors. And I vetoed trend-intensive art."

"The other art is trend intensive?"

Mitch shrugged. "According to my decorator." He moved to the chair and ottoman. "This," he patted the chair, "is the most comfortable seat in the house. Great view of the city lights, too. Want to try it?"

Although it was armless, the chair was big enough for two. "No. Aren't I still here because you're too injured to start your own bath? If you're feeling better, I—"

The phone rang, effectively interrupting Elaine's bid to escape. Mitch headed toward the cordless phone on his nightstand, but the limp he'd acquired earlier slowed him down. The machine picked up moments before he did. From the living room, they could easily hear a woman's voice being recorded.

"Aren't you home *yet?* When you get in, call me. Right away. Don't do your little whiskey and the city lights routine, okay? I need to talk to you about—"

"I'm here." Mitch lifted the receiver, ending the recording and Elaine's ability to hear the woman's side of the conversation. She'd recognized the voice immediately, though. M.D. Whoever-She-Was apparently had detailed knowledge of Mitch's habits.

Whiskey and the city lights, huh? Elaine decided to leave him to it.

"I'm going," she mouthed across the king-size bed.

"Hang on," he said into the phone. "Elaine." She turned around. "Give me just a minute, and I'll be done here."

Elaine could hear M.D.'s distinctively low-pitched voice uttering something along the lines of *"No you won't."*

"It sounds like you have some…business to take care of," she said, gesturing to the phone, trying to keep her tone as neutral as possible. "Really, I think you should ask your friend to come over and help you. It's best to have the comfort of people you know well when you're recuperating." Elaine smiled as sweetly as she knew how.

Covering the mouthpiece of the phone, Mitch said, "If you knew my sister, you would not link her and comfort in the same sentence."

"That woman tonight? M.D.—that's your sister?" The relief was towering. Monumental. Seductive.

"Yes." His expression was entirely too guileless to actually be guileless. "Why?" he asked, "Who'd you think she was?"

An audible voice emanated from the receiver. Mitch returned briefly to his call, and Elaine waited by the side of the bed, the angel on her left shoulder urging her to beat this scene before he got off the phone, the devil on her right ordering her not to move a muscle. She waffled for a good half a minute while he listened to his sister, and all she could think was *Too bad he's not wearing a suit,* because it was much easier to write him off as an uptight lawyer when he dressed the part than when he turned fudgy-brown eyes on her, mouthed *I'm starving,* and rubbed his flat belly *under* his Ralph Lauren Polo shirt.

Run now! Save yourself, the angel commanded. She might have obeyed if the devil hadn't already decided: *Fat chance.*

Fifteen minutes later, Elaine agreed to start the water in his bath, but she told him he had to get into it all by himself.

Muttering that an injured man deserved more sympathy, Mitch began to remove his shirt while she was still in the bathroom, and he not-too-subtly winced to let her know the rib she'd fractured made disrobing a painful experience.

Elaine edged toward the door. He could yowl like an injured tomcat; she wasn't getting her fingers anywhere near his naked torso.

She was about to leave him on his own when suddenly the two-person-wide double-jetted Jacuzzi reminded her of how much she'd taken for granted when she was married and living in Lake Oswego. The home she'd shared with Kevin was not far from here, actually. She'd had a Jacuzzi, too, and a hot tub on the deck, and a chrome blender from Williams-Sonoma that had cost over two hundred dollars. The blender had been her last Christmas gift from Kevin. She'd used it to frappé his favorite colognes the day she'd found out he was cheating on her.

She'd never been much of a *things* person, and yet it was hard not to miss some of the goodies she could no longer afford even to think about. Too bad she'd been a wife back then and not simply a girlfriend. Girlfriends got all the perks without any of the grief. Her problem was that she'd always had "standards." The kind that ruled out a casual trip to Morocco with her weekend lover.

For several seconds, Elaine looked at Mitch, really looked. Most women would consider him a real hot catch.

What if she weren't so concerned with concepts like commitment and fidelity and that dangerous, 1950s fantasy—forever? What if she relaxed her values just a bit, for just a while? She watched Mitch struggle to remove his shirt, and knew what she wanted to do....

Wordlessly, Elaine walked over, grasped the hem of Mitch's shirt and pulled it over his head in one fluid motion. She reached for the button of his jeans next and in a swift, surprisingly efficient move, unzipped the fly. Looking him straight in the eye, she pushed the denim past his hips until the pants fell to the tiled bathroom floor.

His boxers were next.

Mitch's hand covered hers, halting her. He raised his brows, questioning. Elaine paused temporarily, noting the shallow rise and fall of his broad, hairless chest. As he opened his mouth to speak, she placed her fingers gently over his lips. His eyes widened. The boxers dropped to the floor.

Taking his hand, she drew him to the tub, compelling him to step into the warm water and sit down. Locating a bar of soap, she knelt and dipped the bar into the water, grazing the top of Mitch's thigh before rubbing the soap sensuously across his shoulders and over the wide expanse of his superbly muscled back. She scrubbed rhythmically, left to right and back again then circled around to his chest.

Elaine knew his eyes were on her, following her; she felt the full weight of that questing gaze, but resolutely concentrated on what she was doing, pressing the soap against the rippling muscles of his lower abdomen. His inhalation grew labored. On the exhalation, hot breath stirred her hair.

Elaine dropped the soap.

Her gaze locked with his. One smooth brow arched. He smiled, leaned forward and lifted his hand from the water, reaching for her. She smiled, too, as she reached slowly, deliberately for the soap....

* * *

"Damn!"

Elaine jolted. She blinked rapidly, trying to focus. Mitch struggled with his shirt, cursing from deep within its folds. Though his ribs were wrapped in a brace, his bared stomach showed not a speck of spare flesh. The ripples looked just like they had in her fantasy. Heat coursed through Elaine's veins. If she wanted to, she really could walk over, help him off with the shirt and turn her fantasy into reality. If she wanted to...

Mitch jerked impatiently on the shirt, hurting his sore ribs and sucking in a breath. His stomach muscles contracted.

"Would you mind helping me with this?" He sent out a muffled SOS.

Elaine's mouth went dry.

He was close enough to tickle. Temptation beckoned. She could take a big fat bite out of life, or cut and run. It was up to her. Steam rose from the Jacuzzi, inviting her, for once in her life, to take the plunge.

Heart throbbing, she stepped forward, grasped Mitch's shirt and pulled it over his head and arms. He emerged with his hair ruffled, exasperated with himself, but grateful to her. He looked, she thought, adorably disgruntled.

Elaine tried to hand him the shirt, but Mitch ignored it; instead, he held her arms, looking down at her. "Thank you," he murmured.

"You're welcome." Knowing she sounded like Clint Eastwood, she cleared her throat. "I'd better go."

He continued to stare without releasing her, and at this moment nothing about him seemed familiar. "Not yet."

Confusion whirled and eddied inside Elaine. "Yes." She heard the urgency in her own voice. "I should go right now."

"When I get out of the Jacuzzi, it'll be too early to go to sleep."

She patted his arm. "Not if you soak a good long time." Stepping away, she laid his shirt on the sink and backed to the door. So much for taking a bite out of *life*. She'd pick up a Snickers bar on the way home.

Mitch shrugged. "Okay. Have you changed your mind then?"

"A-about what?"

"Wanting to know what happened the night I took you home."

Her heart thwacked against her breastbone. An hour ago, she had wanted to know very much what had happened that night. An hour ago, she had been dying to know. Now she thought about Jack Nicholson and that line from *A Few Good Men:* *"You can't handle the truth."* No, she couldn't. God, she really couldn't.

"No. That's all right. I like mysteries."

His eyes narrowed. He took a step forward. "I don't believe you."

Elaine continued to back toward the door. "It's true. Mary Higgins Clark, Sue Grafton—I can't get enough." She bumped against the door frame. "Well, see ya."

Turning, she walked rapidly through the apartment, grabbing her purse and escaping the town house before she changed her mind and asked him to *show* her what they did that night.

For the next two nights, Elaine tossed and turned in her bed. Lust, apparently, wreaked havoc on REM sleep. If she hadn't known better she would have said Mitch's pheromones were on her pillowcase. Over and over again through the night, she replayed the invitation she'd seen in his eyes as he stood near the Jacuzzi, shirt discarded, holding her lightly and daring her to stay. She knew she should let the thoughts go, simply let them go, chalking her interest up to one of those things a person wanted in life, but didn't need. Like Christian Dior underwear or Godiva chocolate; when you stopped thinking about it, you didn't miss it. Trouble was, she couldn't stop thinking about Mitch.

So, come Monday morning, Elaine had scheduled an appointment with a fertility specialist and a lunch date with Adair Konigsberg Jensen. Adair was the queen of Portland society.

She went everywhere, had a startlingly wide circle of acquaint-ances, and if she didn't know someone, she could usually get all the dirt on them, anyway.

Fortunately Adair knew Mitch well. Elaine had first met Adair two weeks after moving to Lake Oswego with Kevin and joining a chichi boating club, even though she and Kevin didn't own a boat. Adair had been married to Jason Konigsberg at the time, one of the premiere plastic surgeons in Portland. Un-fortunately the faithless doctor had fallen in love with one of his liposuction patients four years after marrying Adair, a fact that left his wife fuming and her friends shaking their heads, because as far as anyone knew Adair could attribute her own pencil-thin thighs to the Stairmaster, not a vacuum treatment. But go figure men.

Adair had hired Mitch Ryder to handle her divorce, and ac-cording to the other gals at the yacht club, she had come out smelling like a rose, with nothing but praise for the "brilliant" lawyer who had taken such good care of her. There had even been a rumor floating around among the yacht set that Adair and Mitch had dated.

Adair was remarried now to a gastroenterologist, but it seemed a good bet that if anyone could shed a little light on Mitch's love life, it was she. So Elaine called and asked her to lunch, hoping that if Adair and Mitch had actually dated, the other woman would be willing to dish a little. Gossip was not Elaine's usual style, but she wanted to know whether Mitch was currently dating, and if anyone would know, it was Adair.

On her lunch break, Elaine changed out of her work uniform and into a designer dress that was a leftover from her days as a would-be boater's wife. She rushed over to Higgins, a swank eatery in downtown Portland and was there when Adair swirled in.

"Hi, doll!"

Elaine rose for a careful press of cheeks that was guaranteed not to disturb the brunette's perfect makeup. "Hi, Adair. Thanks for meeting me on such short notice."

"Oh, sweetie, of course! All the girls have been wondering what you've been up to since you left the club. That awful blonde your ex married wore a thong to the July Fourth regatta, can you believe? No cellulite, I'm sorry to report, but no class, either. No one has nominated her for the Christmas lights committee, I want you to know, although I think Janelle Traynor signed up for her spinning class at the gym."

Elaine felt like her head was spinning before Adair was halfway through. All that information, and they hadn't even sat down yet. She cleared her throat. "I wouldn't want Stephanie to be excluded from the Christmas committee on my account, Adair. I hope you'll pass that on to everybody."

Adair put a beautifully ringed hand over her chest. "You are so salt of the earth."

Elaine smiled. Yeah. So salty she was planning to pump for information a woman she hadn't seen since Kevin got the yacht club membership in the divorce settlement. "Shall we sit down?"

They ate organic Caesar salads with alderwood-smoked salmon and were waiting for dessert by the time Elaine mustered the chutzpah to steer the conversation around to Mitch.

Adair lifted a waxed brow. "Sweetie pie, wasn't he your ex's attorney?"

"Yes, he was. They're in the same office. I was just wondering if you could tell me anything about him. Sort of fill me in on what he's like outside the courtroom, you know. The reason I ask," *is that I'm lusting after him,* "is that he's my new landlord."

Adair's eyes widened. To avoid a lengthy explanation, Elaine said, "It was a coincidence."

"A co-inkydink?" One of Adair's endearing traits, depending on how you looked at it, was that she used cutesy word alterations. "How bizarre!"

"Yes, it is. Truly a bizarre...co-inkydink." The waiter arrived bearing warm marionberry cobbler topped by a scoop of cinnamon-scented vanilla ice cream. Elaine waited while he set the attractive dish between them, offered new silverware and topped up Adair's decaf. When he left, Elaine leaned forward, "To tell you the truth, Adair, I'm a little concerned about my future. I mean, I'm single now, and I have to protect myself. What do I know about Mitch Ryder except that he's a very tough opponent in the courtroom?"

Adair dipped a spoon delicately into the ice cream. "Sure he's tough, but that's good if he's on your team."

"Yes, except that I don't have a team. I mean, I wonder how he treats women in general, outside the courtroom, you know?"

Adair smiled. "Honey, Mitch Ryder is a mensch, no question." She spooned up drippy marionberries. "But underneath, he's a real huggy bear, too. I'm surprised he's still single."

"Really." Now they were getting somewhere. Elaine's guilt over having lunch with Adair chiefly to get information about Mitch yielded to overwhelming curiosity. She decided to pick up the tab for the meal as amends. And to let the other woman have the entire cobbler.

"You know," she said, "there was this wild speculation during your divorce from Jason."

Adair looked up from her dessert, perfect brows spiking. "Oh?"

"Nothing derogatory. But some people said they thought you were actually dating Mitch."

"Oh, that." Adair shrugged. "I was."

"Ah." Even though Elaine had known it was a possibility, she was surprised. And not thrilled. Suddenly she wished she hadn't decided not to eat dessert. "So, what happened?"

"Between Mitch and me? We only went out a couple of times. I was still in a mourning period, of course, so I couldn't get serious about anyone. Mostly I wanted it to get back to Jason that I was already dating. He was all hot and bothered over that twit with the thick thighs. I wanted him to think I got myself a real catch."

"Oh."

"Are you dating anyone yet?"

"Me? No, no. No."

Adair shook her head. "Well, you should be." The brunette regarded her knowingly. "So why all the curiosity about Mitch, sugar pie? Are you interested?"

Elaine felt a trickle of sweat between her shoulder blades. She eyed the cobbler, wanting the sugar escape, but took a deep breath instead.

Yes, she was interested in Mitch. Her first priority was to have a child, and she didn't want a man—any man—to interfere with that. But neither could she ignore what was rapidly becoming the strongest physical desire she'd ever experienced. He made her stomach muscles shiver. Who would have guessed? It's not like she'd lusted after him over cocktails at the company Christmas parties. Well…maybe she'd lusted a little.

Adair was watching her curiously, a smile blooming on her still-pink lips. It was a friendly, mischievous smile, nothing sly or calculating about it; just one girlfriend understanding another.

Slowly Elaine smiled back. "Okay," she said. "So I'm interested."

Chapter Six

It was a warm September evening, with a sky the shade of pale lavender-blue that made one think of walking the dog or going for a jog or pushing a girl on a swing. Not that Mitch could remember ever pushing a girl on a swing. Not even his ex-wife before they were married, when they'd jogged together in the park.

Tapping his fingers on the desk rather than on the keys of his laptop, where they should have been tapping, Mitch stared out the window of his home office. He had a good view of the greenbelt and a mini forest of trees that gave the hundred-and-twenty-unit town house complex in which he lived a homier feeling. Tonight he stared without appreciating the view, however. He was restless, disturbed by his recent actions and frustrated by his inability to concentrate on the brief he was trying to read. Normally work absorbed him completely.

It had been two days since he'd tried to seduce Elaine into…what? The finger tapping accelerated as he shook his head. The truth was he had no idea how far he'd intended to take the flirtation. If she hadn't left, would he have tried to get her into the Jacuzzi? Would he have tried for something more?

Reaching for the bottle of Heineken next to his computer, he took a long swallow and grimaced. The beer had grown warm; no hope for distraction there, so he set it aside. Mitch knew he was no saint when it came to women; he'd had his share of intentionally short-term relationships. He'd never been seriously irresponsible, however, which is what disturbed him about his actions with Elaine. Everything he knew about the woman told him it was hands-off entirely. Yet he continued to test the waters, wading in deeper and feeling frustrated when she backed away.

Rising, Mitch carried his beer to the kitchen and poured it down the sink. He didn't remember eating lunch today, but there was nothing in his refrigerator save for butter, a loaf of his favorite corn rye for breakfast, several jars of preserves his mother had sent him as part of his Christmas present last year, a jar of pimiento-stuffed olives and more beer. Very different from Elaine's refrigerator.

The problem with Elaine, he decided, opening a cupboard to investigate the contents, was her kitchen. Her refrigerator had "Future room mother" written all over it. That was not his future, though. He'd made the wife-kid-dog decision a long time ago, and he knew he'd chosen correctly for him. He and Elaine were walking two divergent paths. He only wished she didn't walk hers with such an enticing sway of her hips. Which meant he owed her an apology. No matter how tempting it was to tease or flirt with her, he owed it to both of them to practice restraint, because no matter how attracted to her he was, their life together would be a mess—the kind of mess he spent most of his time trying to clean up for others.

When the doorbell rang, Mitch slapped shut the cupboard and headed for the living room. He opened the door to M.D., who stood with a disgruntled expression and two large white bags that smelled distinctly like Mexican fast food.

A pencil-slim blue skirt and white blouse already bearing a

smudge of red sauce suggested M.D. had come straight from work. "What are you doing here?" she demanded, brushing past him with her bags and heading immediately for the glass table in what his real estate agent had called a kitchen nook.

"That sounds like my line," he said, closing the door and following her in. "But I'll play along. Where should I be?"

M.D. dumped the bags on the table and put a hand on her hip. "At your office. I went there first."

Mitch checked his watch. "It's after seven."

"Yeah, on a Monday."

He frowned. Clearly the implication was that he worked all the time. "I think you're confusing me with you."

His sister snorted. "Right." She pulled two heavy-looking oblong items from the bag. "Ground beef or shredded?"

"Shredded." He accepted the burrito, but shook his head. "Do you ever eat anything that *doesn't* come wrapped in paper?"

"Sure. Steak."

"I'd like to represent your arteries when they decide to sue you."

"I'll give them your number. So, why weren't you at the office?"

Grabbing a couple of cold beers and the jar of olives from the refrigerator, Mitch helped his sister set the table, such as it was. He tried to remember the last time he'd served an actual meal here, something that didn't come in a box with microwave instructions. Probably never.

"If you'd bothered to say hello properly," he said, answering M.D.'s question to distract himself from his own troubling thoughts, "you would have noticed that I am an injured man."

M.D. took a bite of the burrito while she was still standing. Another blob of hot sauce stained her blouse. "Where? You don't look injured. Are you being represented?"

As M.D. was a corporate rather than accident attorney, he ignored the question. "I hurt my ribs a couple of nights ago.

Then I slipped getting out of the bathtub and sprained my ankle.''

His sister shot him a look. "You sound like a girl."

"Thanks for the sympathy." Mitch popped the tops off the beers and sat down. Unwrapping the burrito, he grabbed one of the dozen or so packets of hot sauce M.D. had gotten for the two of them, but didn't start eating. He'd lost the desire.

His moods were normally as predictable as the tide, but not for the past few days. It surprised him. Even his ex-wife had said she had nothing to complain about regarding his temperament. In fact, life with him had been too sedate for Jeanette's taste. They'd both just turned twenty-five when they'd married. Mitch had been focused on hard work and establishing himself. His young wife had held other expectations. Jeanette had wanted life to feel like a roller-coaster ride, not a merry-go-round. They'd divorced amicably after three years, and to tell the truth, Mitch couldn't recall ever wondering if he ought to have tried harder.

Frowning now, wondering if his general attitude toward the dissolution of relationships was part of the reason he hadn't tried harder to change during his own marriage, Mitch watched his sister squeeze a puddle of blood-red ketchup onto a bag of Tater Tots. "You'll be a great mother someday, Em," he said. "You'll never fight with your kids over where to eat."

M.D. chewed a ketchup-soaked spud and nodded. "You got that right." She didn't take his comment any more seriously than he intended it. They both knew M.D. had no intention of having children…any more than he did. The Ryders weren't huggy-kissy-squeezy family people. Just weren't. It might have been nice, though, to be an uncle. Connected to family but from a distance so that he wouldn't be expected to do the touchy-feely stuff. He wasn't the Great Santini, but affection was not his strong suit.

He watched his sister wolf down her dinner. "Do you ever think about having a family? You know, you could have a wedding, a nice dress, flowers."

Abruptly, M.D. stopped chewing. "You really *do* sound like a girl." She plucked a napkin, wiped her mouth and studied him. "What's with you?"

Mitch shrugged nonchalantly. "I'm wondering if the family's going to die out with us."

Scrunching her napkin, M.D. tossed it onto the table. "Excellent. This is exactly what I want to talk to you about." She pushed the rest of her burrito and the potatoes to the side. "Vicki is moving to Portland."

"You told me that the other night. I said I'd pick her up at the airport. What does this have to do with what we're talking about."

"Vicki is family. At least she thinks she is."

Mitch focused on lacing his burrito with hot sauce. When it came to his sister and their stepmother, affecting a neutral demeanor was, he'd found, imperative. If there were two people on the planet more different than M.D. and Vicki Ryder, Mitch hadn't met them yet. "And?" he asked, trying to nudge M.D. closer to her point.

"And the other night I thought you'd pick her up at the airport, drop her at the Hilton, she'd go shopping downtown for a few days and we'd take her back to the airport."

"But it's not going to happen that way?"

"She wants to stay with me."

Mitch made a gesture that said, *Yeah? So?*

Clutching the sides of the glass tabletop, M.D. leaned far forward. "She...wants...to stay...*with me.*"

Mitch had to smile. "Vicki isn't that bad—"

"She wants to move in. She's not considering this a little vacation from Dad. She wants to move to Portland permanently! And she wants us to be 'roommates.' So we can have 'girl time.'" M.D. pounded the table with a fist. "What the hell is girl time?"

"Okay, calm down. First of all, Vicki is not going to move here permanently." Although Mitch wasn't sure she'd run immediately back to their father, either. Unlike the Ryders, Vicki *was* a touchy-feely type. Mitch often wondered how she'd stayed with Daniel Ryder—or with him and M.D. for that matter—for over two decades. "She's uncertain, Em, probably a little scared. She's never struck me as a highly independent woman. She probably just wants a little moral support while she figures out what she wants."

"She's already figured it out. She called me this afternoon from her lawyer's office. She's filing for divorce."

Mitch felt the surprise slice through the center of his stomach.

"She was going to ask you for advice, but she didn't want you to have to take sides."

A surge of anger supplanted the surprise. Vicki and his father may not have been the perfect match, but she'd managed to hang in there with him for nineteen years, which was more than anyone else had done. Why wasn't Daniel fighting to save this marriage?

"What do you want me to do?" he asked his sister.

"I want you to invite Vicki to stay in your duplex."

"The vacant unit isn't finished yet."

"Well, finish it!"

Mitch took a long, slow swallow of beer. Hell. His sister sounded frantic. Now was not the time to tell her he was thinking of selling the duplex altogether. Or at the very least turning it over to a property management company.

The less contact he had with Elaine, the better.

"I really can't work on the place right now, Em. I'm working on a lot of cases, and with these ribs—"

"Hire someone. *I'll* hire someone." M.D. ran restless fingers through her short hair. "Look, I don't dislike Vicki. I can see the woman's good points. But we were never able to live together. Never. She can't stay with me, and when I said I'd help her find an apartment, she said no, she wants to be connected to family. She wants to feel—I don't know—" M.D. waved a hand in the air. "Cozy. Your duplex will connect her to family. So, please, go make it cozy." She put her hands together in prayer position. "I am begging you. Do this for me. SMS—save my sanity!"

Sitting back in his chair, Mitch looked from his sister's anguished face to the large, untouched burrito in front of him. He thought about being around the duplex and Elaine. Heartburn set in.

"All right. I'll hire someone, and Vicki can move in until we get this whole thing with her and Dad straightened out." And he would do his best to stay out of the way.

M.D. released a profound sigh. "Thanks, Mitch." She sat for a moment, a relieved smile on her face. "Can I have some of your shredded beef?"

"You picked a fine time to leave me, Lucille." Sitting in a wicker chair on her front porch, Elaine warbled the old Kenny Rogers' ditty then kicked her feet up onto the porch rail and sighed. Gordon was out of town on business, and if ever she'd needed her friend, it was now.

She had been sitting here in the glow of late afternoon, reviewing her first set of donor profiles for the past hour.

Visit number one to the fertility clinic had proven that quality DNA was available for a price. It was unsettling to meet the potential father of her child all alone on her front porch. A few facts on a sheet of paper was as close as she was ever going to come to knowing her baby's daddy. If Gordon were here, he could have lightened the mood.

"I can do that, too, though," Elaine muttered, picking up one of the donor information sheets that interested her the most. "So," she said, forcing a smile at Mr. 10876, "what's your sign?"

She tried to laugh, but couldn't dredge up enough humor to overcome her trepidation. She was queasy with nerves and a serious bout of uncertainty. She hadn't told her parents or brother yet what she was planning, but she would this weekend. Maybe the more she talked about her plans, the more certain she would be to go through with them. Right now that was her biggest fear: that she'd chicken out of using alternative insemination to conceive, that her biological clock would time-out and that she would never have a child. She had no illusions that her family would wholeheartedly approve her decision, but she needed support and advice, and they always came through on that score.

Holding the sheets of paper on her bare thighs, Elaine tried to clear her teeming mind. Craving a few moments of peace, with no concerns save for what was going on in this present moment, she watched a butterfly then a bird and then a delivery van. The van was maroon with the words Rooten's Fine Furniture painted in a yellow arc across its side. It pulled up right in front of the duplex.

Two young able-bodied men hopped out, opened the rolling rear door and pulled down a steel ramp. One of the men jogged up to the front porch.

"Are you receiving the furniture delivery?" he asked Elaine.

"No." Surprise kept her from saying anything else for a moment. Had the unit next door been rented? Before she could summon a further response, she saw the young man's gaze travel the distance of her raised legs. Admiration registered on his smooth-skinned face.

His appreciation was flattering, but she was more amused than impressed. Having him ogle her was rather like having one's kid brother escort her to the senior prom.

"I haven't purchased any furniture," Elaine said.

"You must be unit A then," he said, referring to the delivery order he withdrew from his pants pocket. "My delivery's for unit B."

"There's nobody in unit B."

The second deliveryman joined them on the steps. Like his partner, he was moderately burly—a smidge older, though, which still made him young enough to be Elaine's…very baby brother. The two young men hovered over her as if she had the answer to their delivery dilemma while she sat in her chair with her sperm donor stat sheets on her lap. That's how Mitch found them when he pulled up in his shiny new truck a scant thirty seconds later.

Dressed in an expensive suit, his dark hair perfectly trimmed and brushed back, he strode up the front walk, his stern eyes on Elaine the entire time. She smelled his clean aftershave the moment he joined the three of them on the porch. He walked easily, evidence that his bruised ribs were no longer bothering him.

Dapper at almost 5:00 p.m., Mitch looked like he was on his way to work, not like he'd just come from there. He looked, Elaine acknowledged, entirely too yummy. She had always admired a man who wore a suit well. The delivery twins looked like boys in comparison.

"I hope I haven't kept you waiting. Have all of you been here long?" Mitch's first statement sounded entirely cursory, and the question had more than a mere ring of displeasure. He never took his eyes off Elaine, even when one of the boys asked whether they should begin unloading. Even as they got to work and Mitch's gaze followed the same path theirs had— along her raised, bare legs to her sandaled feet and up again. Her response to his perusal was entirely different, however, from her response to the boys. With Mitch evaluating her legs, her skin shivered with gooseflesh. Her stomach and chest filled with heat.

Darn it, he'd done it again—upset her thermostat, made her feel hot and cold at the same time.

A carved cherrywood dresser, decidedly feminine in style, was the first item off the truck. The boys brought a ramp to set over the porch steps. Mitch turned briefly to note their progress, then turned again to Elaine. "I'm going to open the door and show them where to put the furniture. I'll be right back. Wait for me."

Elaine said nothing, but she knew she had no intention of following his directives. Mostly because she wanted to. She wanted to wait right where she was, not move a muscle until he came back to talk to her. She wanted to know who was moving in and why he knew where to put the furniture. She wanted to know entirely too much, and she definitely wanted him to look at her again like he might ravish her here on the front porch.

The moment he entered the front door of the neighboring apartment, she stood, ignored the cramping in her legs and hobbled into her house. But she left her door open...

Mitch knocked on the frame of Elaine's screen door a few minutes later, amazed by his irritation at the two movers next door. They were merely kids doing their jobs, but the way they'd been standing over Elaine when he'd first arrived, eyeballing her terrific legs, simply annoyed the hell out of him.

He was here to wipe the slate clean with her: to put their relationship in clearer terms. They were landlord and lessee. Acquaintances, and that was it. He'd already decided to turn the duplex over to his friend at Portland Property Management on Monday, and from here on in, that company would handle any problems Elaine had with her apartment. Any problems Vicki had, too. And he would get back to his law practice, pick up a little community work, play more tennis before the weather turned. This winter he'd get back into cross-country skiing.

And he'd date. He'd date the right kind of woman for him; the kind with whom divorce would never be an issue because neither was marriage. Good plan.

He waited rather impatiently outside Elaine's door then knocked again, louder.

"Come in," she called from inside.

Mitch walked in, assailed immediately by a sense of home. A savory, hickory-scented aroma emanated from the kitchen.

He announced himself, and she said, "I'm in the kitchen, I'll be out in a minute." A cabinet opened and closed. Mitch moved to a couch upholstered in a nubby ivory fabric with a pale green and lavender throw folded over the back. He imagined sitting down, putting his feet up, and the image was inviting but he was too restless to relax. He wandered toward the small dining area and hovered by the oval-topped table.

In the kitchen, a bell dinged, an appliance door was opened, and Mitch realized Elaine was using the microwave. He checked his watch. Almost five o'clock. On his own, he rarely got around to dinner before seven, and that was on an early night.

He squelched a sudden urge to ask her to have dinner with him. That was not why he was here. He was here to—

A stack of glossy pamphlets lying on the coffee table caught his eye. Bending forward, he took a closer look. The top pamphlet was titled *New Concepts in Fertility* and bore a photograph of a pregnant woman holding a flower in front of her protruding belly. Next to the pamphlets was a sheaf of papers. Picking up the stack, he held it close to his face, his eyes widening, his heart beginning to throb. *Donor 1086,* he read. *Twenty-six-year-old male, blond hair, blue eyes...prelaw Stanford...favorite breakfast: toasted bagels with cream cheese and strawberry jam...*

What the hell?

Mitch shuffled quickly through the next few sheets. *Twenty-four-year-old male...brown hair...drinks coffee...loves water sports...*

Twenty-eight-year-old Ph.D. candidate...birthmark on right thigh...pizza fanatic...

Mitch swore three times in rapid succession. Elaine Lowry was going to get pregnant by a personal ad.

She'd been serious about this. She was honest-to-God going through with it, may *already* have gone through with it.

"Sorry to keep you waiting. I was starving." She swept in from the kitchen dressed in white shorts, a red tank top, her hair in a ponytail...

...and those perfect bare legs making him think of lazy summer sex when all you had to do all afternoon was make love...

He shook his head, hard. He had something to say here, and she wasn't going to like it.

"Bacon, lettuce and tomato." She raised a plate with two thick half sandwiches. Mayonnaise oozed between the lettuce and toasted white bread. "The more I tell myself to eat health food, the worse my diet gets. Are you hungry?"

Hungry? Mitch felt his anger mount. How the hell could she think about food right now? He raised the papers. "Who's the winner?"

Elaine's eyes narrowed, and she felt like kicking her own rump when she realized what he was holding and that it was her fault for leaving such personal information lying in plain view. Then again, she wasn't plotting a Pentagon takeover here; she was simply trying to have a baby.

Brushing past Mitch as if the papers in his hand were no more personal than the *TV Guide,* she sat cross-legged on her couch with the plate on her lap. Carefully raising her packed sandwich to her lips, she looked at Mitch's angry face and shrugged. "I'm not sure yet. What do you think?" Then she took a big bite of her BLT.

The funny thing was, as casual as she was trying to be, she really could have used some advice here. And it occurred to her that an objective Mitch might have some good insights about people and relationships.

Wiping mayonnaise from the corner of her mouth, she said, "I'm kind of leaning toward the English major who raises Golden Retrievers."

For a moment Mitch only looked at her. Then, with a scowl as black as the tips of his polished shoes, he shuffled through the papers until he found the correct sheet. "Number One-Four-Five-Seven?" He read. "English major…twenty-two years old…junk food junkie…loves Orville Redenbacher's popcorn. Enjoys visiting amusement parks on the weekends." Mitch raised the white page while pinning Elaine with a glare. "Why don't you adopt him? You'd be killing two birds with one stone."

Elaine shook her head in disappointment. "That's not funny."

"Am I laughing?" He shook his head. "Nothing about this is funny. I can't believe I'm standing here talking to someone who is contemplating buying sperm from some kid who, unbeknownst to her, might be impregnating half the women in Portland."

"Arbitrary exaggerations are not going to help." Elaine had no intention of admitting it now, but the likelihood of the donor impregnating other women in the same general geographical area had started to make her very uncomfortable. With that thought, she set the sandwich on the coffee table. She needed reassurance. She needed someone to get excited, hold her hand and plan with her. Because she was scared that, if left on her own tonight, she might talk herself out of the best plan—the only plan—she had for making a baby.

Horrifyingly, she felt tears spring to her eyes. Immediately she looked down at her clasped hands, trying to squelch the tears before Mitch could see them. Fear and longing quarreled inside her, each trying to win, and her emotions refused to be shushed.

Mitch watched Elaine's shoulders begin to quiver. He saw tears drop from her face to the bare legs she'd crossed on the couch. His frustration didn't dissipate; it mounted.

As a divorce lawyer, he was used to women's tears. Having grown up with a sister, he was even used to the monthly march of the hormones. But those were noisy affairs, and Elaine's weeping was, well, *weeping*. Quiet, heart-wrenching, almost… hell…noble.

He didn't know what to do.

Scraping a hand through his hair, he swore, realizing he was doing a lot of that lately. "All right, look, I'm sorry. I didn't realize you had your heart so set on this One-Four-Five…" He forgot the last digit.

"Seven," Elaine choked out.

He scowled. "Right. Seven." Elaine kept her head down,

so he couldn't see her expression. With great reluctance, he glanced again at One-Four-Five-Seven's sheet. What did she see in this guy? What was so terrific about his gene pool? So he liked amusement parks; did that qualify him to be a father? Not that he was actually going to be one, Mitch reminded himself somewhat smugly. He felt like pointing that fact out again to Elaine, but he didn't want to keep repeating himself. Instead, he said, "I knew an English major in college. Walked around with his head in the clouds half the time. No sense of reality."

Rubbing her nose with the napkin she'd brought for her sandwich, Elaine looked at him over the top of it. "*I* was an English major," she informed him and burst into tears again for no obvious reason.

The noisy, not-noble kind of tears this time.

Chucking the idiotic donor pages, Mitch strode to the sofa, sat down and pulled Elaine into his arms. He had no idea whether she wanted to be there or not, but he held her to his chest, feeling her little fists trapped between their bodies, feeling her face pressed to his increasingly damp shoulder.

Though he was used to seeing a woman cry, he wasn't used to doing much more than nudging a box of tissues her way. He had no idea if he was doing this correctly. Probably he should say something.

"No one will blame you if you forget this whole idea."

The crying turned into a wail. Or maybe it was a growl. She shoved away from him, hard, gave him an extra sock in the shoulder, unfolded her legs and stood. "Does the concept of a biological clock *completely* escape you?" She gestured broadly, glaring at him with outrage. "You and your male plumbing! Can you try to put yourself into a woman's shoes for *five seconds* and think about what it's like to have this drive, this, this *hunger* to be a mother, to start a new life in your body and hold a child to your breast, to believe that's why you were put on this planet and then to know that if you don't do it soon you are going to be totally out of luck *because your ovaries are shrinking every second?!!!*"

She stood over him, breathing hard, beautifully furious and obviously demanding a response. Mitch was still trying to get past the holding-a-child-to-your-breast image.

He stood. "All right, I still don't understand this. If you wanted a child so much, why didn't you have one when you were married?"

"Because I wanted it to be right for both of us. I had a picture of the perfectly happy family in my head, and it didn't include a reluctant husband." Using the napkin again, Elaine blew her nose noisily. She wagged her head in what appeared to be disgust. "Expectations can absolutely ruin your life. I should have done exactly what I wanted to."

Mitch frowned heavily. It was common knowledge at the firm that Kevin's second wife was glowingly pregnant. Did Elaine know?

Mitch studied Elaine. It wasn't difficult at all to imagine her glowing with pregnancy.

"Are you honestly ready to raise a child on your own?" A thought occurred to him, and he narrowed his eyes. "Or is your family in support of your decision?"

Mitch saw her gaze dance away. He recognized the uncertainty in her eyes before she looked at him squarely again, but with a confidence that was obviously strained. "This time," she said pointedly, "I'm not waiting for anyone's approval."

Walk away, the voice inside his head advised him sagely. This was not his business, and she didn't want his interference, anyway. So she'd be a single parent, on her own, possibly with no emotional or financial support.

Not his business.

Of course, he knew what a disaster single parenthood could be from the child's perspective, but that was still *not his business.*

"All right." Giving her a wide berth, he strode to her front door. "You know what you're doing." She was a big girl. She hadn't asked for his protection or advice. Didn't want it; didn't need it. Fair enough.

Mitch put a hand on the screen to make his escape. This was as good a way as any to end their association. He was going to be smart for once where she was concerned. He would go home, get out of his suit, grab a beer, put his feet up. His stepmother would move into the duplex this weekend, Elaine would choose a sperm donor and he wouldn't have to know about any of it, except from a very safe distance.

He looked back at Elaine briefly. "Call Portland Property Management if you need anything," he said gruffly. "Same company you worked with before." *Before I was enough of an idiot to think you needed my help.*

Elaine nodded at him, a barely perceptible jerk of her head, and not before he noted the flare of surprise in her light hazel eyes. He ignored the sudden, infuriating feeling that he was abandoning her.

Returning the nod as abruptly as she had delivered hers, he pushed open the screen and walked away.

Chapter Seven

If she didn't want his interference, why did she feel abandoned?

Elaine stood in her living room, fairly certain she was, at this very moment, entering pcri-menopause, because she felt a little nuts, she really did.

Mitch had turned the duplex over to a property management firm. He hadn't returned her call earlier in the week when she'd phoned to inquire about his rib injury. He was no longer going to try to talk her out of becoming a parent through artificial insemination. He was severing their ties, which was exactly what she wanted.

She was happy. No more Mitch Ryder equaled a greatly simplified life for Elaine Lowry. Thank goodness. *Thank goodness.* You betcha.

She refused to even entertain the stupid bereft feeling that was, at this moment, assailing her. She was hormonal and couldn't count on her feelings to be rational. But she could count on her actions.

Reaching down to the coffee table, she picked up the plate with her sandwich, ignored the protest in her tummy and took a big bite of the BLT. Dinner. Exactly what she needed: A little protein, a little fat to keep her brain cells operating in peak shape.

She took another bite, ignoring the plump and utterly incomprehensible tear that rolled down her cheek.

She barely heard the screen door open, again.

Mitch stepped halfway across the threshold, a tall well-clad container of smoldering frustration and annoyance.

Elaine turned her head, her mouth full of food, eyes swimming.

With one hand Mitch held the screen door open for himself; with the other he gestured impatiently. "Aren't you even remotely curious what happened the night I took you home from the Heathman?"

Elaine stopped chewing. Her heart leaped to her throat. No way was she going to be able to swallow the sandwich in her mouth, so she shrugged.

A rather long moment passed, during which Mitch and Elaine's gazes seemed locked. Letting go of the door, he walked all the way inside the apartment, not stopping until he was directly in front of Elaine. He stood before her, his eyes unfathomable. Elaine watched his chest rise and fall beneath the perfectly tailored suit. A soundless sigh.

"Why am I here?" He appeared to be asking the question of himself and of her.

She tried to mumble "I don't know," but around the sandwich the sound emerged, "I—oh-oh."

Irony infused Mitch's expression. He took the plate from her and set it on the coffee table. "Chew and swallow," he told her, not without humor. Once she had dispatched her bite of sandwich, he asked again, his voice lowered until it was almost a whisper, "Tell me why I'm here."

She had no idea, and she couldn't think with his face so

close, his gaze so steady and searching. "You tell me," Elaine whispered back.

When his fingers threaded through the upswept hair at the nape of her neck, she didn't resist in the slightest.

He kept his eyes open—and so did she—until the moment his lips touched hers. From first brush, the kiss packed as much intensity as any kiss she'd ever experienced. His hand cupped the back of her head, holding her close, ensuring the thoroughness of his exploration. When the embrace ended, his fingers slid slowly away, leaving her hungry for his touch again.

Mitch looked as intent when the kiss ended as he had when it had begun.

"Now we both know why I'm here," he said. The breath he took was deep and ragged. "Let's sit down."

Elaine's legs felt about as solid as grape jelly, so sitting sounded like a good idea. Nodding, she led the way to the couch.

She perched rather hesitantly toward the edge of the cushion. Mitch seated himself more squarely, but not too close, and he didn't touch her. When the silence persisted beyond the length of time her wired nerves could handle, Elaine spoke first. "I'm not sure what to say. That—" she gestured to the spot where they'd stood during the kiss "—was unexpected."

"For me, too. I hadn't planned on kissing you again." He didn't sound exactly happy about it.

"Again?" A lump formed in Elaine's throat. "Then, that night…"

Mitch's brow rose. After a moment, the tiniest curve tickled his lips. "Ah, yes, that night." He shook his head. "Tragic that you have no memory of it. A fact which I suppose should threaten my masculinity."

She didn't even bother to fill the pause. Her whole body had started to quiver at the end of the kiss. Her pupils were probably still dilated. He knew exactly how much he had affected her. And he liked it.

When she refused to indulge him, his smile grew. Leaning back, he crossed his arms over his broad chest and nodded slowly. "That night," he said, picking up the thread, "we did kiss."

A thousand butterflies beat in Elaine's stomach. "What else did we do?"

The moment she uttered the question, Mitch's eyes darkened a shade. His smile inched just a bit broader, and Elaine felt the heat from the look he was giving as if her blood had been set on fire.

I knew it, she thought. *That's why I'm having all these feelings for him now. We did have sex.* Before Mitch, she'd only had one sex partner in her entire life. To her, the words "casual" and "sex" were mutually exclusive. So naturally her body responded to him the moment he came near. It was a Pavlov's dog kind of thing.

As Mitch's posture became more relaxed and his expression more roguish, Elaine's awkwardness intensified. Unconsciously she inched farther toward the edge of the sofa cushion. When Mitch leaned toward her suddenly, she almost tumbled off.

"How badly do you want to know?" He looked like a pirate, calculating and wicked, as he studied her. "More to the point. What will you give me for the information?"

Elaine blinked. "But you just gave me the information," she blurted then realized her error. *He* hadn't told her; her body had. To his quizzical gaze, she explained, "Obviously something happened or you wouldn't think you had information worth dangling in front of me."

"Mmm." His eyes narrowed. "That's true. So what you have to decide is whether you're interested in the details."

"What kind of details?"

"Where? When? How often?"

"How often?!"

He nodded, adding, "And what you said. You do like to chat."

Elaine stood, and it wasn't easy, because her knees were

knocking like canastas. "That's not true! I never—" Her eyes narrowed. "You're teasing me."

"Am I?" He grinned. A full, beautiful, unrestrained grin.

Slowly Elaine's knees stopped knocking; her heart, however, pounded harder. "Aren't you?"

He shrugged.

Elaine crossed her arms. "All right, what do you want?"

Mitch patted the cushion beside him, nodding his approval when she sat. "Do you remember Christmas 2002?"

She frowned. "Christmas? What does that have to—" *Ohmigod. Yes, she did remember...*

He nodded. "I thought you might."

The legal firm at which both Kevin and Mitch worked had hosted an open house Christmas party that year. The office had been packed with lawyers, secretaries, family and other guests. The lawyers' personal offices had been open to encourage a cozy, personal feeling, and Kevin had been in his element— schmoozing, leading personal tours, pouring drinks.

Elaine had been left to fend for herself in the crush of bodies, which she'd done agreeably for the first two and a half hours, but then she'd wanted nothing more than to escape the beautiful people, the relentless smiles, the chitchat.

She'd found a closed office, knocked and, receiving no answer, cracked the door to creep inside. The room had been dark, but the huge windows at the far end revealed a sparkling view of Portland at night, illuminating the winter evening and beckoning to her. Sighing with pleasure and relief, Elaine had moved to the window, intending simply to stand and gaze out, when a voice made her jump.

"Are you lost?"

Mitch had been sitting in his desk chair, also staring out the window. When he'd spoken from directly behind Elaine, she'd yelped, whirled around and tangled a high heel in an electrical cord. Mitch had leaped from his leather swivel chair to reach for her as she began to fall. Elaine had grabbed him too hard, sending him sprawling back into the chair...with her on his lap. All in all, the whole thing had seemed reminiscent of a Cary Grant-Katharine Hepburn movie.

Mitch watched the memory register in Elaine's eyes. He recalled exactly what it had felt like to hold Elaine on his lap and in his arms. He remembered the trembling in her body, the way her soft lips formed a stunned *O* in the shadowed light. He remembered that, before he'd escaped to his office, watching her had been the only enjoyable part of the evening.

Sometimes he wondered whether he'd agreed to represent Kevin in his divorce from Elaine partly to ensure that she would remain off-limits.

"That night in the office," he said to her now, hearing his voice roughen, feeling his muscles tense as the answer became hugely important. "Would you have let me kiss you?"

Elaine's shock was apparent. Her lips parted, closed, and she swallowed. "That's it? That's what you want to know?"

He'd had no idea when he'd first started the game that this was the question he was going to ask. Now he nodded. "That's what I want to know. The truth for the truth. Nothing less."

Elaine's breath quickened. The Christmas party was so long ago. She knew she could claim to recall only the broadest actions of that night, but not her thoughts, not her feelings.

Nothing less than the truth.

Mitch's eyes and voice compelled her. Nothing, however, prodded her more than her own feelings and her curiosity about how he would react to her answer.

"I would have let you," she said, her voice surprisingly even.

From a distance, there would have been no visible change to Mitch's demeanor, but seated near him on the couch, a mere half foot away, Elaine saw the satisfaction in his eyes, the almost imperceptible nod of assurance, the flash of purely masculine victory.

He reached for her hand and stood at the same time. "Walk me to the door, Elaine."

"What?" She resisted, but he tugged her along while she

protested. "Do what? That's not fair, you—you big traitor! You as good as lied. You're supposed to tell me—"

As they neared the door, Mitch turned without warning, pulled her hand until she tumbled toward him, and wrapped his arms around her. Without asking permission this time, implied or expressed, he lowered his head and kissed her as thoroughly as she'd ever been kissed in her life. A breeze from the open door swirled around them while Elaine felt a heat inside that promised to reduce her to cinders.

He broke the kiss when he was good and ready, which seemed to be an eon later, certainly enough time for a new world to be created. She became aware of his hands on her back, supporting her. His face was only inches from hers. "Nothing happened the night I took you home," he told her, his voice a velvet caress. "I helped you take off your shoes and put you to bed. Then I left. If we had made love that night," he said with a confidence that could have moved mountains, "you would have remembered."

Later, Elaine wondered how she'd kept herself from falling when he let her go. Or how she'd refrained from calling him back as he walked out the door.

Elaine's OB-GYN worked Saturday mornings. A true convenience when Elaine had to schedule an appointment and didn't want to miss work. A pain in the rear, however, on this Saturday morning when she wanted nothing more than to lie in bed, reliving yesterday evening and avoiding all reality.

The reality was that her baby plan was moving forward.

"Dr. Crandall would like you to start charting your cycle this month so that we'll be ready to go as soon as you choose a donor." Megan, Dr. Crandall's nurse practitioner, phoned early Saturday morning to advise Elaine. "When a woman over the age of thirty-five decides on alternative insemination, we don't like to waste even a single useful cycle."

The implication being, of course, that a woman over thirty-five might not have that many more "useful" cycles left. Elaine murmured something agreeable into the phone.

"Do you have an ovulation predictor kit?" Megan asked.

"No. I thought I'd take my temperature."

"Temperature and other physical markers are all helpful, but the kits are simpler and more reliable." She named a brand Dr. Crandall recommended. "Use the first day of your next cycle as a starting point, and notify us when you've chosen a sperm donor. We'll be ready to go as soon as you are." Elaine identified the sound of paper shuffling then Megan added, "Oh, Dr. Crandall also wanted me to mention a class you might be interested in. It's called New Baby Care. It's given several Saturdays a year, and it's terrific for picking up the basics in baby care." She named the registration fee. "That covers two people, so you can come alone or bring someone."

Thanking the other woman, Elaine returned the phone to its cradle on her nightstand and hunkered down against her pillows. Her next logical step would be to throw on some clothes and run down to the drugstore to buy the recommended kit.

She glanced at her clock—9:22 a.m. She bet she hadn't slept more than a couple hours all night.

Sliding lower beneath the sheets, Elaine stared at the ceiling and recalled last night's kisses one more time. Her whole body tingled, but tingling nerves were not enough to halt her plans. Mitch wasn't a family man. He dissolved family ties; he didn't cement them. And not that she wanted to beat a dead horse, but a woman with a child in her heart would be foolish to ignore red flags when they were waving in front of her face. Been there, done that.

It took great self-discipline to push off the quilt, get out of bed and begin the day, leaving her memories—and her fantasies—behind for now.

By 10:00 a.m. Elaine was showered, dressed in a long-skirted sundress and sandals and antsy to get out of the house. She had a slice of toast in her mouth as she pulled her front door shut and locked it and hadn't even let go of the knob before a petite woman with ivory skin and big blond hair styled like one of Dolly Parton's wigs pounced on her.

"Hi, darlin', I'm Vicki LeBeau, your new neighbor." Vicki spoke with a lilting southern accent that matched her appearance perfectly. She stuck out a beautifully manicured, bejeweled hand. Elaine didn't even have the chance to lower the toast. "Goodness, what's that in your mouth?" Vicki asked, large blue eyes widening beneath expertly penciled brows. "Please don't tell me that dry ol' cracker is your breakfast?" The curvy blonde tsk-tsked. "You girls worry too much about your figures. A crust of bread's no way to start the weekend. Why don't you come over to my place?" She plucked the toast from Elaine's mouth and grabbed her hand, hauling her next door.

Elaine stumbled along, disoriented, as if she'd stepped out of her apartment and into someone else's conversation. "Have you moved in already?"

Vicki sounded like an exotic bird when she laughed. "It wasn't hard. I just opened the door and stepped in! All I brought with me was a few suitcases and my stainless steel cookware. I drove down from Bellevue. That's just outside of Seattle, have you ever been there? See, at first I was going to fly, but then I said to myself, 'Vicki, honey, you are going to *need* a car if you are intendin' to nurture your independent spirit in a new city.' And I am intendin' to, so I did drive my car. Also, I got to bring all my stainless steel this way. I simply can't cook on anything else, can you?"

Elaine was breathless after the bubbling monologue, even if Vicki wasn't. They were in Vicki's apartment before Elaine could inhale deeply enough to respond.

The exquisitely furnished room was a perfect expression of the ultrafeminine blonde. A love seat in a pastel floral print sat cozily in front of the brick fireplace, which had been painted a soothing cream. The walls were coated in palest blue. Beautifully framed watercolors and a Thomas Kinkade that looked like the real thing hung on the robin's egg walls.

"This is lovely," Elaine said, thinking of the plain off-white walls in her living room. "But, um, Vicki, if you only arrived this morning, how were you able to decorate?"

"I didn't, honey." Vicki's laugh trilled again. "My stepson did it all for me, bless his heart. He knows what I like. Once he knew I needed a place to stay, he was so helpful, and, well, I suppose I did act the teeny weeniest bit helpless about this move, but it's so *big!* Emotionally speaking, that is. I mean, I'm leaving my husband, and I've been married longer than I was single. You girls today are so independent. I took a quiz in *New Woman* magazine last month, and I flat-out failed 'Can You Live Alone And Like It?' So this is kind of like going to college for me!"

By the time Vicki finished this last monologue, they were standing in her kitchenette. There hardly seemed to be room for her beloved stainless steel pots and pans, but Elaine watched, fascinated by the exuberant, ageless blonde as she began immediately puttering about the small space, placing a fry pan on the two-burner stove, pulling eggs, bacon, green onions and a block of cheddar cheese out of the refrigerator.

Mentally tallying the grams of cholesterol she'd consumed since embarking on her health food regime (and subsequently craving every fat-soaked snack she could get her hands on), Elaine knew she should stick to her dry toast and her errands this morning. She was sure, however, that Vicki would be wounded if she begged off of breakfast. That was no way to begin a relationship with one's neighbor. So when Vicki brought out cornmeal, white flour, buttermilk and a stick of butter to make cornbread, Elaine resigned herself to a week's worth of lemon-dressed salads to compensate for what she was about to eat and asked what she could do to help.

Soon she was companionably whisking eggs, grating cheese and greasing a cast iron muffin tin as per Vicki's instructions.

"So your stepson went apartment hunting for you?" Elaine asked while Vicki stirred cornbread batter with a fork. Bacon sizzled and popped in a small skillet and even the nutty aroma of the raw batter made Elaine's stomach growl.

"Well, it wasn't much of a hunt." Vicki grinned, more than willing to chat again now that breakfast preparations were well under way. "I mean it was kind of the obvious place. Don't get me wrong, though, I am *so* grateful to Mitchell for offering me his little pied-a-terre and not even charging rent until I get my finances sorted out. I did insist on paying something each month, though. Family's got to look out for each other, but of course Mitchell and M.D. are really Daniel's family and my stepfamily, and I don't want to take advantage."

Elaine's head swirled. She actually felt a bit faint. "You're Mitch's stepmother."

Vicki nodded as she poured batter into the muffin cups. "Didn't I say that right off?"

No. She hadn't. Over the next half hour, though, while they waited for the muffins to bake, Elaine learned enough about Mitch and his family to make her feel like a voyeur.

"Mitchie was twelve and M.D. was seven when Daniel brought me home. We'd already gotten ourselves married in Vegas, *not* by Elvis or in one of those horrible drive-thru's," she stated adamantly, shuddering at the thought. "I knew I was gonna be a momma to Jack's kids, and no way was I gonna let my wedding day remind me of ordering a Big Mac. Becoming a momma was serious business to me. I wasn't a whole lot older than the kids, to tell you the truth, but I figured they'd been without a momma and I'd been without a family so long that we'd just take to each other like chicks to feed."

With her hands cupped around a pretty china teacup she'd unpacked earlier that morning, Vicki inhaled the bergamot aroma of her favorite Earl Grey tea and sighed regretfully.

"It didn't happen that way?" Elaine surmised.

Vicki shook her head. "Not hardly. Their momma is a journalist and loves to travel. She'd left when M.D. was still a tiny little baby, and by the time I entered the picture M.D.'d already decided she didn't need a momma, and she didn't want one."

Vicki toyed with a lace doily that covered the creamer. "She never has changed her mind."

The genuine sadness in Vicki's voice made Elaine wish she had some words of comfort to impart, but from what she remembered about Mitch's sister, she and Vicki were about as different as Laurel and Hardy. "What about Mitch?"

"He wasn't too much better at first, but then I think he started to feel sorry for me." The timer on the oven buzzed, and Vicki rose to check the muffins. "About a year after I moved in, I was ready to move right back out again because I was just so frustrated. We never ate together as a family, no one would go to church with me, I couldn't discipline the kids worth squat."

She broke open a muffin, sniffed the steam, pronounced them done and fired up a pan to make the omelets. "I think Mitch must have overheard me talking to his daddy and telling him I was going to leave, because the next day he had himself and Emmy all dressed up and sitting at the breakfast table, and he told me, serious as can be, that they needed to go to church that day." She chuckled at the memory. "That boy could always get to my heart."

"Are you and Mitch close now?" It was impossible to pinpoint Vicki's age. There were times—when she laughed, for instance—that she could be Mitch's date and no one would blink an eye. There were other moments, though, when Vicki looked weary, and Elaine would have guessed that she was on the evening side of fifty.

At first glance she looked like she belonged on a chintz sofa, with a fluffy white dog snuggled against her and a cutesy mixed drink in her hands. Yet now she was toiling in the kitchen at her own insistence, and she looked just right here, too.

Confidence infused Vicki's movements as she made the omelets. The same could not be said of her voice as she replied, "I don't think you could call me 'close' with any of those danged Ryders. They're all so blasted independent! But Mitch is always there if I need him. For the easy things, anyhow."

Elaine frowned. "The easy things?"

Vicki shrugged. "I appreciate this place, don't get me wrong, honey. But giving material things is easy when you've got them. Givin' your heart—that's a whole lot harder, and that is not something any of the Ryders has been too successful at." Her tone had turned bitter. Instantly she put a hand over her lips. "I shouldn't have said that. I'm talkin' too much. Oh, it's just all so danged frustrating! I spent twenty years thinkin' I could be a good enough wife and a good enough stepmomma so they'd forget whatever upset 'em so bad that they stopped lovin'. But you can't change a person's basic character. I learned that in therapy, and it's why I'm here. Nothin' and nobody is going to make Daniel Ryder open up and get seriously vulnerable. The eggs arc ready."

Elaine blinked at the segue. Suddenly Vicki was a crystal ball to Elaine's own future. Both women had only narrowly escaped a sterile, emotionless life. Neither knew if her new life was going to be better. Only one thing seemed sure: they'd both concluded that being alone by choice was better than being alone in a relationship.

"I like my eggs soft," Vicki said. "The Ryders like their eggs practically dehydrated, so I been eatin' them that way for years, but I can't stand a dry omelet, or dry anything. Is that okay with you?"

"Yes, fine. Thanks." It was funny, the way Vicki kept referring to "the Ryders," as if two decades in a relationship with them still didn't qualify her as one. Why was connection to another person, to a family, so hard to achieve?

Elaine loved her immediate family—her mother, father and brother. She'd always assumed that creating a family of her own would be a simple matter of falling in love, having children, making sure everyone knew he or she was loved. It wasn't that way, though. Connection, true connection, took place between souls, and there was no formula for making that happen. Still, she hoped…

"Did you ever think about having a baby of your own?" she asked as Vicki slid the omelet onto a plate.

After a moment's surprise, Vicki's upturned lips expressed a wealth of irony and sadness. "You bet I did. But Daniel didn't want any more kids, and now it's too late. I've already started my change."

Elaine's heart beat too hard. Briefly, she closed her eyes. Yep, like looking into a crystal ball.

Vicki transferred half the omelet onto a second plate, adding a corn muffin and a handful of strawberries she'd pulled from the fridge. As she set the plates on the table, a knock sounded on the front door. "I'm not expectin' anybody," she murmured, frowning. "You get started," she told Elaine. "I'll be right back."

Vicki was gone only a few minutes. When she returned to the kitchen, she held a long gold box and wore a bright, mischievous smile.

"Well," the blonde drawled, her original cheer restored. "This here's proof that I most certainly do talk too much. 'Cause I can see I should have spent a lot more time askin' you about yourself instead of jabberin' on about me." She held out the gold box. Elaine stared at it dumbly. "It's for you," Vicki urged, nudging it into Elaine's hands. "The young man who delivered them tried next door then came here when you weren't home. I signed. Hope you don't mind."

"For me?" Elaine was still frowning. A clear label with white lettering read The Enchanted Florist. She hadn't received flowers in years.

"Aren't you going to open it?" Vicki was bouncing on her toes, as giddy and enthusiastic as a sorority girl. "Do you want privacy?" she asked as an afterthought, trying to be polite yet so clearly disappointed by the possibility of missing the unwrapping that Elaine had to laugh.

Once she'd eased the lid off the box, both women gasped. Settled inside were a dozen long-stemmed pink roses interspersed with another dozen miniature yellow buds. Elaine removed the envelope tucked into the bouquet, flipped it open and read the card inside.

"To memories. Losing them…and making them." There was no signature to the card, but Elaine didn't need one. She blushed from her head to her toes.

Vicki leaned forward to peek at the note. "How romantic! Are they from your beau?"

Elaine looked up, having trouble at first in applying the question to herself and Mitch. "What? No!" She resisted the urge to fling the flowers aside. The box felt like it was on fire, teasing her, daring her to keep breathing normally. "I don't have a beau." How could she possibly explain her relationship with Mitch to his stepmother? "The flowers are a joke."

"A joke? Who sends roses as a joke?"

Elaine shifted uneasily. "Some people."

Vicki appeared confused at first then scowled. "But that's like blasphemy. Roses are the universal symbol of love."

"Yeah, well…" She fit the cover onto the box again, overriding Vicki's protest that the bouquet—joke or not—ought to be trimmed and arranged in a vase right away. "Look," Elaine pointed out, "each stem is in its own little vial of water. I'm sure the flowers will be fine 'til I get them home." She set the box on the floor next to her feet and took a stab at shifting Vicki's focus. "Mmm, I'm starving, and this all looks so delicious." She took a bite of the omelet and rolled her eyes. "This is perfect, Vicki."

Reluctantly, Vicki sat, but she wasn't about to let the topic of romance drop. Not with twenty-four velvet-petaled roses egging her on. "Do you date much, Elaine?"

Elaine leaned over her plate as she coughed. "Date? No." She wiped her mouth with the linen napkin Vicki provided. "No. I'm recently divorced."

"Oh. How recently?"

"It's been official for nine months, but it was over quite a while before that."

Vicki stopped eating. Her eyes lit with the kind of zeal only an inveterate matchmaker would experience upon hearing that someone's marriage had ended. "Well, you are definitely ready to start dating then, aren't you? A woman as lovely as you, I bet there are men falling all over themselves to court you and send you roses—real ones, not joke ones. You know," she said, warming to her subject, "I bet my stepson would know somebody. He works in a big office downtown just bursting at the seams with lawyers. Why, I bet if I asked him—"

"No! Absolutely not." The couple bites of omelet Elaine had managed seemed to swell like sponges in her stomach. "I mean, thank you very much, but no. No men."

Vicki leaned across the table to touch Elaine's arm. She nodded. "I understand. I told myself the same thing the day I left Dan. But if we women stop believing in love, who's going to keep romance alive? You certainly can't count on men to do that. Besides, honey, you're young and you're resilient. I can see that in you. You can't stop believing in love."

"I believe in love. I'm just not interested in men at this point in my life." Elaine infused the statement with as much finality as she could, and thankfully, that seemed to do the trick.

Vicki went stone silent. Her heavily fringed blue eyes blinked several times. Then her brows lifted, and she breathed, "Ohhh!" She nodded. "Well, my heavens. I read about this in *Cosmo,* I think. Or was it *New Woman*?" Her neat brows drew together as she tried to remember. "Anyhow, it was an article entitled 'The New Backlash of Divorce.' That part I do remember."

Breaking open her muffin, Elaine halfheartedly began to butter it while she waited for Vicki to convince her that a disinterest in dating was merely a temporary response to her failed relationship.

"According to the article," Vicki continued, "we women spend our formative years watching fantasized versions of love in the movies and reading fantasized versions of love in books, so naturally we develop certain expectations about romance. Know what I mean?"

"Mmm-hmm."

"And then we meet a man who fits the picture in our heads of what a man should be, and—*boom!* Before you know it, we've gone and married ourselves a fantasy, not a real man at all. We marry our *expectations,* see what I mean?"

"I think so."

"And then when the reality turns out to be something completely different from what we wanted, we get all frustrated and disillusioned."

"Naturally."

"Right! It's perfectly natural to be all disgusted and upset when Mr. Right turns out to be Mr. Giant Mistake. Why it's enough to turn you off of romance all together."

"Sure is." Elaine bit into her buttery muffin with growing pleasure. Maybe Vicki wasn't going to try to talk her into dating, after all.

Ignoring her own breakfast, Vicki folded her arms on the table and bobbed her head. "Which is why it's totally understandable that you'd become a lesbian."

Corn muffin crumbs blew across the table as Elaine choked. Vicki brushed a crumb off her bosom and patted Elaine's arm. "It's all right. According to the article, for some women it's just an experimental phase until they can stand the sight of a man again. But for others…" She shrugged. "I've been to church every Sunday since I was old enough to walk through the doors, but I'm not here to judge, and I don't think anyone should."

Elaine tried to form a reply, but her vocal cords were in shock.

"We all deserve companionship, no matter what. Right?" The doorbell rang, and Vicki rose. "Be right back." She sent Elaine a beatific smile. "You eat up now." She exited the kitchen then poked her head back in. "By the way, I saw the movie *Kissing Jessica Stein.* I thought it was very nice." She disappeared again.

A moment later, Elaine heard her open the door then exclaim, "Mitch, honey! What a nice surprise."

Elaine hung her head. *Oh, no.*

After a few murmurings from the living room, Vicki reentered the kitchen with Mitch following behind. Standing next to the petite blonde, he appeared even larger and stronger than usual. Wearing a soft V-neck pullover that emphasized the width of his shoulders and exposed a sprinkling of dark chest hair, he appeared surprised but not at all unhappy to see Elaine. Planting himself stolidly inside the femininely appointed kitchen, he cocked his head in acknowledgement and smiled. How could a man dedicated to dissolving marriages manage to make a woman feel safe just by looking at her?

And Elaine did feel safe. Foolishly, ridiculously so.

I am not a woman meant to be alone, she thought, and for the first time in months the notion no longer frightened her. It was simply a fact. She was meant for marriage, family. Love.

How she was going to find that and keep it was another story.

Mitch's brown hair looked damp, which meant he'd showered recently and that put all sorts of ideas into Elaine's head. She looked down and toyed with her omelet.

"I know you two know each other," Vicki said in lieu of introducing the landlord to his tenant. "Mitch, you're in time for breakfast."

"I've eaten, Vicki."

"Well, corn muffins and a dish of strawberries, then." His stepmother bustled about, preparing a midmorning snack. Elaine watched her, seeing clearly that she loved the mom role she'd never completely satisfied. She and Vicki weren't so different.

Pouring a small amount of real cream onto the strawberries, Vicki said to Mitch, "You're just in time to help me out, too."

He arched a brow. "How?"

"Well, you know me. I'm just a terrible matchmaker."

"That's true," he said, accepting the bowl of fruit. Since

there were only two chairs at Vicki's small table, he leaned against the kitchen sink and winked at his stepmother. "You are a terrible matchmaker. I can't think of a date you ever set up that didn't end in combat."

"Oh, you!" Vicki flicked her hand at him. "That is not true."

"Who's your victim this time?"

"Elaine."

Elaine's gaze flew to Mitch. He stopped eating, raised his head and stared at her. "Is Elaine agreeable to this?"

Vicki answered. "Of course. Elaine is a special case, though, which is why we need your help. I'm so new to Portland that I hardly know anyone yet." She resumed her seat, took a bite of the now lukewarm eggs and chewed. Unfortunately that didn't break her stride. "You, on the other hand, work in that nice big office with all those lovely people. Didn't you tell your father and me that a hotshot new attorney joined your firm?"

Mitch's brow knit in confusion. "Sydney Corey."

"And I believe you mentioned that Sydney is single?"

"Yeah." He shook his head. "Vicki, Sydney is a woman."

Vicki nodded enthusiastically. "I know."

Mitch regarded his stepmother warily. "...who likes other women."

"I thought you mentioned something about that." She clapped her hands. "Isn't this lovely?" She reached over and took Elaine's hand, which was currently frozen around her fork. "I'm so pleased to be part of your search for fulfillment." She looked up at Mitch. "Lots of women become lesbians after divorce, you know. That's something you should be aware of in your line of work. Why, after talking to Elaine and seeing how comfortable she is with it, I may become one myself!"

Chapter Eight

*Oh, Lord. She was going to have to perform the Heimlich
again.*

Mitch became the second person to choke in Vicki's kitchen
that day as he gagged, presumably on a berry. And, actually,
now that she took a good look at him, his face was nearly as
red as a strawberry. Surprising herself, Elaine smiled.

Vicki slapped her strapping son-in-law on the back. When
he stopped coughing, he stared at Elaine, eyes bugged wide.
For a moment she thought he might truly believe…

Mitch had entered the kitchen with his usual confidence,
causing her, also as usual, to quiver like jelly inside. Now he
was the one off-kilter. A curl of sneaky enjoyment swirled
through Elaine.

Carefully dabbing her mouth, she folded her napkin and set
it on the table. Slowly, as if she didn't have a care in the world,
she bent to pick up her roses.

Smiling at her hostess and her landlord, Elaine approached
them. ''Thank you so much for breakfast, Vicki. You're an

excellent cook.'' Leaning forward, she placed a relaxed kiss on the other woman's cheek. When she pulled away, she stared Vicki comfortably in the eye. ''Thanks for being so understanding about…everything. I hate to rush off, but I have a couple of appointments today.'' She hugged the flower box close to her chest. ''I'd better put these in water before I head out.'' Turning to the man standing speechless before her, she murmured, ''Good to see you again, Mitch. You do seem to have an alarming tendency to swallow the wrong way. Maybe you should look into that, if you don't mind my saying. Bye now, you two.''

Elaine turned and strolled out of the apartment, leaving two silent Ryders behind her. She was barely able to contain her laughter.

By eight that evening, she was home again, sitting on her couch, reading the instructions to the ovulation predictor kit she'd bought on her doctor's instructions. What a day it had turned out to be.

After visiting the drugstore, she'd headed for her parents' place in West Linn, making a brief stop at Zupan's beforehand to pick up a very rich, very expensive chocolate-raspberry mousse cake. It was her father's favorite, and Elaine had chosen it with an ulterior motive. As soon as she decided on a donor, her pregnancy plan would be all systems go. It was time to tell her family what she was about to do, knowing the whole family would be in attendance for a late-summer BBQ.

Even under the influence of sugar grams approaching the three digits, it hadn't gone quite as well as she'd hoped.

Elaine stared at the instructions of the predictor kit, reading them over in English and then, for the heck of it, in Spanish. Then she tried to make them out in Japanese, which she had never even studied. It was better than having to think.

No one, it seemed, in her exceptionally loving, always vocal, wonderfully supportive Jewish family was going to shout, ''Mazel Tov!'' when she chose her donor. They seemed to understand how desperately she wanted a baby, and she'd ex-

pected their questions, of course. She hadn't, however, anticipated their blatant misgivings.

Elaine sighed. She felt as blue this evening as she had rosy
and bright this morning.

When the doorbell rang, it took several moments to push up
off the couch. For some reason, the sight of Mitch on her doorstep didn't particularly surprise her. She'd thought of him on
and off all day, had even wished he was the kind of friend she
could call for a phone hug.

Nudging open the screen door, she offered a wan smile. "Hi.
Come in." She turned to walk back to the couch. Mitch followed her in.

Plopping onto the sofa, Elaine slumped against the cushions.
Mitch watched her with his hands on his hips. Without a word,
he went into her kitchen, opened the refrigerator and a drawer
and returned with her last pint of Ben & Jerry's and two
spoons. Seating himself next to her, Mitch pulled the lid off
the ice cream and handed her a spoon.

She looked from the chocolate-caramel swirls to Mitch.
"This is exactly what I need."

"I know." He tilted the pint toward her.

"How do you know?"

"I've seen your freezer. Also, you had Cherry Garcia on
your breath the night I kissed you."

"I did not."

He shrugged. "Maybe not." Scooping his own spoon into
the container while she hesitated, he said. "Dig in, Lowry."

They ate in silence for several spoonfuls. "I've decided to
take back my maiden name."

"Good."

"It's Rozel."

"Elaine Rozel." He nodded. "Good name."

They'd left the front door open. Soft summer air made ice-
cream eating the perfect activity.

When Elaine had eaten enough, she scooched down into the

cushions and toyed with her spoon. "Have you ever felt like you fit in completely with a group of people?"

Mitch swallowed his last mouthful, took her spoon and joined it with his in the half-empty container. He reached for a section of newspaper lying on a corner of the coffee table then glanced back. "Is this today's?"

She waved. "I'm done with it."

Pulling it forward, he set the ice cream on the paper and turned so that he faced Elaine squarely. "Explain."

Her brow furrowed. "I went to my parents' house today. They live in West Linn, so on the way, I drove past Marylhurst College, and I saw a group of girls out for a jog. They looked *so* young. They must have been freshmen. I thought, wow, they have everything ahead of them. And then it hit me that freshman year of college is the perfect time of life, you know? Because you don't even have to be certain of where you're going yet. Just being there, exploring your life, you're already right where you're supposed to be. And I watched them jog by, and I was smiling, and then suddenly I got so sad. When I got to my parents' house, it got worse."

Mitch rested an elbow on the back of the couch. She had his full attention. "Why?"

She tried to explain how she'd felt when she'd walked through the house and into the backyard, where everyone had gathered for the barbecue. Her brother, Sam, and their father stood near the grill, arguing good-naturedly over how much charcoal it took to make an adequate fire. Her mother and sister-in-law, Carolyn, knelt by the edge of an inflatable pool, coaxing Sam and Carolyn's daughters to come out before they shriveled like prunes. And Elaine had stood there, looking at the faces she'd known for years, remembering what it had been like to be seven and ten like her nieces, the center of your own world and of your family's. She'd looked at Sam and Carolyn and at her parents. They had all had a job, a purpose, and no doubt about where they fit into the family.

"But you had a doubt?" Mitch asked.

"Not about how they see me. Oh, it's hard to articulate."
She looked up from under her lashes. "It probably sounds like
your garden-variety identity crisis. Woman gets divorced, won-
ders *Who am I now?*"

Mitch moved his hand from the back of the couch to the
back of Elaine's neck. He leaned closer, studying her face.
Slowly, he shook his head. "There's nothing 'garden variety'
about you."

Elaine took a breath. If she had been a garden, she would
have said the sun had just burned her right down to her roots.
The sizzle rising inside her weakened her legs; it made her
stomach quiver and her arms feel like rubber. Mitch's eyes
locked on her lips again. She asked herself whether she was
going to pull back, and the answer came swiftly: *no way.*

She inched forward, relaxing her lips into what she hoped
was an irresistible pout. She could smell a hint of chocolate
from the ice cream on his breath and felt her heart pound with
the anticipation of kissing him.

Mitch stroked his thumb along the side of her jaw. His
fingers remained buried in the hair at her nape, but he didn't
pressure her, opting to wait until she moved nearer. Elaine was
ready for their kiss—oh, boy, was she ready—and she was
determined to make it a *real* kiss this time, in which she was
a full participant rather than being caught by surprise. This
could be, a small voice inside her suggested, the most mind-
blowing kiss of her life.

Only when they were close enough to feel each other
breathe, did Mitch bend his head toward hers. They kept their
eyes open, and as they moved toward contact, Mitch whispered,
"No identity crises for you, Elaine. Never doubt it. You're a
vibrant—" He placed an agonizingly light butterfly kiss on her
cheek. "—beautiful—" The corner of her mouth was tickled
by his tongue, and when he pulled away to speak, she thought
she would burst. "—lesbian."

He swooped down for the real thing then, a kiss as rich and
full-bodied as the finest wine. The hand at the nape of her neck

slid up to cup the back of her head, their mouths angled and opened and…

It took Elaine a moment to realize what he'd said. Speaking was out of the question, so she balled a fist and socked him in the arm.

"Ow!" he complained against her mouth, but loosened his hold enough for her to pull back.

Prepared to scorch the man verbally for toying with her, Elaine took one look at the maddening, sexy grin that crawled across his face and knew they were even. She'd teased him; he'd teased her back.

"Did you know all along?" she asked, her tone indicating that she would be miserably disappointed if he said yes.

"I know you better than you realize."

"Oh." She could have brought up the choking fit. She could have mentioned that his eyes had bugged out so far, they'd risked popping from their sockets. But why squabble?

There were other ways to show Mitch Ryder that he didn't know her really, yet. At all.

Slipping a hand between them, she placed it on his chest, right over his heart. That might not have been enough to make his blood pump faster…except that her hand was under his shirt instead of on top of it.

Mitch's skin was warm. His chest, smooth and muscled. Smiling up at him, she slid her palm to the right, exploring his pecs, making a leisurely journey until she came to the small hard nub in the center. Resting her left hand on his thigh, she found that delicious place where his neck curved into his shoulder and used her tongue and her teeth to mark the spot while her fingers proved beyond a shadow of a doubt that a man's nipple could be every bit as sensitive as a woman's.

His heart pounded so hard it almost bounced her hand off his chest. Mitch's breathing became audible. "Elaine…" he began raggedly, but she was through talking.

"Quiet," she commanded a moment before she rose up so their mouths were level.

And the kiss she gave him absolutely was the most mind-blowing kiss of her life.

She was in control for untold moments, until Mitch turned the tide. Hands went everywhere, lighting fires that lips put out…almost. Mindlessly, it seemed, Mitch began to press Elaine forward to lie on the cushions, but Elaine pressed back until he was lying flat and she was on top of him. They kissed and touched some more, and finally Elaine lifted her head. She was breathing like she'd run the Portland-to-the-Coast marathon.

"I haven't made out like this since the back seat of Todd Ellenstien's parents' Cutlass in 1984," she panted.

Something flared in Mitch's eyes, and the hand on her back moved confidently down to cup her buttocks. Under her shorts.

"You've *never* made out like this," he growled, pulling her against him and proving it.

They almost rolled off the sofa.

Somehow managing to keep one hand under Elaine's top while she returned the favor, Mitch sat them both up. He looked her seriously in the eye. "Well?"

Licking her lips, Elaine nodded. "Give me five minutes." Untangling herself, she got up.

"Make it two," Mitch said, and she headed, not quite steadily, for the bathroom.

While she was gone, doing whatever a woman did before a man ripped off her clothes and hauled her into bed, Mitch sat up, raked shaky fingers through his hair and exhaled long and loudly to slow down his heart. Damn, she was going to kill him.

Elaine Lowry was turning out to be the biggest surprise of his life.

He was thirty-six, and he'd seen enough divorces—including his own—to know that the only relationships he wanted began and ended without hearts becoming involved. His heart was not involved now. He and Elaine liked each other, but liking wasn't the same as loving. What surprised him was that Elaine was willing to take it to the next level without a declaration of anything—love, like, some kind of commitment. She was surprising the hell out of him, making it almost impossible to read her, because he was so hot he could hardly think straight. And maybe he should. Maybe he should use this breathing space to—

"Was that fast enough?"

He looked up. Elaine stood in the hall, wearing a long T-shirt with a huge happy face on the front. Her feet and her legs up to her thighs were bare; even with the rest of her covered by one hundred percent opaque cotton, Mitch was sure he'd never seen a sexier sight in his entire life. If he didn't take her to bed soon, he was likely to damage himself permanently.

Standing, he walked toward her, feeling a bit too much like a panther on the hunt. Reaching for her hips, pulling her toward him, he couldn't deny a rush of proprietary satisfaction as a shiver ran through her. Mitch lowered his head to kiss her, but paused short of her mouth. "He's staring at me." He nodded to her breast and belly.

Elaine looked down at the big iron-on smiley face. "This was the first shirt I saw."

Shaking his head slowly, Mitch murmured, "I hate an audience." Then he reached for the hem of the tee....

She slept like a cat.

Mitch stood by the side of Elaine's bed, clad only in the jeans she'd helped him discard last night, and watched the woman he'd made love to smile and stretch in her sleep. She extended both legs out straight beneath the light covers, flexed her arms, then curled happily back into a child's pose.

He wanted to dive back in bed and have his way with her all over again. Or let her have her way with him. It had definitely been reciprocal.

It had definitely been amazing.

He glanced at the clock and shook his head slightly. It was nearing 9:00 a.m. on Sunday morning. He hadn't slept past seven even on a weekend in ten years. Generally he was out of bed by five, had his workout, a shower and was seated at his kitchen table or in his home office by six-thirty to catch up on work. Caffeine was unnecessary; he'd had early-morning insomnia since he was a teenager.

Today he'd slept until a couple of vociferous birds outside Elaine's bedroom window had awakened him. He'd opened his eyes to find himself lying on his side even though he'd been a back sleeper all his life. One of Elaine's knees had been wedged between his. Her head had rested on his arm, which had gone numb from elbow to shoulder, and his free hand had held the curve of her hip. As far as he could remember, he hadn't made a conscious decision to sleep here. All he knew was that it would have seemed unnatural to leave.

He had no idea what she planned to do with her Sunday, but if it was up to him, they'd spend it together. And he had several notions about what they could do…

First, though, he wanted to get her away from the duplex, from the interested eyes of his stepmother. He didn't want an audience, didn't want questions, didn't want commentary about him and Elaine. He simply wanted her. And a whole day with her.

Moving quietly, he exited the bedroom, intending to make a small pot of coffee to help Elaine wake up. They needed to shower and sneak away soon, while Vicki was at church, and he had no doubt that his surprisingly reverent stepmother had already found a house of worship to visit. If her habits hadn't changed over the years, she would stay for coffee hour after the service, which gave him time to lure Elaine away with the promise of a late breakfast in Charbonneau.

The coffeemaker was in plain sight on the kitchen counter. Easily locating the filters, Mitch grinned when he found her stash of coffees; she had enough varieties to go into business for herself. She'd even written comments on the bags, like "Makes a great mocha" and "Yummy iced." Mitch smiled at the labels. And now he knew two of her weaknesses—sugar and caffeine.

The image of her arching back and gasping in shock during a certain moment in their lovemaking last night encouraged him to amend his estimation: now he knew *three* of her weaknesses.

He was gathering mugs, sugar and spoons when he remembered there was a half-eaten pint of ice cream sitting on her coffee table from last night. Swearing, he hustled to the living room. Thankfully his mental image of thick, sticky puddles of melted chocolate ice cream were unfounded. The paper he'd placed beneath the carton was wet and limp, but the carton itself was intact and the table didn't appear to have suffered much.

He stooped to clean the minor mess, moving aside a small collection of papers and a long, narrow box that looked vaguely pharmaceutical. Not that Mitch was particularly interested, or particularly nosy, but his glance fell immediately to the printed words, "Ovulation Predictor Kit."

It took a moment for the meaning to sink in. He shuffled through the papers and saw that they were how-to instructions. A dark foreboding tightened his chest. Before he'd arrived last night, Elaine had been looking at the instructions for some device that was going to tell her whether she was *ovulating*?

The sexual assertiveness that had surprised—and delighted—him last night took on a different color now. Yesterday he'd seen a side of her he'd never anticipated. Today he knew why.

His hand fell to his side, but he held on to the small box. Courteously, he had shut the bedroom door…so his lover could sleep undisturbed until the coffee was ready. It opened now, emitting Elaine, clothed in another of her extra-large T-shirts, her thick hair mussed from sleep—and play; her drowsy eyelids were half-shut. She leaned against the door frame.

"You were right." A smile that was wholly fun and flirtatious widened her lips. "I've never made out like that."

Stretching her arms overhead, she reminded him of what was beneath the cotton. "I'm starving. Are you?"

The predictor kit felt hot in Mitch's hands. Had she used birth control last night? She hadn't said so; he'd just assumed that was what she was doing when she excused herself to go to the bathroom. His jaw tightened as his teeth ground together.

"We didn't use a condom." Not the greatest morning-after line, but he was so angry he could barely speak.

Elaine blinked at him, ostensibly not comprehending him at first. Then—and he had to give her credit for this—she actually blushed.

Sheepishly, she shrugged, crossing her arms in front of her. "No. I didn't think about that. I'm…fine. I mean, I'm sure I am. Are you?"

"Yes. But you're supposed to ask *before* you go to bed with someone new."

Someone new. Elaine frowned at the words and at Mitch's tone. She'd awakened this morning so replete, so supremely relaxed and content…and a little bit giddy…that she wasn't quite certain her feet touched the ground when she walked. Mitch, on the other hand, looked like…well, like he was about to be a really big butthead. "Are you angry with me or you?" she asked.

Mitch felt himself glaring. Good question. He was angry at her for using him to further her plans and desires, and with himself for falling for it. "I just fail to see how an obviously experienced woman could 'forget' to ask her partner to use protection. You're not a kid, after all."

Uncrossing her arms, Elaine planted her fists on her hips. He should have quit at "obviously experienced." She could take that as a compliment. The "not a kid" part he could stuff. She hadn't even gotten naked for her GP since the divorce. This was a poorly chosen moment to remind her that she was no longer twenty. "Am I missing something here? Did you *offer* to use a condom? 'Cause speaking of experience, you're not exactly wet behind the ears."

Her point must have penetrated, because he didn't respond right away. After a couple of beats, he grunted something that sounded like "okay" then raised a long slender box. "I found this."

As he was still a good ten feet away from her—and her eyes were no longer kids, either—Elaine leaned forward and squinted. "That's my ovulation predictor kit." She must have left it on the coffee table last night, which was a little embarrassing, but why was he angry—

Oh, no. He didn't think… He couldn't—

"I suppose it's pointless to ask whether you're on birth control."

He did. He thought she'd made love to him in order to get pregnant! Elaine's eyes narrowed as she viewed last night's passionate lover in a whole new light. She opened her mouth to ask him how a generally intelligent man could be such a gigantic boob, but quickly reconsidered. That was easy. Way too easy.

Consciously relaxing the muscles that had stiffened throughout her body, Elaine took a deep breath and let it out on an ingenuous sigh. Clasping her fingers loosely in front of her, she shrugged and giggled. "Caught me. You know how badly I want to get pregnant, and you happened to drop by, and, well…" She gestured to the kit. "I am ovulating. It'd be a shame to waste it, right? And those kits are expensive! You don't want to have to buy them month after month after month." She rolled her eyes. Hurrying on before he could give voice to the explosion building behind his expression, she cooed, "A woman dreams about who the father of her children will be, you know, and I've always hoped my babies' daddy would be a big…strong…masculine…*arrogant…condescending…FATHEAD!*"

Striding forward, she planted herself in front of him and pressed her knuckles to her hips again, if only to keep them from connecting with Mitch's jaw. "What do you think, that I'm so desperate I'd trick someone into getting me pregnant?

You think there's so little sperm in the world that I need yours? A man who is *totally* unsuitable?''

''What do you mean? I'm as suitable as those donors you were looking at.''

''You are not. They *want* to do this.''

Mitch sneered. ''Anonymously.''

''So? At least they're willing to help.''

''Willingness,'' he huffed. ''That makes them more suitable than me?''

Elaine held up a hand. '''Scuse me. Are we arguing because you think I want you to get me pregnant or because you think I don't?''

Mitch tried to reply, but stumbled to a halt. He had to admit it: life was a whole lot easier when he'd thought she was a lesbian.

What the hell was the matter with him? Why was he arguing with her? ''You did use birth control, didn't you?''

He watched her face get red. She didn't have to answer; he knew he'd accused her unjustly. The awareness was a weight on his chest.

Visibly controlling herself, Elaine walked to the front door, opened it and said, ''Goodbye.''

Mitch cringed. For a man who made his living by being verbally astute, he hadn't done too well this morning. Was there any way he could salvage this day?

Setting the boxed kit on the coffee table, where maybe he should have left it to begin with, he said, ''I made a mistake.''

Elaine cocked her head. ''Really? I didn't notice. G'bye.''

''Elaine—''

''Mitch,'' she interrupted. *''Go...now.''*

Frustration burned in his gut and tightened his muscles. Admittedly he had ruined the morning. Admittedly he hadn't clearly thought his accusations through. He'd stopped thinking clearly the moment he'd touched her last night. Obviously, touching her again was not the answer, not if he wanted to get his head straight. That left two options: talking or leaving.

One look at Elaine told him talking was out of the question. As for leaving…

"Don't wanna," he said. Besides, he didn't have his shoes. And he wasn't wearing underwear.

She scowled ferociously. "Too bad. I want you out."

Mitch took a few steps toward her. Slow ones. He didn't want to upset her. "No, you don't."

"What? Now you're telling me what I want?"

He took another step. "Naw."

"Mitch, I am getting really…really…angry."

He believed her. Her eyes flashed like bottle rockets.

Two more paces, and he was standing right in front of her. He bent toward her.

"What," she asked tightly, through a clenched jaw, "do you think you're doing?"

He smiled. "*Showing* you what you want."

Her nostrils, he noted, flared when she was peeved. "You arrogant, egomaniacal—" she began.

Up close and personal, he could see the outline of her body beneath the T-shirt. "Are you wearing underwear?"

That stopped her for a good two seconds. "—shallow, insensitive, supercilious—"

"No, I didn't think so." He kissed her then, burying the words with his lips. He held her face first, gently, but his hands ached to be filled with more of her. No point in trying to hide it, he rationalized, moving one hand up to cup the back of her head while allowing the other to explore the lush round curve of her butt.

Responding immediately, his body surged against his jeans. *Nope,* he realized, *no panties.* He knew she was coming around when her hands clutched his bare back hard enough to cause pain and one smooth, bare leg raised to wrap around his.

Chapter Nine

Elaine shifted, wondering how in the world cold oak had managed to seem perfectly comfy only moments before.

Fishing around with the hand that wasn't trapped beneath Mitch, she groped for her T-shirt on the living room floor. Where had they—

"You're lying on it." Mitch answered the unspoken question.

"Oh."

He moved so she could retrieve her shirt. Eschewing modesty—hardly appropriate after the past twelve hours—she sat up, drawing the shirt over her head and tugging it into place. At least they'd exhibited enough self-restraint to close the front door.

Mitch sat up beside her. Modesty didn't seem to be an issue for him at all. He ran his fingers through his hair, bent a knee and hung an arm over it. Without turning her head, Elaine snuck a last peek at his nude form. Beautiful. Lightly tanned and not a spare inch of flesh to spoil the musculature.

Stretching her own legs out straight, she clasped her hands, resting them on her knees. "Mitch?"

"Hmm."

"This time we *weren't* using birth control." He tried not to stiffen. She could feel him trying. "On a reassuring note, I am ninety-nine percent certain that I'm not ovulating."

Since she was no longer looking at him, she couldn't see what he was thinking, but his thigh flexed. Twice. Hard. That didn't seem like a good sign.

He made a guttural noise that sounded like throat clearing, but may have been an attempt not to choke. "About what I said...before—"

"You know what?" Elaine interrupted. "We don't have to talk about that." Finger-combing her hair into place, she endeavored to sound both modernly casual and upbeat. "Really. We're good." Turning toward him then, she reached out to pat his knee, but somehow, now that she was partially clothed, the move seemed too forward.

Mitch's arched brow formed a question mark to punctuate his somber expression. "Really?" He sounded doubtful.

Smiling brightly, Elaine bobbed her head. "Absolutely." Her knee popped as she stood. She was too old for sex on the living room floor.

Making sure the hem of her long tee was smoothed over her thighs, she gazed at the man who had, in one night and half a morning, given her the greatest physical pleasure of her life.

She was too old for sex without love.

"What time is it?" Elaine squinted at a miniature grandfather clock perched on one end of the mantel. "Is it that late already? I've got to go." She started toward the bedroom, deliberately not turning around as she heard Mitch get to his feet and pull on the jeans he'd discarded earlier.

"Go where?" he said, masculine displeasure evident.

"I have a brunch date."

"Cancel it."

"I can't." She refused to break stride as she gathered clothes in her bedroom. Mitch was only halfway down the hall as she scooted into the bathroom. "Hope you don't mind if I shower first." Consciously endeavoring to control this moment, she shut the door on any comment he cared to make and raised her voice to be heard through the wood panel. "Help yourself to anything you want in the kitchen. I'm busy the rest of the day, but let's talk sometime this week. Okay?"

"So was he gone by the time you came out of the kitchen?"

"Yeah. Wouldn't you have been?"

Gordon scooped up the last of his goat cheese and artichoke heart frittata and gave the question some thought while he chewed. "No," he decided. "I'd have hung around pathetically, hoping to pry out information about where you were going, with whom you were going to be and—if you were seeing another male—whether his waist was larger than mine. But that's me."

Elaine leaned back in her chair, raised her face to a perfect midday sun and smiled. "Why can't I fall for an uncomplicated man like you?"

Gordon chortled, the same chortle he'd had since grade school. If she could have, Elaine would have frozen this moment in time, sitting with her best friend at an outdoor table at Papa Hayden's, listening to the usual weekend bustle on NW Twenty-Third and watching Gordy contentedly add to the waistline he perpetually bemoaned. Simple. Easy.

"So, have you 'fallen' for him?"

Uh-oh. "It's an expression."

Gordon frowned at her over a glass of chardonnay. "I would prefer that you plead the Fifth, rather than answer my questions with platitudes. After all, this is me you're talking to, the only soul who knows you wore a girdle under your homecoming gown."

The waiter arrived, affording Elaine a minute's breathing space while he cleared their plates and took their dessert order.

Gordon refused to let her sit in peace for long. "Come on,

'fess up. If you weren't so committed to home, hearth and headaches, spit up and sleepless nights, would you be able to have a relationship with this guy?''

Amazing how swiftly a body could respond to a thought. There had been a time last night—a couple of times—when Elaine had pictured her near future with Mitch: laughing at a movie, snuggling as the weather changed, making love again— maybe next time at his place—and her body had felt awash in comfort and safety and excitement. Now the mere suggestion of "future" made her cells dance a jig.

"I'm thirty-seven, Gordon—"

"You look young."

"Thank you. And I intend to live the rest of my life the way that *I* want, instead of twisting myself into a pretzel so some man can stay in his comfort zone.''

"What is his comfort zone?''

"I don't know. But it isn't home, hearth and headaches. I can tell you that.'' She recalled Mitch's expression when he thought they might have risked pregnancy. He'd been furious.

In her heart of hearts, she knew she had been falling for him. That frightened her enough to make her draw a line in the sand. "Mitch was…a crazy night of passion. That's all.''

"That's 'all'? I'd pull my own wisdom teeth for a night of passion.'' He eyed her askance. "Suddenly you think they're so easy to come by?''

"That's not what I meant. I meant that Mitch Ryder is my walk on the wild side. A one-time ride on the giant roller coaster. You know? Go once and you're exhilarated, but ride it too many times and you'll upchuck your lunch.''

"An excellent analogy.''

"I know.''

The waiter dropped off a gorgeous slice of Sacher Torte and two espressos. Papa Hayden's was famous for its desserts, but suddenly Elaine felt a bit queasy.

While Gordon dug into the cake, she plowed through the large shoulder bag she'd set by her feet.

"Look," she said, clearing a space atop the table and arranging the papers so Gordon could see them. "This is the list of donor profiles. I've narrowed the choices down to a couple of pages. Help me pick one."

Gordon's eyes had barely had a chance to focus before he and Elaine were interrupted by a lilting southern drawl. "Elaine, is that you? 'Course it is. Well, my goodness, somehow I wasn't expecting to run into you today! My, isn't Portland a small world?"

It was if you were foolish enough to pick a restaurant on NW Twenty-Third Street, the brunch capital of the city.

Trying not to cringe visibly, Elaine summoned a smile for the stepmother of her own personal roller-coaster ride. She liked Vicki, but now was not the time to introduce the woman to Gordon. Elaine knew her friend would love to continue talking about Mitch. Meeting his frilly blond stepmother—and, oh Lord, M.D., too—would only add fuel to Gordon's fire.

"Hi, Vicki." Elaine folded her hands primly and nodded up at the other women, hoping her manner would bring this to a quick end. "Out shopping?" Vicki, her hands full of shopping bags bearing the names of eclectic boutiques, stopped in front of the table. Mitch's sister stood beside their stepmother, also carting bags, but looking less than thrilled.

"We've walked our poor feet to the bone this morning!" Vicki exclaimed. "I simply lose track of time when I'm on a mission."

"Mission?"

"Finding all the little knickknacks that turn a house into a home. And buying an outfit or two for Emmy." To M.D.'s acknowledging grunt, Vicki responded, "It's a stepmother's prerogative to see her daughter in a dress occasionally." Vicki turned toward Gordon, obviously expecting an introduction. When Elaine complied, reluctantly, the effervescent blonde said, "Are you Elaine's beau?"

Gordon was charmed instantly. He stuck out a hand and when Vicki took it, kissed her creamy white knuckles. "Actually," he leaned forward as if about to share a secret, "no. I'm the gay male friend she can hang with while never having to leave her comfort zone."

Vicki stared, speechless for a moment, then broke into a beautiful grin. "What a delicious idea. I may have to get me one of you!"

"Join us?" Gordon gestured to the empty chairs at their table.

Elaine tried to kick him, but bashed her toes into the table leg instead. "Ow!" She turned her grimace into a feeble smile when they all turned to her. "Charley horse."

No second invitation was necessary for Vicki. She dropped her bags beside the nearest chair. "We could certainly use a coffee break."

"I could use food." M.D. peered at Gordon's plate. "What's that?" Her eyes rolled when he told her. "Oh, my God. Is it good?"

The women were seated and ordering desserts before Elaine could think of a way to save herself. She sensed her ship was about to suffer a fatal blow when Vicki looked at the papers on the table and murmured—somewhat belatedly, Elaine thought, "Oh, dear. What are we interrupting?"

"Nothing," Elaine insisted, reaching for the papers to stuff them into her purse and keep a private matter private, but Gordon, the rat, beat her to them.

"As a matter of fact, you arrived at the perfect moment. We can definitely use your help." Blithely he ignored the narrow-eyed, clench-jawed glare Elaine sent him. "We were just about to pick a donor."

"Donor?" Vicki beamed approvingly at Elaine. "Are you involved in a charity function?" Enthusiasm made her wriggle in her chair. "That's something I know *a lot* about. I was on the sponsor selection committee for the Bellevue Belles City Beautification League. I had a knack for picking the people I knew would dig down deep when the time came and give, give, give."

Gordon wagged a finger at his new friend. "That is exactly the kind of discernment we need." The big lug was so obviously enjoying this, Elaine wanted to reach over and smack him. "Although," he continued, "this may be a bit outside the realm of your previous experience. You see, Vick…M.D.… Elaine isn't working for a charitable organization. Her needs are a little more—" he tilted his head thoughtfully, "mmm… personal."

Elaine closed her eyes. "Oh, dear God."

"You know the term 'biological clock'?" Gordon continued. "Well, Elaine here has a clock that's been tickin' like a time bomb." He raised his fork and swung it like a crazed pendulum. "Tick-tick-tick-tick-tick-tick-tick. So she's decided— with my whole-hearted support and blessing—to shun romance, eschew the fable we call 'true love.'" He set the fork down, earnestly leaning across the table. "And to get herself knocked up by a stranger with good DNA. Make sense?" The women bounced their gazes from Gordon to Elaine like spectators at a Wimbledon final. "Your mission, should you choose to accept it, is to help me help her. Ladies, it is our solemn duty, no less than our privilege to help our girl here pick a sperm donor." He sat up straight and smiled. "It ain't the Bellevue Belles City Beautification League, but you know what they say." Gordon winked at Elaine. "Charity begins at home."

The Pick-A-Daddy Party was about to begin.

How Elaine had allowed this debacle-in-waiting to progress so far, she didn't know. Perhaps because Vicki and even M.D. had shown great empathy for her desire to have a child? Perhaps because having witnessed Vicki's earnest enthusiasm, she'd feel positively churlish rejecting the woman's participation now? And perhaps because Vicki and Gordon were teaming up to prepare the food, so if nothing else they'd eat well while they discussed the relative merits of Donor One-Two-Six-Three versus Donor One-Zero-Four-Two.

She was due next door with her donor ID forms in five minutes. In addition to Vicki, Gordon and, surprisingly, M.D., Elaine's friend Bee Bee would be in attendance. Gordon and Elaine had met Bee Bee in college, and though she'd never been married, Bee Bee had outstanding "loser" radar; she could pick out the one guy in a thousand guaranteed to be a liar, cheat or all-around flake. It was agreed that whomever Bee Bee chose, Elaine would dismiss instantly.

Drawing a brush through her hair, Elaine gave her reflection a final okay, grabbed the papers off her dresser and headed for Vicki's. An ivory lace top that hugged her body and a sheer floral skirt with a flounce at the hem afforded the look she was after: demure yet confident. Maternal yet stimulating. PTA mom meets *New Woman* cover girl.

When Elaine stepped outside, the clear, balmy evening felt more tropical than Pacific Northwestern. It would have been a lovely night for summer sex. But that was neither here nor there. She hadn't heard from Mitch since this morning, and once she was pregnant, a tawdry night of pure sexual bliss would be in poor taste. More than likely, her trysts with Mitch were a done deal.

Ignoring the protest of her newly awakened inner lover, Elaine focused on the task at hand. Decide on a donor. Make the choice. Take the plunge. That was the name of the game this evening. It was the first step on the road to her dream. No time left for distractions. Focus, focus, focus.

Taking a deep breath, she knocked on Vicki's door.

Everyone was assembled. The party was already in motion.

Dressed in a colorful fiesta dress with tiered ruffles, Vicki embraced Elaine with the arm that did not have a giant margarita at the end of it.

"*Hola,* sugar pie! Come on in. Gordy and I decided on a Mexican theme. Here." She placed the frosted glass in Elaine's hand and ushered her in. "Oh, I'm so excited we're doing this! Imagine, in a few more months we could be planning a baby shower!" Elaine took a large swallow of the very strong margarita as Vicki announced, "Look who's here, everybody. The guest of honor has arrived!"

Bee Bee waved to Elaine from the love seat, a huge grin on her gamine face as she raised a copy of *Baby* magazine. M.D. sat in an attractive but uncomfortable-looking white wicker chair, tapping a foot, her characteristic nervous energy apparent even as she nursed a margarita. Taped to the brick fireplace behind the women was a banner printed with colored markers. It read: Daddy Pickin' Party.

In front of one window, where a spider ivy formerly resided, hung a piñata in the shape of a huge…male… *Oh, my sweet baby Jesus!*

"Is everyone present and accounted for?" Gordon emerged from the kitchen carrying a platter of nachos and looking suspiciously like Vicki, in a multicolored mariachi-style shirt atop insanely snug black trousers. "Marvy! We've got food, we've got drinks and we've got a little lady lookin' for Mr. Right in a test tube. Is this the way to spend a Sunday night or what?"

Elaine gaped. This had to be Gordon's brainchild. Vicki's apartment looked like a set from *Dirty Dancing: Havana Nights.*

Vicki clapped her hands. "All right, y'all. Have a seat around the coffee table. We're going to begin." Reaching behind the love seat, she brought out a box filled with what appeared to be brightly patterned notepads, a large poster and who knew what else. "Gordy and I decided that games might be a good way to start—don't you roll your eyes at me, M.D. Ryder. These here are games purposefully designed to awaken our dormant intuition. Now." She dug into the box, withdrawing the glossy poster board. "This first game," she said, holding the board so they could all see it, "is a lot like Pin The Tail On The Donkey."

In the egg roll game, during which participants pushed labeled hardboiled eggs across Vicki's floor with their noses, Donor 0940 was in a neck and neck finish with Donor 1385.

Using the prominent shnoz she'd steadfastly refused to alter despite her mother's heartfelt urgings, Bee Bee nudged 1385 to victory.

At the edge of the Persian rug, she raised her arms in a vee. "I knew it! I knew this guy was a winner." She pointed to Elaine, who sat on the floor, pink highlighter poised above the donor ID sheets. "Mark him down."

Giggling from the effects of her second industrial-strength margarita in under two hours and the insanity of the evening in general, Elaine put a wobbly fluorescent line over the potential future father of her child. "All right. We've narrowed the field to five, ladies and gentleman."

It hadn't taken Elaine long to give in to the mood of the evening. Now, in her current giddy state, the idea of choosing donors via Vicki's adaptation of parlor games seemed almost reasonable.

"Let's pick a winner from this group," she said, becoming almost eager.

Over M.D.'s enthusiastic cry of "Once more unto the breach, dear friends," which seemed to have nothing to do with the activities at hand and everything to do with the amount of tequila Gordon had poured into the margarita mix, the doorbell rang.

"I'll get it." Vicki stepped over the bodies of players trying to roll their eggs back the other way.

Drawing a bright pink baby on her paper, Elaine bounced her legs to the music pouring from Gordon's portable CD player while Vicki opened the door.

"Mitch, darlin'," she drawled in an accent that had thickened with every sip of the drinks she and Gordon had apparently started before the others arrived. "Well, fancy this. Look, ever'body, it's Mitch!"

Elaine froze at first following Vicki's announcement then whipped around so fast, she got a crick in her neck.

"Let's see now." Vicki put a finger to her lips. "Who don't you know? Um, Gordon? He's on the floor over there, eatin' the egg. And Bee Bee. She's…oh, my, look at her go." Vicki wagged her head. "That girl is an absolute athlete with her nose."

"Vicki." Mitch's tone was as dark as his expression. "What is going on?"

The blonde turned to her stepson. "We're havin' a party, silly. Want a taquito?"

"I thought you asked me to come over to check the faucet in your bathroom."

"Oh, that's right. I did mention that it has a teeny leak, didn't I?"

"You said you thought the plumbing was about to burst and begged me to look at it tonight."

Vicki nodded seriously, her pretty blue eyes wide. "Yes, and here you are. You are so predictable." She patted his arm. "Which makes you *such* a good landlord." Raising a hand, she waved broadly. "Gordon, are there any more eggs? Mitch needs an egg."

"Vicki. I don't want an egg. I— What the—?"

Mitch seemed to take it all in then—the hats, games and noisemakers littering the floor, his own sister standing with one foot raised on a chair and her arm straight out while she wielded a margarita glass like a sword and spouted something he vaguely recognized as Shakespeare. He saw a hanging piñata that looked so much like a portion of male anatomy he couldn't imagine what else it could be, and he saw Elaine, sitting rather demurely in front of the coffee table, a shiny, cone-shaped foil hat atop her head and her brow marred by an uneasy frown. Then his gaze lifted and he noticed for the first time the sign above the mantel: Daddy Pickin' Party.

"What the hell is going on in here?!"

Vicki cringed. "That was far too loud, sugar." She walked away.

Mitch's outburst didn't seem to faze anybody. *He* was fazed, though. He was confused and suspicious and…

He strode toward Elaine since his sister and stepmother

seemed to have gone crazy, and he didn't know the other people.

"Hello," she said quietly when he reached her. Her brow remained puckered.

"Hello."

"You came to fix the plumbing?"

Mitch crouched next to Elaine so she wouldn't have to crane her neck. And because he wanted to get closer. "Ostensibly. But I doubt there's anything to fix."

"Why did Vicki invite you then?"

An empty margarita glass sat on the coffee table. The pupils in Elaine's doelike eyes were dilated. Mitch had an impulsive urge to kiss her to see if she tasted like tequila. He hadn't kissed her in hours. After she gave him the boot this morning, he'd wondered if he was ever going to kiss her again.

"Maybe," he said, answering her question, "she thought the party needed another man to even things out."

"No." She wagged her head. "That wouldn't be it." Elaine pursed her lips in deep thought.

She was adorable. Mitch let his eyes wander over her lush breasts, cupped beautifully by the lace top, but not as beautifully, he recalled, as when his hands had cupped them. That sight had imprinted itself on his mind; probably indelibly.

Elaine's gaze shifted to Vicki and then back to Mitch. Her eyes widened and she leaned forward to tap his knee with a forefinger. "I wonder," she said in a rasp that was too loud to be a whisper, "if she knows what we did?"

Mitch smiled. In that moment, Elaine looked and sounded like a teenager concerned that she may have been caught necking by her parents. A slightly inebriated teenager. Then he realized his stepmother probably had seen his car sometime between last night and this morning—or why would she have hauled him over here for this…this…

"What is this?" he asked Elaine, realizing he still wasn't sure precisely what he was witnessing here, other than a gathering of people with really bad taste in party decorations. "What is a 'Daddy Pickin' Party'?"

Elaine smiled almost mischievously then shook her head. "You won't like it if I tell you."

"I'll like it less if you don't."

Elaine raised a sheet of paper, one he recognized, except that now the printing had bright pink lines over it. He barely stifled a curse.

Elaine slapped the paper onto the table again. "See? I knew you'd react badly."

"I didn't say anything."

"You made a face." She pointed at him. "You're still making it."

"This is incautious."

"Oh, but last night was cautious." Elaine reached for her drink, looked inside the empty bowl, shrugged and returned the glass to the table.

Mitch wasn't going to quarrel with her about last night. Or this morning. He didn't want to argue about it; he wanted to repeat it. What he did not want was to vie for her attention with a nameless, faceless Donor One-Three-Five-Seven. What he did not want was for her to become a mother the way she had planned, never mind why.

"I can't believe my sister is party to this," he growled, glancing around for M.D. *Traitor,* he wanted to add, but refrained.

"Emmy won Pin the…Tail…on the Donor," Elaine informed him blithely.

Mitch was speechless. There had to be some way to talk sensibly about this. But not, he realized, unless he got her away from his crazy family and her equally nutso friends.

"You want to come back to my place?"

Butterflies took flight in Elaine's belly. Back to his place. Only the two of them. She pictured an evening of smooching and cuddling. Of his incredibly warm palms heating her skin. Of snuggling into his neck. It was that pheromone thing.

Mitch waited for her answer. She took a deep breath and blew it out on the word. "No."

"No?"

"It wouldn't be right." It wouldn't be smart. Not if she wanted to keep her heart in one piece. "The party is in my honor," she said. "They're trying to help me."

Mitch glanced to where Gordon was peeling M.D.'s hard-boiled egg over M.D.'s fervent protests and Bee Bee was once more nudging her egg to victory. "You'd get more help from a Ouija board."

Elaine lowered her brows reprovingly.

The staccato clap of Vicki's hands curtailed further discussion. "Time for our last game, everyone. This will determine our final round of donors, and then over coffee and a scrumptious Kahlua cheesecake, we will decide on a daddy for Elaine's baby. All right now, get ready for the artichoke toss!"

Mitch looked at Elaine. He didn't have to say a word to communicate his opinion. Raising her chin, she glanced away.

When he stood, Elaine forced herself to sit still and let him go. She expected to hear the sounds of his leaving, but Vicki clapped her hands again. "Who's playing?"

Elaine nearly jumped when the first response came from right beside her. In a less-than-festive but resolute voice, Mitch announced, "I am."

Chapter Ten

Garbed in a tank top and cotton shorts, Elaine sweated to a Crunch abs, butt and thighs workout video. She was less interested, however, in whittling her measurements than she was in working out the anger she'd been lugging around since last night's daddy pickin', party poopin' fiasco.

She completed a set of squats and grunted rudely when the superhumanly fit video instructor suggested she had another ten reps inside her. Elaine had worked all day after a sleepless night. Maybe she should stop crunching her muscles and start crunching potato chips.

Swigging the water she'd set on the coffee table and reaching for the remote, Elaine pressed rewind to watch Ms. Perfect Tush workout backward.

Elaine had been furious since last night. After the artichoke toss, they'd all sat down to choose a donor, and Mitch had shot down every prospect Elaine had. Every single one.

Which, of course, was not surprising.

What was surprising was that he got everyone to agree with him.

On the profile sheet, one donor had reported that he played flamenco guitar and loved eggs and chorizo for breakfast. Mitch had whistled. "Lotta cholesterol in that sperm."

One donor was a vegetarian marathoner who had run across the U.S. barefoot. Mitch had pronounced him "a skinny loner with bad feet" and tossed the sheet over his shoulder.

Another donor's profile stated that he was a Phi Beta Kappa law student, top of his class, volunteered one day a week to tutor ESL students in computers and English and had written a term paper entitled *Hummable Mozart.* "An anal retentive perfectionist," Mitch had clucked sadly. "I hear that's genetic."

The others had started giggling, and then Bee Bee remembered an article she'd once read about a doctor who had substituted his own sperm for the donors' and no one found out until after who knows how many babies had been born, and now there were all sorts of siblings running around with the weird doctor's DNA. Then everyone began speculating on other potential mishaps until finally Mitch piped up again with, "But none of that's going to happen to Elaine. Is it?" And they'd all looked at her with wide, worried eyes.

So now, in addition to being furious with Mitch, Elaine was also completely disheartened. Her former confidence—which she'd clung to a bit too tenaciously, perhaps—seemed to be melting like candy dropped on hot pavement, and she was having a devil of a time scooping it up again. Not even Gordon had done anything to refute Mitch's dramatic caveats.

Tossing the remote control onto the sofa, Elaine stomped to the door to let more air into the apartment. Whether courtesy of her workout or her emotions, she was burning up.

She jerked the door open as Mitch raised his hand to knock on it.

They stared at each other.

"Hello," he said.

"Hello," she returned.

They stared some more.

Dressed in his business suit missing only a tie, Mitch appeared to have come directly from work. European tailoring enhanced his innate air of authority. She imagined his clients emerged triumphant nineteen times out of twenty, and that the few who didn't blamed themselves and not him.

When he raised a large white paper bag with a savory aroma emanating from it, Elaine felt like poor client number twenty. "Dinner," he said, watching her closely. "Shrimp curry, spring rolls and broccoli and beef with fat noodles. Can't remember what they called that one."

"Not hungry."

Following the mandate "Never let 'em see you sweat," Mitch showed no surprise. Nor did he back down. "You don't like Thai?"

Elaine stood with one hand on her hip, the other on the doorknob she refused to release. "Actually," she intoned, "I'm more in the mood for eggs and chorizo. Get my drift?"

Lowering the bag with good grace, Mitch smiled. "I think so." He nodded to her athletically attired body. "Have a good workout?"

"It was okay."

"So my plan was to bring dinner, you'd invite me in and we'd talk."

She gave him nothing. Dead eye.

"Alternatively, you invite me in, and I eat and run."

Still nothing. Elaine wondered if it would be awful to admit she rather enjoyed chinking *his* armor for a change.

Mitch squinted, getting serious. "What'll it take to get me through this door? Did I mention I had the restaurant throw in a couple scoops of coconut ice cream?"

She paused a minute more. "All right. We'll have dessert. Then you'll leave."

"You're a tough customer."

Elaine turned and let him follow her in. Briefly she debated showering and changing, then thought better of it. This wasn't a date. She'd said he could stay but a short while. She would stick to that. Even if her top stuck to her.

"Have I told you how sexy it is to see a woman sweat?"

She'd have told him to stuff the canned compliments, but his eyes revealed his seriousness.

Elaine took a seat at the dining table.

"You really want to start with the ice cream?" Setting the bag between them, Mitch opened it. "I know you're angry. If we start with the spring rolls, you'll have more time to chew me out."

The aromas wafting from the open bag made her stomach growl. She had done a lot of squats. "Did you bring plum sauce?"

Mitch dug through the bag, producing a small plastic container of sticky sauce. Elaine examined it. "There are chopped peanuts in there." She loved it when the sauce had little peanuts.

Picking up the small containers that obviously held ice cream, she rose to put them in the freezer and returned with plates and silverware.

Silently, Mitch opened all the containers and waited for her to serve herself. He sat at the table, watching her as she opted to use the chopsticks the restaurant had provided. "I like watching you eat."

"Oh, that's sexy," she said, having bitten into a shrimp. "Just what I always dreamed of—a man who likes the way I chew. Tell me if I dribble."

Warm laughter loosened more of the strain between them. "I didn't say that's *all* I like. Besides, eating is much more than chewing, Lainey. It's the way you hold those slender pieces of wood." He nodded to the chopsticks. "Like they're extensions of your own arms. The way you raise them to your lips. And close your eyes when you take the first bite." His voiced lowered to a subtle caress. "It *is* sexy. Don't underestimate the power of something as primal as a meal."

Hell. Elaine set her chopsticks down. Now he was seducing her over spring rolls and sticky rice. Calling her "Lainey." Dabbing her lips, she tried hard to avoid the sight of his smile; she didn't need this kind of confusion in her life. She'd already decided it…they…would never happen again. "Maybe I should start chewing you out now."

His eyelids half lowered. "You could. But will you respect yourself in the morning?"

She nodded. "I think so."

"I did say I'd let you take a few shots, didn't I?" He sat back. "Go ahead."

"I'm not going to sleep with you again."

He arched a brow.

"Ever," she clarified, folding her arms. "Not today, not tomorrow. Not ever again."

Something flashed in his eyes. Anger? Challenge? But then, surprising her, he simply shrugged. Reaching into one of the boxes, he pulled out a spring roll and dipped it into the container of sauce near her plate. "Yeah, I wasn't too crazy about the sex, either. Too much noise."

Unable to resist a well-baited hook, she asked, "Noise?"

After Mitch took his bloody sweet time swallowing, he nodded. "The truth is I'm not used to that degree of… vocalization."

"'That degree'?"

"The grunting." He pointed the spring roll. "The hollering."

"I did not grunt!" She hoped to God she hadn't hollered, either, with Vicki right next door, but it was a possibility.

Mitch shrugged. "Well, that 'uh-mmmm' sound you made. I thought that was grunting."

"That was a moan. 'Uh-mmmmmm' is clearly a moan."

"Oh. A moan." He nodded broadly then frowned in concern. "Were you in pain?"

"No. A *pleasurable* moan."

"Ah." Reaching toward her, he dunked a new spring roll and winked. "Good to know. At least one of us enjoyed it."

Elaine wanted to hit him. She wasn't a violent person, but she would have loved to at least throw something at him. "I didn't say the sex wasn't great—"

He grinned.

"But we can't have a relationship. I've never had sex without a relationship before, and I don't think it's right for me."

The smile slipped from his face. "We have a relationship."

Elaine regarded him doubtfully. "Relationship means 'the state of being related or interested. A kinship.' *Webster's New Collegiate Dictionary.* You can look it up. I did."

"You looked it up?"

"Yeah. I'm anal, okay? I admit it. But at least I'm not confused."

Mitch picked up the carton of rice and slapped a huge sticky portion onto his plate. "I'm not confused. You're saying all this because of the kid thing. What you persistently refuse to acknowledge, however, is that I'm trying to help you, like any friend would. A friend does not let another friend walk into a barbed wire fence without saying, 'Hey, look. There's a barbed wire fence.'"

Grabbing the rice, Elaine handed him the broccoli beef. "See, this is exactly what I mean. You still view my having a child as a mistake. You and I are totally incompatible. It's a good thing I decided never to sleep with you again."

Mitch stared at his tablemate long and hard. "Oh, we'll sleep together again. And I did not say having a kid was a mistake. Having a kid *with a stranger* is what's asinine." He set down the carton of food and wiped his hands. "Unless you're looking forward to answering the question 'Mommy, who is my daddy?' with 'I don't know, kid, but he sure liked chorizo.'"

Elaine scrunched her paper napkin, threw it onto the table and spoke through gritted teeth. "I have told you and told you, my baby's father will not be a total stranger."

"Hmm. You must not have looked up *that* word, then."

"And it is not asinine," she said, refuting his other attack. "Not if it's your only option before your last egg *calls it a night*. You know what your problem is? That these men are empathetic in a way you can't understand. They're sweet and giving."

Pushing his plate away, Mitch rose, looking incredulous. "'Sweet' and 'giving'? Who are you getting sperm from, the Easter Bunny? Elaine, these guys are getting paid."

"They don't do it for the money. They do it because they want to help. They understand the significance of their act."

"My God, you're a hopeless romantic."

Elaine stood. "You're a cynic!"

They faced each other across the table, breathing hard.

Mitch's eyes flashed. "Are you as hot for me right now as I am for you?"

"Totally."

Their gazes remained locked while they decided what to do. It didn't require Dr. Phil to tell them that more sex would solve nothing. On the other hand…

Mitch took a step right. Elaine's heart beat faster.

Then, in a moment of absolute clarity, her life with Mitch flashed before her. In a few months, maybe a year if they lasted that long, the sexual *oomph* would be history; they'd have quiet dinners in restaurants that served steak and vodka gimlets, and Elaine's fertility would have dropped another twenty percent.

"No," she said, taking a sidestep that countered his. "Nothing's changed. We're still…wrong."

A cloud of displeasure darkened his face, and she expected another rebuttal, but Mitch was through arguing. He nodded once, almost imperceptibly, then took several long, telling strides to the door, his body vibrating with restrained emotion. If he had to fight the urge to look back, he won the battle, because he stalked across the threshold and disappeared into the evening.

Elaine was less successful with the war raging inside of her, but she refused to regret her decision. She couldn't.

Her stomach churning, she left the table. Retreating to the living room, she threw herself onto the sofa and hugged a pillow.

She had just sent away the most exciting lover she'd ever had, and she was no fool. That kind of chemistry didn't come along every day. It was no comfort to Elaine that she knew she could fall for Mitch and fall hard. Mitch, whose eyes and whose humor warmed her to her toes. Mitch, whose touch made her shiver with goose bumps.

But falling for the man would not bring her a happy ending.

One of her all-time favorite daydreams involved taking her child to Disneyland for the first time. Seeing his or her little face light with wonder at the sight of Cinderella's castle and the Main Street parade and a life-size, walking Winnie-the-Pooh....

But the part of the dream she enjoyed the most was when she met her husband's eyes above the head of their child, and the two of them grinned and held hands, knowing they would do this again in a couple of decades or so, next time with their grandchild.

Knowing, too, it would all go by in the blink of an eye.

And when she was very, very old and her skin was pale and soft again, though crinkled with age, Elaine would look at her husband and together they'd remember the parents they'd been...and the lovers. In a hushed, timeless moment they would stare into the mirror of each other's eyes, and the past would seem as near as yesterday.

Curling onto her side, pulling the pillow close to her chest, she closed her eyes to let the daydreams carry her away, and if they were heaven then hell was surely the aching gap between the wanting and the having.

Four days later, Elaine was curled on the sofa again, but this time she was sound asleep, thanks to a liberal dose of extra-strength cold medicine.

She'd spent most of the week concentrating on the new computerized filing program at work. Her own life, including her need to make a decision about a donor, had been temporarily shelved.

Now it was raining, the weather a constant, pattering reminder that time marched on, summer turned to fall…and plans had to be realized or lost forever.

Two days ago she'd come down with the nasty cold that was going around the office. Even though she was physically miserable, Elaine had to cop to a secret relief that she was too sick to worry about anything more pressing than orange-flavored zinc tabs vs. cherry.

Insistent knocking on her front door roused her…slowly. She'd come home early, changed into her favorite pajamas and conked out. That had been around three. Lifting her head and her wrist, she squinted at her watch—six-fifteen.

"Coming," she croaked, pushing off the couch and shuffling to the door. Her poor head was pounding. "Hold your horses, hold your horses," she muttered, but when the door swung open, she squawked out a happy, "Sam!" Rising to her tiptoes, she flung her arms around her brother's neck.

"I hear you're sick," he said in the warm, deep voice she loved. "I brought chicken and matzo ball soup."

"You angel." She sniffled. "That's exactly what I want." Easily taking his hand, Elaine led him into the apartment.

"Cute jammies," Sam said as he followed her in.

Through the windshield of his car, Mitch watched Elaine hug a tall, slender man with dark hair. She seemed thrilled to see him.

Jealousy choked Mitch like a hand around his throat. He hadn't seen Elaine in four days, and in fact he hadn't come here today intending to see her; he'd come because a pipe in Vicki's bathroom really had burst this time. Now he had an overwhelming desire to storm Elaine's apartment.

All week he'd tried to concentrate on work, not something he'd ever had to worry about.

Exiting the car, he strode up the steps to Vicki's place. According to his stepmother, who enjoyed giving him daily play-by-plays on her new next-door neighbor, Elaine's baby plan was temporarily on hold due to the cold, but also, according to Vicki, who'd heard second party via Gordon, because Elaine was having second thoughts about using artificial insemination. Gordon reported that it was the mad doctor story that had gotten to her.

As he raised his fist to rap on Vicki's door, it suddenly occurred to Mitch that Elaine might have found another way to achieve her goal. A more...hands-on approach.

He froze.

With his hand still raised, he looked toward Elaine's door and shook his head, almost laughing at the ridiculous notion that Elaine might actually look for her donor among her friends or acquaintances. She wasn't the type to have casual sex. For any reason. She might *think* she'd had it with him, but what they'd done hadn't been casual. Not for her. In some ways, he knew her better than she knew herself.

Again he started to knock on Vicki's door. Again he paused.

Maybe he ought to stop in next door, though, to make sure she wasn't experiencing any of the plumbing problems Vicki was suffering through. Elaine might not want to bother him, after all, given the way they'd left things.

Mitch took a step toward the other apartment. Vicki opened her door, stopping him in his tracks.

"There you are," she said. "I thought I heard someone out here."

Turning reluctantly toward his stepmother, he saw that Vicki was ready to get down to business, dressed in pale blue overalls, a long-sleeved cotton top, and a kerchief she'd tied headband-style around her hair. Plumber attire, Vicki-style.

"I've got franks 'n beans bubblin' on the stove and a red-potato salad in the fridge. That seemed to fit the plumbing theme, don't you think? I hope your plumber gets here soon. I don't want the beans to dry out."

"Vicki, you didn't have to cook. He's coming over here after hours expecting to work, not have a picnic."

"I know, sugar, but everyone's got to eat." She grabbed him by the elbow. "Come in and tell me all about your day while we're waiting."

Mitch didn't have much of a choice. It was either sit down and talk to Vicki or explain why he was hell-bent on going next door. He wasn't sure he wanted to explain that to himself, much less to his ever-curious stepmother.

An hour later, Rick, the plumber, had finished the dinner Vicki prepared and was poking around her bathroom. Vicki was cleaning up in the kitchen and Mitch was standing way too close to the living room wall, listening for sounds from next door.

It was freaking humiliating, that's what this was. He grimaced, utterly disgusted with himself. He was going to wind up on the front page of the *Oregonian* as some nutso stalker. If Elaine had decided to cull for donors among her friends and acquaintances, that was her business, and of course she hadn't asked him, because she knew he'd say no in a heartbeat.

But the fact that she was willing to throw away all that was brewing between them—that ticked him off.

"Mitch, honey, I made some pecan sandies. You want— Mitch? What are you doing, sugar?" Wiping her hands on a dish towel, Vicki stared at her stepson with some concern and a lot of curiosity.

"Uh…I'm…listening."

"What for? Isn't Elaine's living room on the other side of that wall?" There was nothing naive in Vicki's question. Her expression was fraught with humor.

Mitch could practically hear the police megaphone: *"Step away from the wall, sir."* He nodded to Vicki. "Yeah, yeah. I wanted to see if I could hear any…plumbing sounds."

"There's plumbing in that wall?"

"I thought there might be."

"I guess that's why you're a lawyer, then, and not a plumber."

Vicki's knowing expression gave Mitch a lot more respect for his stepmother's acuity.

Waving her dish towel toward the chintz love seat, Vicki suggested, "Let's sit down."

Mitch hesitated briefly, but ultimately followed her. He liked Vicki, had never experienced the unease his sister had always felt in their stepmother's company. He knew Vicki had tried earnestly to become a mother to the two Ryder offspring she'd inherited when she'd married their father. When she failed to create the warm relationships for which she'd hoped, Vicki had settled for a friendly but distinctly nonmaternal bond with her stepfamily. On some level, Mitch felt guilty for his and his sister's reticence. Their own mother had bailed out of the family when he and Em were still asking for the crusts to be cut off their peanut butter and jelly sandwiches.

Carla Ryder hadn't enjoyed motherhood as much as she'd enjoyed travel and being entertained by her friends in a variety of glamorous locations around the world. She needed color and change the way other people required food and water. Mitch hadn't seen his mother for three years; they spoke on the phone only occasionally. It was Vicki who celebrated birthdays and holidays, Vicki who remembered to send a postcard when she and Mitch's father went on vacation.

She looked at him now the way he imagined an interested mother might look at her adult son—with concern and gentleness and a calm perceptiveness.

She wasted no time on a preamble. "I know you like Elaine. I *know* it," she said, holding up a hand when he opened his mouth to utter a denial. "You've never asked my advice before, and I've never offered it. But, darlin', I'm going to tell you now. Choosing to live your life without making a family of your own is like deciding to be a car with no engine. I don't pretend to know you well," she said matter-of-factly. "You've never let me. But I know more than you think. You and your sister are very much like your daddy. So confident and sure. And so hard on the people who love you.''

Mitch had not anticipated his stepmother's candor or the steel that supported the compassion in her gaze.

''Elaine is a smart woman. She's decided to go after what she wants, no matter what. She'll never have to regret her choices, the way some women do.''

Some women. ''What do you regret?''

Vicki's smile conveyed her sadness and a hint of apology. ''Putting all my efforts into a family that never really wanted me to begin with. Believing that would be enough.''

She must have seen the pain and the immediate, conflicting desire to defend himself, because she placed a hand on his arm. ''Feeling like family can't be forced. When it's something you want, though, you shouldn't settle for less. Your daddy didn't want any more babies, and by the time I realized you and your sister didn't want another momma, it seemed too late for me.'' She shook her head. ''That wasn't true, though, 'cause I wasn't even Elaine's age yet. I was just afraid to start over.'' Her hand slid to his, and she gave his fingers a gentle squeeze. ''And by that time, I loved the three of you. I knew you needed *someone,* even if she wasn't a momma, exactly, and maybe even not quite a wife.''

''What do you mean? I thought things between you and Dad—''

''Are between me and Daniel. Your daddy knows where to find me if he wants to have a real conversation, 'stead of lecturing at me like I don't know the difference between 'sit down' and 'come here.' But that's enough about that.''

Vicki stared at Mitch levelly, and he had the feeling she really wasn't going to say any more about her marriage. Besides, he had his own amends to make, apparently, without worrying about the relationship between his father and stepmother. Mitch rubbed a hand across the tension in the back of his neck then stood to pace the room.

''I never realized you felt that way,'' he began, feeling awkward, wishing this could emerge as smoothly as one of his final summations in court. When he knew what was hanging in the balance, when he wanted to win, words came easily. In this moment, however, he wasn't sure what was at stake; he merely sensed there was something he could lose—a something he couldn't even define—if the words didn't come out right.

Vicki watched him patiently, appearing not to expect a thing, which made him sweat harder. "Maybe," he began again, "maybe we needed a mother, and we just didn't know it."

Almost immediately, it seemed, Vicki's eyes sparkled with tears, but not before Mitch's own words hit his gut like a fist. Had he ever considered Vicki's need for family? No.

Mitch took for granted that his family consisted of the people to whom he was related by birth and whom he saw more than once every ten years—his father and M.D. He'd never expanded his view beyond that narrow definition. He'd never felt the need.

What was a 'family'? At thirty-six, shouldn't he have defined that for himself by now?

Shoving his hands in his pockets, he stood deep in thought, unaware of Vicki's approach until she laid a hand on his shoulder. "At least I've always known what I wanted. I'm grateful for that. It would be a real shame to look back and realize you didn't even know what you wanted until it was too late."

The plumber, Rick, entered the living room before Mitch had a chance to respond. "'Fraid you won't be able to use your bathroom sink tonight. I had to shut off the water in there." He smiled apologetically at Vicki. Nearly old enough to be his mother, she'd won him over nonetheless with her southern hospitality and award-winning red potato salad. "When I come back tomorrow, I'll dig into your wall to see if there's been any leaking behind the plaster. Will someone be home during the day? It could take awhile."

"Tomorrow? All day? Oh, my." Vicki frowned prettily. "I didn't know you worked on weekends, and I want to be accommodating, of course, but actually I—"

"Yes." Mitch answered for his stepmother. "Someone will be here."

"Mitch, sweetheart." Vicki leaned toward him and lowered her voice. "I have a hair appointment with one of the busiest stylists in the city. If I cancel without twenty-four hours notice—"

"Don't cancel it," Mitch said. "I'll be here."

Rearing back a bit, Vicki gazed at her stepson. "Oh." Turning to Rick, she said, "Well, I guess everything is set then." With a blooming smile, she took Mitch's arm. "Imagine my stepson giving up his whole Saturday…just for me." Glancing up at Mitch and smiling approvingly, she winked.

Chapter Eleven

Saturday's sky dawned blue and white, with puffy clouds and crisply clean air, the streets having been washed with rain most of the day and night before. Mitch let himself into Vicki's place at 8:45 a.m., ready for Rick's appearance at nine.

Vicki had already left. Since they both knew Mitch had an ulterior motive for being here, he'd sent Vicki off on a "spa day," whatever the heck that entailed. He was simply glad he could approach Elaine today without an audience.

A restless night had afforded him ample opportunity to think about what he wanted and why. *What* he wanted was a commitment from Elaine to hold off—for a while, at least—on her baby-making plan. *Why* he wanted that was straightforward: so they could explore their relationship further.

He figured she'd want more of a commitment than that, but after thirty-six years of ambivalence toward anything domestic, he couldn't turn into Ward Cleaver overnight. Maybe he couldn't turn into Ward Cleaver ever. He did not consider it a copout to attribute some traits to DNA.

But if Elaine could accept that he was willing to *think* about starting a family, then their relationship might have a chance. She needed to give him time to get used to the idea, time for them to be a couple first.

He wasn't one hundred percent confident, but neither was he unduly worried, that she would respond positively to his overture.

Proceeding to the kitchen in Vicki's apartment, Mitch deposited several bags onto the counter. Proving he was not averse to domesticity, he'd brought breakfast—bagels and cream cheese from Holy Bagels!; doughnuts, cherry Danish and bear claws from The Cakery; coffee and, in the event that Elaine was still on her health food kick, an apple bran muffin from Wake Up And Smell The Coffee.

Setting the java into the microwave for reheating, Mitch decided to wait until 9:00 a.m. before he knocked on Elaine's door. It was a weekend, and he was, after all, unexpected. He watched the digital clock on the microwave roll to eight-fifty then eight fifty-two…eight fifty-five…eight fifty-eight…

Good enough. He pressed the start button to heat the coffee.

By the time the microwave dinged, Rick had arrived and Mitch was good to go. Leaving a bagel and a couple of doughnuts on a plate for the plumber, he set off, balancing the paper cups of coffee in a cardboard holder and grabbing the three bags of baked goods. As he stepped outside the apartment, he narrowly escaped a collision with a tall blond man coming from the direction of Elaine's apartment. Dressed in casual pants and a loose-fitting top, the man gave the appearance of being younger than Mitch, but it was hard to tell. The untailored clothes, bright blue eyes and a smile as bleached as his hair made him look like the sprouty, California yoga type who could be eighteen or thirty.

"Hey, man," he said, nodding hello and pointing both index fingers, like twin pistols, at the paper cups. "Caffeine. Good idea. Gotta get some. Not awake yet." Flashing another hey-peace-man grin, he sauntered down the porch steps, unlocked the bike he'd tucked behind the bushes and pedaled away.

Mitch stared at Elaine's door. *It was nine o-damn-clock!* What the hell was she doing with a man in her apartment—a man who didn't use pronouns—at nine o'clock on Saturday morning? A man who *wasn't* the man in her apartment Friday night?

Needing a moment to come up with a logical explanation, Mitch stepped back inside Vicki's apartment. He tended to jump to conclusions where Elaine was concerned. That wasn't good. Inviting two men to her apartment in…what?…twelve hours wasn't *necessarily* suspect.

Unless you were a woman admittedly looking for someone to father your baby.

Juggling the food bags, Mitch jerked the door open again, prepared to walk next door and accept Elaine's explanation regarding the man who'd been in her apartment last night *and* the one this morning. He'd trust her word.

But she'd better understand that monogamy was important to men, too. Contrary to some women's beliefs you couldn't expect to have outstanding sex with a man one night and then interview two other guys to see if they wanted to father your kid. It was weird. He wasn't going to have sex with her if she kept doing that—

"Pardon me! Sorry, sir. I wasn't expecting that screen door to open."

Mitch stopped dead, trying not to move at all while the coffee settled in the cups. He looked at the man who'd nearly run into him. Twenty-five, maybe twenty-six years old… dressed in blue slacks, green shirt, blue tie, looking like he'd just polished himself from head to toe. Dark hair, light eyes, almost as broad-shouldered as Mitch…all right, he *was* as broad shouldered.

The words *Can I help you?* nearly made it to Mitch's tongue, but the younger, handsomer man pointed to the bags of baked goods. "Wow, that smells good. I bet someone's going to be happy to see you.'' Smiling his perfect, I'm-an-ad-for-the-power-of-tooth-bonding smile, he bade Mitch, ''Have a good morning,'' and continued to Elaine's apartment.

Elaine's. Apartment.

The young man—correction—the *boy* rapped strongly but politely on her door, turning his head once to nod at Mitch, who still stood there, staring, carrying his breakfast treats like he was the Pillsbury Doughboy.

Unwilling to be caught staring, Mitch ducked into Vicki's apartment. Again. He left the door open though—oh, yes he did—to eavesdrop.

He heard Elaine answer the knocking.

Heard her say, ''Hi. You must be…let's see…you're Chris, right?''

And Chris said, ''I hope I'm on time.''

And Elaine answered, ''On the button.''

And the screen door banged, and Mitch wanted to slam Vicki's door in response, but he didn't intend to give Elaine the satisfaction.

Instead, he sat on the couch to crack his knuckles and think. The hell with her explanation, he decided, he wasn't going to ask for one. Pulling a bear claw from one of the bags, he ate it mindlessly, spent some time brooding then polished off a chocolate doughnut with sprinkles.

Three men. The count had now risen to *three,* and the last one had worn a suit. Plumbers didn't wear suits. Neither did electricians, phone guys or cable TV personnel.

He wasn't stupid; he could put two and two together and come up with three potential donor daddies.

Squeezing his fist hard enough to break his knuckles, never mind cracking them, Mitch reached for the apple bran muffin then realized he was acting like…a girl.

Rising, he hollered to Rick that he was leaving and would return in an hour or so. Then he stepped onto the porch, intending to head to the gym for a good mind-numbing workout.

"Whoa! Hey, sorry. Guess I wasn't expecting that door to open again."

Once more, Mitch almost collided with the young man in the suit, who very solicitously put a steadying hand beneath Mitch's elbow. "You all right?"

Mitch glowered. "Yes, I'm all right."

The youth nodded. "Okay. You have a good day, sir."

Sir. Disgusted, Mitch watched the younger man jog down the porch steps. The little pisher acted like he thought Mitch was eligible for a senior citizen discount.

Looking toward Elaine's door, Mitch revised his precious plan. Striding to her apartment, he rapped loudly.

Elaine blew her nose, glad her guests were gone so she could indulge all the I've-got-a-cold sounds she was too ladylike to perform in public. She'd felt better after last evening's chicken soup and a good night's sleep, but midway through her recent appointment, the bug had taken hold again. Now all she wanted was a cup of tea, her favorite pillow and a Meg Ryan video.

When an insistent knock sounded on the door, she groaned. Hoping it was simply Chris, back with something he'd forgotten to tell her earlier, she pasted on her company smile and opened the door.

"Everything all right over here?"

The first thing Elaine noticed about Mitch this morning was that he looked like a pissed-off cop—stiff and accusing.

The second thing she noticed was actually about her. As always when she first glimpsed Mitch, her heart started pounding, but this morning it settled pretty darn quickly. Surreptitiously, she glanced at her watch. It took only fifteen seconds or so for normal rhythm to be restored. She didn't even feel dizzy or giddy or especially excited, the way she had the past few weeks. That was progress.

Perhaps the spell was over. Her mind had told her body, "Forget about him," and her body had listened.

"What's up?" she asked.

Mitch's eyes darted to points behind her. "You tell me." His jaw was so tense, his lips barely moved. "Are you alone?"

Elaine leaned against the door, studying him. "Yes." He looked positively suspicious. Folding her arms, she narrowed her eyes. "Why? What's it to ya?"

"May I come in?"

Elaine spent a long moment pretending to ponder. In reality, she was far too curious to say no. "It's starting to drizzle again," she noticed aloud, and for no particular reason. Then she looked down at Mitch's shoes. Expensive brown loafers coordinated well with beige slacks that looked a bit too stuffy for the weekend. "You can come in," she told him. "You have to take off your shoes, though. I mopped the floors this morning."

She hadn't mopped in three weeks, and she'd never asked anyone to take off his shoes. But she liked throwing him off guard; it put them on more equal footing. So to speak.

Doing as she asked, Mitch braced a hand on the door frame and slipped out of his shoes. He wore very nice socks, which seemed in keeping with the fact that he paid great attention to detail. She had a sudden image of him shopping for them, concentrating very seriously as he chose colors and styles. The picture was oddly endearing, and a little buzz of attraction flew through her. She swatted it away.

"So, what can I do you for?" she asked, following him in and hoping he wouldn't mind having this conversation with her recumbent, because her cold really was getting worse.

Standing in the center of the living room while she flopped onto the sofa, Mitch braced his hands on his hips and announced, "I was at Vicki's last night."

He stopped there, as if that single bit of information should mean something to her. Since it didn't, Elaine prompted, "And?"

"I arrived at approximately seven-oh-two."

She dipped her head. "Okay." Elaine blinked, feeling woozy.

On the other side of the coffee table, Mitch began to pace. ''What were you doing at seven-oh-two, Elaine?''

This must be what it felt like to be in a *Dragnet* episode. She thought a moment. ''Um, I was two minutes into an episode of *Friends*?'' When he scowled, she waved dismissively. ''How should I know what I was doing at seven-oh-two? Why do you want to know?''

Immediately Mitch stopped moving. He looked at his subject and his next words, spoken slowly but sharply, truly surprised her. ''I saw the men. The one last night and the *two* this morning. Who were they?''

Elaine was so mystified by this odd meeting, she couldn't seem to work up a healthy resentment over his highhandedness. Instead of demanding to know what he was doing watching her apartment, she shrugged. ''The man last night was Sam, and the two this morning were Ocean and Chris.''

''Ocean?''

''Right.''

Mitch grimaced. He could feel a bad moon rising. Was he supposed to stand around while Elaine and some kid with 1970s recessive genes made children they would, no doubt, name Meadow and Skylark? ''All right,'' he said, ''I'll do it.''

Elaine gazed dumbly for several seconds, and he thought she hadn't heard him. Then she shook her head. ''Do what, exactly?''

''The same thing you were going to do with the others.''

''Eat chicken soup, have a Shiatsu massage and buy a water purifier?''

''What are you talking about?''

''That's what I was doing with Sam, Ocean and Chris. Not all at once, though. I had the soup with Sam, Ocean gave me the massage and Chris sells water purifiers. What were you talking about?''

It took Mitch a moment to replay his encounters, plugging in this new information. The men weren't auditioning to be daddies? He felt an uncomfortable heat creep up his neck. ''I, uh…'' He backpedaled quickly. ''What kind of water purifier are you thinking about?''

Elaine narrowed her eyes. ''Mitch.''

''Do you like bear claws?''

''Mitch!''

Raking a hand through his hair, he explained. ''I saw three men come to your apartment between last night and this morning. Naturally I assumed you were interviewing donors.''

Elaine's whole head felt like it could explode, and she knew she couldn't blame the sensation entirely on her cold. ''*Naturally* you assumed?''

''It's not entirely unreasonable. Vicki said you'd become uncomfortable with the thought of an anonymous father, so when I saw the men coming and going, I assumed you'd decided to pursue this face-to-face.''

Though Elaine hated to admit it, Mitch was right; his conclusion was not entirely unreasonable given the circumstances. ''Sam is my brother,'' she said. ''Ocean is a friend of his who does Shiatsu massage to stimulate the immune system, and—'' Her head began to swim. ''You'll do what the other guys were going to do?''

Mitch felt his heart pound harder than it had during his single attempt at the Hood to the Coast marathon. ''You're not interviewing donors?''

''You'll do what the other guys were going to do?''

He hadn't meant to say that. He'd come here intending to convince her that a relationship between them deserved a fair shot. But he'd meant to caution her, too, that he still wasn't certain about kids, or even marriage. Because that was honest…that was candid…that was…

He looked at Elaine, staring at him with those wide, lake-hazel eyes. She was dressed in loose pink pants with a tie at the waist and a pink T-shirt that exposed her creamy, lightly freckled skin. With her hair piled on her head in a ponytail, she looked a little like Pebbles on *The Flintstones*. Except that she was older and a lot sexier, and she made him crazy.

"You really want a baby?" he asked, and, of course, she nodded her head. Only one more breath passed before he said, "Then I'm the man to give it to you."

When Elaine came to several seconds later, Mitch was kneeling by her side, holding her hand and stroking her forehead. Not only did he look worried, she could feel his concern through the touch on her brow.

"What happened?" she murmured.

"You tell me. I thought you passed out because I shocked you, but you're burning up."

Elaine blinked at him. "You did shock me."

The smile he flashed was brief. "Are you sick, Lainey?"

Her brows lowered. "That's the second time you've called me that. No one calls me that."

"No one except me, then. Does it bother you?"

She shook her head, but a traitorous quiver ran through her. "Oh, no," she groaned. "Not again."

In his concern, Mitch sounded almost gruff. "What do you mean 'not again'? Have you been experiencing chills? Fever?"

"Both," she grumbled.

"How long?"

Ever since I met you. So much for her brief reprieve. One word—Lainey—and she was covered in goose bumps again.

Before she could guess what he was doing, Mitch scooped her up in his arms and carried her to the bedroom. Laying her on the unmade bed as easily and gently as if she were porcelain, he drew the sheet and blanket up to her chin, tucking the material a bit too carefully around her. She felt like a mummy.

"Stay put," he ordered, heading toward her bathroom.

She grunted, her teeth chattering. As if she could get out of these covers without a pair of shears. In any case, an overwhelming fatigue seemed to glue her to the mattress. She was suddenly exhausted. So much so that she couldn't organize her thoughts and longed to give into the drowsiness. There was definitely something she wanted to ask him, though…what was it?

Oh, yeah. Why did he want to father her baby?

The next time Elaine woke up, a very attractive polished woman wearing a white blouse and tan slacks and carrying a black bag was walking out the bedroom door with Mitch. They conversed in soft tones that made their words unintelligible to Elaine. She tried to call out, but her throat was so sore, only a thin hiss emerged before Mitch and the woman proceeded out of sight.

Mitch returned several moments later with a steaming mug and a smile when he found Elaine awake.

"Who was that?" she croaked, wincing as she felt the full force of her sore throat.

"Better take these." Setting the mug on the end table, he handed her two aspirin and a glass of water previously placed by the bed.

"Who was that woman?" Trying not to hurt herself, Elaine spoke in a whisper, but she grimaced anyway.

"Swallow first," he said, urging the water and pain relievers to her lips. When she did, he said, "Julia is a doctor. She thinks you caught a flu that's been kicking butts around town. She prescribed aspirin for the fever, zinc, vitamin C and rest."

"She makes house calls?"

"I represented Julia in her divorce. She left some heavy-duty throat lozenges. Take one." He popped a lozenge through its silver pouch and held it out.

Elaine wrinkled her nose when she saw the brand, but took the lozenge, anyway, and it made her throat happily, if temporarily, numb. "So, have you helped everyone in Portland split up?"

"I don't help them split up. I help them not kill each other over who keeps the bone china."

Elaine couldn't argue that. Not once during her divorce from Kevin did she ever feel threatened by Mitch Ryder's influence on her wily ex. Quite the contrary.

Mitch sat on the edge of the bed, his hip touching hers through the quilted spread he'd added to the stack of covers while she was sleeping. "I took a couple of classes in mediation and relationship counseling. Which is why I can't understand why I get so nuts with you."

"Nuts?"

"I'm usually very sensible. Not impulsive."

"That's no fun."

"I'm beginning to realize that."

Mitch leaned over her, and Elaine wasn't certain whether it was her fever or the brush of his chest against the quilted spread heating her up. Either way, her heart started thumping as she wondered what he was going to do...and found out when he plucked her stuffed Tigger from the other side of the bed and tucked it neatly next to her shoulder.

"I'm going to the drugstore for supplies. Julia says you're not going to be going anywhere for the next few days." He nodded toward the end table. "I made a mug of chamomile tea and warm apple juice. Julia thought that was a good combo. God knows why." He stood, and immediately Elaine missed his closeness. Reaching down, he tapped the bridge of her nose with a forefinger. "Don't go anywhere. I'll be back."

She awakened, burning up, two hours later, but with no awareness of the time. Elaine was hardly aware of anything, in fact, save for the clammy cloth on her forehead and the cold, wet towel being stroked rhythmically between her breasts and down her belly. Soothing murmurs accompanied the long, gentle strokes. She moaned. The slow caress felt wonderful, even if it was wet....

She decided not to wake up fully. She'd just lie here and enjoy the feeling a little while longer.

Mitch sat in a dining room chair he'd pulled up next to Elaine's bed. He'd phoned Julia twice more, nearly panicking when Elaine's temperature spiked. He'd followed Julia's instructions to the letter, but no amount of reassurance from the capable doctor had been able to calm the thumping of his heart. He'd never known caring for someone could be this exhausting. And not the physical caring *for,* but the emotional caring *about.* If anything happened to Elaine…

Leaning forward with his head almost between his knees, Mitch took deep breaths. He'd made a mistake. He'd been rash. Uncharacteristically rash.

He couldn't donate sperm, not for anyone. Even Elaine.

Especially Elaine.

Lifting his head, Mitch watched her sleep…face turned toward him and still flushed…eyelashes resting delicately on her cheeks…mouth open slightly as she breathed…tiny rivulet of drool trickling down…

Elaine was not a doll he could stop thinking about when they were no longer in the same room. She was real. She deserved his honesty; deserved to be taken seriously. Like it or not, Mitch knew he had to talk to her as soon as she woke up.

He had to tell her he was rescinding his offer.

"Oh." Awake but aching from the flu that had sneaked up on her the night before, Elaine pulled the bedcovers over her chin and stared at Mitch. She'd fallen into a feverish stupor so quickly after his original announcement that she hadn't had time to figure out how she felt. Now, fewer than twenty-four hours later, he was reneging on his proposal to father her child. Maybe she was still delirious, but the disappointment was towering.

Wrinkling her nose at the tray of eggs and toast he'd brought her first thing this morning, she tried to ignore the sickening thud in her stomach.

Mitch had made her breakfast then paced the floor while he'd spoken to her, explaining that his original offer had been "precipitous" and that he'd since had time to reason it through. Now he stood before her, gazing down, waiting for a response.

Determined not to bare her feelings until she had time to examine them in private, Elaine forced a small laugh. "Sure,

I understand. I thought it was weird when you said you wanted to be the donor. I mean, it seemed a little…spontaneous of you.''

Mitch frowned. ''I'm spontaneous.''

Elaine paused. ''Okay.'' She swallowed past the soreness in her throat. ''Anyway, you with a baby in the world—that's actually a hard picture to form.''

He scowled harder. ''I like babies.''

''You do?''

Mitch opened his mouth to reply then snapped it shut. Dropping into the chair, he looked at Elaine, who had brought one hand out from beneath the covers and was nudging the egg with her spoon.

Did he like babies? He wondered. He hadn't been around a lot of them. What would it be like to actually raise one? Kids suffered tremendously in a divorce; he knew that. And parents—the good ones—seemed to go through holy hell, believing they'd failed their children. He did not want to go through that. And he didn't want to hurt a kid in so fundamental a way, teaching by example that life was unpredictable and messy and filled with heartache. Who needed to learn that at a young age? He hadn't liked it. And to this day, his sister had trouble forming relationships. Kids needed to feel secure. They needed to know that the people who brought them into this world would put them first, protect them.

Elaine twirled a loose thread from the bedspread around her finger. ''So, you do enjoy kids, hmm?''

''I… Yeah.'' He could picture a little girl with Elaine's freckles, reaching out her chubby arms to be picked up and hugged. ''Kids need to feel secure,'' he blurted.

Elaine blinked at the apparent non sequitur. ''True.''

Rising, he started to pace, realized that was a bad habit indicating he was about to deliver a speech, and sat down again. ''I'm going to be serious for a minute.''

Deciding not to point out the obvious—that he was often serious—Elaine nodded. ''All right.'' Mitch looked like a bullfighter, getting ready to face off. He was so big and intense; a child probably would feel secure with him, as long as he wasn't scaring them with his bluster. And then she recalled how gently he'd stroked her forehead....

"I did imply that I was prepared to father your child. But you know how I've felt about your plan to raise the child on your own."

"I am perfectly capable—"

"I didn't say you weren't. Capability doesn't have anything to do with this."

"Then why do you persistently doubt my—"

Mitch picked up a piece of toast and shoved it between her teeth. "Chew and be quiet for a minute. I have no doubt you'll be a great mother. That isn't the point. The point is a child deserves to know who his father is. I would want my children to know."

Around the bite of buttered toast, she said, "So this is about the birth certificate? You think 'father's name' should be filled in?"

A spoonful of egg joined the bread in her mouth, though not of her own free will.

"Let me finish," Mitch requested, short on patience.

She extracted the spoon he'd stuck in her mouth and scowled at him.

"This is not about a birth certificate," he assured her. "I'm talking about the child's welfare after he's born. *If* I father a child, I intend to be present in his life. An active influence. I intend," he stated, looking as adamant as she'd ever seen him, "to be married to my children's mother."

Toast and egg lodged in Elaine's throat. With effort, she swallowed. "You want to get married again?"

Mitch crossed his arms, puffing his chest out and drawing his chin in. "You sound shocked."

"I am shocked. You said wanting to be married, wanting to have children was all 'ancient history' for you." Of course, that was when *she'd* brought it up.

Elaine felt anger and the sting of rejection take up residence in her chest. What was he saying? Suddenly he was prepared to marry and have children, just not with her?

Sorry he'd ever seen her looking as pitiful and vulnerable as she had last night (and, let's face it, she was no Miss America contestant this morning, either) she yanked the sheet up to her nose, nearly upsetting the breakfast tray.

"Well. I'm very happy for you," she said with prim insincerity. "It's nice to know such *evolved* DNA won't go to waste. My best to you and Mrs. Flintstone...um, Ryder."

A pause followed, during which they both frowned heavily at each other. Finally Mitch stood, picked up the TV tray, returned it to the end table and sat on the bed, too close to Elaine for comfort. She glanced away, intending to tell him she thought he should go now, but he held her chin, turning her toward him. "I intend to marry you. Did you get that part?"

She blanched. "No." For the life of her, she couldn't bring up a single other word.

Mitch released her, but held eye contact. "Any thoughts?"

None coherent. She tried to speak, but managed only to shrug.

From the other side of the proposal, Mitch watched the stunned, unusually silent woman before him. He'd expected a bigger reaction, some enthusiasm. He had just told her she wasn't going to have to do this alone. That he would be there before, during and after. He'd proposed, for crying out loud. And she looked like he'd just told her he had something communicable.

Mitch rose from the bed. What did she expect? A grand declaration, hearts and flowers, a bended knee? He had offered all he could. He was willing to open a door he thought he'd closed long ago. That ought to be enough for now.

"This seems sudden." Elaine's raspy voice poked through his thoughts. "Why have you changed your mind, Mitch?"

He grew decidedly ill at ease, as if he hadn't expected, or didn't want, to answer that question. Elaine was fully prepared to wait through the awkward silence, unwilling to let him off the hook.

Mitch had turned on the heat when Elaine's fever broke, so she wouldn't be chilled. Now he wished he'd opted for air-conditioning. What could he tell her that made sense and was truthful? Not a liar by nature, he especially wished to be truthful with Elaine.

He approached the bed again, but remained standing. "I like what we have going," he said bluntly. "I don't want it to end. I'm thirty-six, I'm a divorce lawyer, I've been married once myself, and the truth is I don't know if I believe love exists in anything other than the minds of people who can't stomach the thought of life without it. I'm not one of them."

Lord, did he *mean* that?

Elaine shifted uneasily beneath the covers. Mitch's statement had to be one of the saddest she had ever heard. And, for someone like her, who had spent most of her life believing in love—hook, line and sinker—it was also one of the most annoying. Particularly as he'd uttered it after proposing.

He began to pace, head lowered, hands absently finding his pockets.

Whoever marries him will have to get used to that pacing, Elaine thought, recognizing his typical way of working through a problem. The truth was she didn't mind the pacing. Actually, she considered it rather vulnerable. It reminded her of her great-uncle Herb, who used to push his lips out, nod and walk a hole in the rug when Aunt Fay told him of some issue she'd usually solved already, anyway.

Still, that fond memory did not prevent Elaine from wanting to answer Mitch's proposal by pitching a soft-boiled egg at his head. Clod! Did he think she would melt into a sentimental puddle because he'd decided to marry her despite the fact that he didn't love her? *Not!* Okay, so she had felt a little rush of excitement in those first seconds of realizing Mitch Ryder was standing before her offering children *and* marriage. If only he'd have shut up after that.

"You know," she said, beginning to feel too fatigued for a conversation of this magnitude, "men who say, 'It's not that I don't love *you*, it's just that I can't love *anybody*,' are usually full of bull." He opened his mouth, but she raised a warning finger. "Don't interrupt. I'm sick, and I'm cranky." She narrowed her eyes. "Kevin proposed to me on a ski trip to Mt. Hood. He was standing about ten feet away, turned, hollered, 'Hey, you want to get married?' and pushed off. I fell halfway down the slope, broke my ankle and said 'yes' on the way to the hospital. I had something a little different in mind for my next proposal." Mitch looked like he was going to speak. She raised her finger. "However. I do want to have a child, and I'm not sure I'm comfortable with the idea of an anonymous donor, anymore. So I might—*might*—be willing to consider your suggestion."

Mitch clenched his jaw. "When will you know?"

"When my throat doesn't feel like a bed of molten lava. Now beat it. But I do thank you for all your help." Flipping onto her side, she pulled the covers over her ear.

The conversation was over for today. For better or worse.

Chapter Twelve

During the two days Elaine stayed home from work to nurse her flu, she watched way too many episodes of *A Baby Story*.

If any TV program could make her yearn for the picket fence life, it was that one. Each episode of the show followed a couple about to have a baby. Invariably the woman glowed, the husband was as excited as his wife about the impending birth, and as long as an epidural was involved, the labor looked a lot like a family reunion. After the birth, the show would get a shot of the new parents holding or playing with their baby and their cocker spaniel in their pleasant three-bedroom, country-decorated home.

It was enough to make a single woman contemplating artificial insemination feel positively lonely.

Snuggled under a crocheted throw, Elaine watched the TV from her couch. On the current episode, Chad and Annie were holding newborn Hughie while eighteen-month-old Kari sat between her parents, babbling at her tiny brother. Annie spoke: "I love having two children this young. Chad's an outstanding father. He wants to hold them and cuddle as soon as he comes home from work.''

''Yeah, I don't like diapers, though.''

Annie giggled. ''No, but you're great with everything else.''

''We want more kids,'' Chad, a youthful thirty-four-year-old announced, and his wife nodded. ''Definitely. This is *so fun*.''

Elaine raised the remote and clicked to Oprah.

Wrapping the afghan around herself, she sat up. Mitch had laid low since she told him to scram, but he'd phoned Vicki to see how the patient was doing. Nothing was mentioned, of course, about his proposal, and, for once, Elaine decided to keep mum, too.

Typically, she used the committee process to make major decisions: phone Gordon and perhaps another couple of friends, present the issue, order take-out, hash over said issue. But this time she knew the choice to take Mitch up on his offer, or not, had to be all hers.

She'd have decided ''yes'' already except for one thing. Marrying a man who practically wrote a prenup before he proposed meant she had to give up her last glimmering hope of having a family like the one on *A Baby Story*. Marriage to Mitch would be steeped in reason and practicality, not starry-eyed dreams. It would be sensible.

She could just see the two of them on *A Baby Story*…

Elaine: ''We've been married since we found out I was pregnant.''

Mitch: ''That was the agreement.''

Elaine: ''I was really ready to have children.''

Mitch: ''And I wasn't completely opposed.''

Elaine: ''So when he offered to be the father, I agreed.''

Mitch: ''It made sense.''

Elaine (nodding): ''We're very sensible.''

Could she stand it? Could she truly let go of the last slat in her picket fence dreams? Turning the TV off altogether, she stared at the dark screen.

The ringing of the telephone made her heart skitter. Perhaps Mitch had tired of waiting for her answer.

The cordless receiver was in her bedroom, so, lugging her afghan with her, Elaine shuffled to the wall phone in the kitchen.

"Hello."

"Elaine? It's Adair. Do you have a minute, sweetie pie?"

"Adair." Tucking the phone between her ear and shoulder, Elaine pulled a carton of grapefruit juice from the fridge. "I've got nothing but minutes. I caught that crummy flu that's been going around."

They chatted about mutating viruses for a few moments, and then Adair said, "Listen, the reason I'm calling, sweetie, is that I have some news I thought you should hear from a friend before it travels down the grapevine."

"Oh, yeah?" Juice spilled onto the counter. Adair's tone had turned ominous. Did she have news about Mitch? The kind of news that might make Elaine decide absolutely, positively not to accept his proposal? The kind of news that might make her poor, virus-ridden body writhe with jealousy?

At their lunch, Elaine had fished for information about Mitch's love life. Perhaps now she was going to get it.

On the other end of the line, Adair sighed. "I'm only sorry it's me who has to deliver these tidings, because—" another sigh "—I know how you feel about surprises."

She did? Even Elaine wasn't sure how she felt about surprises. As far as she could remember, she'd always kinda liked them. "Go on, Adair."

Again the woman exhaled long and noisily, and Elaine began to feel the foreboding in every sigh. Oh, Lord, Mitch was seeing someone else. It had to be that. Even while he was making love and proposing to her, he must be seeing someone else.

The mere possibility brought with it a crushing disappointment. Elaine had trusted his integrity. She realized now, as the mere suspicion of his infidelity hit her like a blow to the chest, that she had trusted him never to hurt her deliberately.

She heard another heaving breath and snapped, "Adair, if you sigh one more time, you're going to make yourself pass out. Just tell me!"

"All right. But remember… Don't blame the messenger." She paused again, more briefly. "Kevin and Stephanie have had their baby. One month early, which I am sure Stephanie somehow arranged because Nordstrom's downtown is having a Fall Fashions sale in two weeks. She probably put Pitocin in her morning smoothie. It took me six weeks to drop the eighteen pounds I packed on with my last baby, but don't you just know Stephanie was back at the gym before the placenta was out, pardon me. Oh, sugar pie, I know this has got to be just bruising."

"Boy or girl?"

"What? Oh. Uh, boy."

"Do you know what they named him?"

"Spencer, I hear."

"Spencer." Elaine tried it out. "Spence. That's a good name."

A moment of dead silence followed. "You're not upset?"

Taking a sip of grapefruit juice, Elaine was grateful to see that her hands, which had started shaking as Adair spoke, were now steady as rocks. "I guess not." She was envious, but she felt that every time she heard of any baby being born. "If you see Kevin at the club, tell him congratulations."

Adair made a sound of disbelief. "You are so…"

"Salt of the earth?" Elaine suggested, tongue in cheek.

"Yes. Truly!"

"Actually, Adair, I think I've just moved on."

Because Adair had also been an ex-wife, she was absolutely sincere when she said, "Good for you."

They spoke of other things for a couple of minutes, promised to meet for lunch or shopping downtown soon, and hung up.

Elaine picked up her juice and walked slowly back to the living room. She sat, ignoring the TV this time as she recalled the relief that washed through her when she realized Adair's ominous news was about Kevin, not Mitch. She trusted Mitch; she really did, and her gut told her that trust was warranted. He might not love her, but he wouldn't cheat. Integrity was part and parcel of his identity. He would be faithful to her, faithful to his family in every way, because to lie or cheat would send him into an identity crisis!

Maybe that type of loyalty was better than what she'd expected before: fidelity based on affection. When she'd confronted Kevin about his affair, he'd said to her, not unkindly, "Our relationship stopped being fun a long time ago, don't you think?"

Yeah, and she'd hated the tiny mustache hairs he'd left on the bathroom sink every morning, but she hadn't taken a lover because of it.

The funny thing was, she hadn't been all that surprised by Kevin's response. On the other hand, she couldn't imagine Mitch saying such a thing and assuming it served as an explanation.

If nothing else, her failed marriage had taught her as much about her own nature as it had about her ex-husband's. All her life Elaine had possessed a romantic bent, one that she now viewed as unconstructive. Even harmful. It was utterly foolish, for instance, to believe a man would stay true to her because he loved her. It must be closer to the truth to believe that a man's loyalty was dependent upon his own intrinsic personality. On a code of honor.

As for her belief in soul mates…

Curling onto her side again, Elaine shivered a bit beneath the warm afghan. What a liar she'd be to say she *didn't* believe that soul mates existed. Truly, she didn't know whether she could live in a world where it wasn't possible for two people to connect fully and deeply, to fall in love and stay in love, forever and ever and ever. It didn't even have to happen to her; she just needed to believe that it was happening for someone, somewhere.

Perhaps for her that special connection would come with her

child. And marriage, if there was a marriage, would be a pleasant accompaniment. Like cranberry sauce at Thanksgiving; it was a nice addition, but it wasn't the meal.

So Mitch would be her...cranberry sauce. Lord knew he didn't want to be the turkey.

Flipping onto her back, Elaine stared at a crack in the ceiling and twiddled her thumbs. A relationship like theirs was bound to have fewer problems than one riddled with love. Fewer problems. That right there was a pretty good reason to marry him. But it wasn't the best reason.

No, the best reason was that for a few moments while talking to Adair, Elaine had pictured Mitch with another woman, and she hadn't liked it. Not one little bit.

Folding an arm behind her head, she remembered that she'd promised to give herself a few days, at least, to make her decision. She knew, though, that it was already made.

Tonight, when she was sure he was home from work, she would phone and tell him that yes, she was willing to accept his proposal...with a few important amendments.

When Mitch walked into the Cup and Saucer at 8:00 p.m. Tuesday evening, Elaine was already seated in a booth, her hands wrapped around a steaming mug of what he assumed was herbal tea, a half-consumed roll of zinc and C lozenges in front of her. It was drizzling outside, and Elaine was dressed in an oversized, bunchy wool sweater and knit leggings to ward off the cold. With her thick auburn hair scraped back into a neat ponytail, she looked like a coed from some college back east, and she fit in perfectly with the Cup and Saucer's wheat grass-and-tofu clientele.

Still dressed in his suit from work, Mitch felt decidedly out of place, but he'd arrived home late, spoke with Elaine briefly over the phone and hadn't wanted to waste time changing clothes. He'd got back in his car and headed immediately for the Hawthorne area eatery where she'd suggested they meet.

When Elaine looked up and saw he'd arrived, she smiled, somewhat guardedly, Mitch thought.

"Thanks for coming," she said as he approached the table. Her voice was still throaty and muffled from the flu.

Mitch frowned as he slid into the booth opposite her. "You're still sick. I could have met you at your place. Or we could have done this another time." Not that he would have tolerated even one more night without Elaine's response to his proposition. In the past two days, he'd snapped at his secretary, who'd snapped back justifiably, had forgotten a lunch date with M.D., who had phoned him from Jake's to read him the riot act through a mouthful of steak, and he'd forgotten—twice— to pick up his cleaning, which was why he'd worn the same suit two days in a row. Staying away from Elaine, giving her space, as it were, was bad enough; knowing he'd proposed and hadn't gotten an answer was just about killing him.

"I didn't want to wait any longer. I've hardly slept in two days." Chin lowered, eyes raised, she looked at him. "Have you?"

"Not a wink." It was an enormous relief, somehow, to mutter the confession. "Are you feeling better? I hope you've been staying home."

The latter part of that sentence sounded more like a directive than a "hope," but Elaine was used to Mitch's benevolent paternalism by now. He was so genuinely protective, she could hardly mind. "I have been staying home," she assured him. "I'm going stir-crazy." Grabbing the roll of zinc lozenges, she removed one, popping it into her mouth. "And I'm becoming addicted to these things." She tossed the roll in her purse.

The waitress stopped by to top off the hot water in Elaine's mug and to offer Mitch a chance to order.

"Have you eaten?" he asked Elaine.

"No, but I've got a stomachache from all the zinc and C."

Mitch ordered two "Portland scrambles" with cottage fries and home-baked scones. Elaine knew better than to argue.

"You're going to make some pregnant woman very fat someday," she told him wryly.

"Pregnant women aren't 'fat,'" he countered immediately in a tone that sounded vaguely scolding. "They're pregnant. A weight gain of twenty-five to thirty pounds is desirable." To her arched brow, he responded, "I've been doing some research."

"Ah." She nodded. Squeezing honey into her tea from a half-used packet on the saucer, Elaine tilted her head. "So are you going to be one of those prospective fathers who watches everything his partner puts in her mouth, monitors her exercise and puts in an appearance at all the doctor visits?"

"I hadn't thought about it," Mitch grumbled. But he had. He'd even pictured a great deal of it over the past couple of days, and, yes, he wanted to be at the doctor visits. All it would take was a little thoughtful scheduling.

The waitress brought his coffee and the scones. Elaine dug into hers right away. "What about you?" he asked, watching her spread the biscuit with butter and raspberry jam. "Do you think you'll like being pregnant?"

"I hope so. I've been looking forward to it long enough. My mother had good pregnancies, so I'm hoping I will, too." One bite of the scone made her shiver with pleasure. "Mmm. I bet I gain more than thirty pounds. I really love food."

Mitch grinned. "I've noticed." Already he'd imagined the cravings a true connoisseur like Elaine might have, and he'd made a list of gourmet food stores open seven days a week. "How much participation do you picture the child's father taking in your pregnancy? Assuming you don't use a donor."

Sweeping scone crumbs from the table to her palm, she dropped them onto a napkin. "Guess I haven't thought about it too much, either." It was a fib, she knew, and not a very convincing one at that, but Mitch accepted it.

"That should give the father of your offspring a lot of leeway then."

"Offspring?" she echoed. "Plural?"

He shrugged. "I assume a woman with a maternal drive as powerful as yours will want more than one child, eventually. Do you?"

Elaine licked her lips. The gray eyes that seldom gave away any secrets pinned her with steady intensity. Yes, she'd thought about how many children she wanted, and yes, in her daydreams she'd imagined their father, her husband, taking an active part in every aspect of their lives. What made her jittery now, what made her want to physically squirm was the secret knowledge that in her weak, least disciplined moments, the husband and father she pictured—had been picturing for weeks—looked and sounded just like Mitch.

"Here we are, two Portland scrambles with potatoes. Can I get you anything else?"

The waitress set bulging plates in front of them, but Elaine really had lost her appetite this time; Mitch never took his eyes off her, even as he answered the waitress. "Thanks, no. We're good."

Left alone again, neither of them made a move toward the food. Mitch waited patiently for her answer then repeated the question, leaning across the table, his voice dropping to an intimate tone. "Do you want more than one child?"

Slowly, truthfully, she answered, "Yes."

Mitch nodded, but his expression yielded little. "When you've thought about those kids, Lainey," he persisted, never raising his voice above a murmur and never looking away, "have you thought yet about having them with me?"

Elaine had the oddest sensation through the silence that followed: time seemed both to race and stand still. She wouldn't have been surprised, had she glanced at her wrist at that moment, to see the minute hand of her watch speeding around the face of the timepiece. Mitch kept on surprising her. At times he was so commanding he bordered on arrogant; at other times, his patience seemed tender and infinite.

Pushing the plate of food to one side, Elaine clasped her hands atop the table. "I've thought about it. That's why I called—because I've thought about your offer *a lot.*"

Reminding herself they were in a public place and that this was an intimate conversation, she spoke softly. "I have reservations. I'd be lying if I told you I didn't. Until very recently you haven't wanted children, and you haven't wanted to be married again. Of course, I know people can change their minds. I've seen that firsthand." She rambled, half expecting him to interrupt, but he seemed to realize she needed to muddle through this out loud. "The other day you said you liked what we had together and didn't want it to end. Well, I like what we have, too. Without the added pressure of my wanting to have babies, I'd say our relationship has gone pretty smoothly so far. I've never been—" she glanced around, then bent forward over her clasped hands "—as sexually attracted to anyone as I am to you." She straightened up again.

Mitch may have tried to remain impassive, but he couldn't help the flash of satisfaction in his eyes. "I figure I may as well be honest," Elaine said. "It's not like we're trying to court each other, after all. We sort of skipped over that part."

Choosing not to dwell on the frown she'd brought to Mitch's face with that last comment, Elaine unclasped her hands, allowing them to drift along the table. Gradually she drew her plate closer as she spoke. "Please understand that I'm not complaining. I think our relationship has a certain raw honesty that was lacking in my marriage. So I feel comfortable—" She smiled. "Well, *almost* comfortable, telling you that—" A deep breath helped her get through the rest of the sentence. She took a deep breath. "I would like you to be the father of my children."

Thunder roared. Cymbals crashed. Trumpets blared.

And that's only what was going on inside Mitch's head. He'd had no idea he would react this way until Elaine spoke the fateful words. He'd thought he would be calm and philosophical. He hadn't expected his heart to stop then suddenly start again with a rush of expectation and excitement and adrenaline. He definitely hadn't expected wanting to lift Elaine off her feet, swing her around and announce to the restaurant that this was his bride-to-be and the mother of the children he'd never expected to have.

The uncharacteristically ebullient urge lived and died in his imagination. Mitch noticed that Elaine had started to eat again, but not with her usual relish. She nibbled at a cottage fry, appearing not to taste it at all. More disturbing, she hadn't smothered her potatoes in ketchup. The waitress had delivered a bottle that remained unopened at the end of the table. With his forefinger, Mitch nudged the bottle a little closer to Elaine's plate. She merely glanced at it.

He shook his head. "What's wrong?" By now, he knew her eating habits well enough to know that something was up.

Elaine appeared relieved that he had spoken. "I was wondering if we should hammer out some of the details now or wait a bit. I guess we could start hammering."

"Details."

"Amendments. Conditions. Except I don't like that word."

"Go on."

Elaine crumbled a corner of her scone, but didn't eat it. "Well, the first thing we should talk about is the idea of getting married. Because I don't want to. Not unless I'm pregnant." She looked at him earnestly, determined to explore the topic now that she'd broached it. "There's no point in marrying beforehand, because neither of us was interested in getting married again to begin with."

Mitch felt his brow dip into frown territory. She wasn't interested in marrying again? That was news to him. He made a conscious effort to keep his expression neutral. "Go on."

"I think the best approach is to wait. See if I get pregnant and if I do, then and only then explore marriage." She paused for his reaction.

"Go on."

The absence of a more direct response seemed to throw her, but she rallied. "Well, if we do decide that marriage is the next logical step, I think a one-year trial period with a detailed pre-nuptial agreement—mostly to protect your assets, but also to hammer out any potential custody issues in the event of our separation and subsequent divorce—would be a very sane pre-caution. Don't you? Because we're not kids, and we've been through this before, and like you said," she gestured to him, "this isn't about love. It's about logic and practicality."

"When did I say—" But he remembered: two days ago when he proposed. "Never mind. Go on."

"That's it, pretty much. Except for the, um, particulars of the pregnancy itself. If you know what I mean."

Mitch glowered darkly. "Go on."

The certitude Elaine exhibited up to now faltered just a mo-ment as she organized her thoughts. "I see it this way. I was already on the path to pregnancy through A.I. I have the doctor and the plan in place. Why throw the baby out with the bath-water? So to speak. Because, you know, there's less margin for error this way. And with the higher probability of successful implantation via artificial insemination versus…the other way…A.I. seems like an excellent idea now that I'll know who the donor is, which was what bothered you about the whole thing to begin with." She smiled. "Shall I go on?"

Mitch felt his body go rigid. *Hell, no.* "I'm not going to make errors," he growled. "And I'm sure as hell not going to make a kid in a doctor's office."

Elaine's glance darted around the room. "People can hear you."

"Good. Because I'd like to take a poll. How many people in this restaurant, I wonder, would think it's crazy for two people who have already made love to conceive a child without touching each other? How much 'sense' does that make?"

Across the table, they stared at each other, Elaine looking

like she wanted to crawl beneath the table and Mitch wanting
to stand atop it and shout. Sense aside, her suggestion, all her
suggestions, cut him to the bone. It had been years, twenty-six
to be exact, since he'd felt the sting he felt now. Rejection—
it was something he rarely felt anymore. He tried never to
expose himself to the possibility.

Mitch would not forget the ten-year-old boy whose mother
had stared at him and his baby sister for what had seemed like
hours one morning in May. The mother had not said a word;
she'd merely smoked a cigarette and stared while the boy and
his sister had fought over whose turn it was to play with a
large stuffed monkey. Finally their mother had risen, stubbed
the last cigarette in an ashtray, and said—and if Mitch lived to
be a hundred he would never forget the words—''This is not
me.'' Then she'd made a phone call, packed a suitcase and told
Mitch to make sure his sister had lunch. When he'd asked his
mother where she was going she had smiled the strange, hu-
morless smile so characteristic of her and replied, ''To play
with the big kids. Tell your father I'll call.''

Once Mitch began to fear his mother wasn't coming back,
perhaps not ever, he'd done more than make sure M.D. got
lunch. He'd made sure they were both bathed well and dressed
well; he'd given Em the stuffed monkey, the best toys, whatever she wanted to keep the peace. He had been petrified that
their father, too, would leave them ''to play with the big kids.''

Gazing at his now cold plate of food, Mitch shook his head.
The memory of that day had protected him, instructed him
through the years. It had filled him with the kind of fear that
kept a child from burning his hand on a hot stove more than
once.

Until now.

He looked at Elaine, who was toying with a Kleenex, lips
pursed as she considered his question. What he saw was not
merely a woman, but a range with every burner on high.

And still he wanted to touch again.

"I didn't mean we can't continue our relationship," Elaine said after considerable deliberation. "I just thought it might be a good idea not to put so much pressure on each other. You have to make love something like every other day for seven days to increase the odds of getting pregnant, and certain times are more optimal than others. So it can become very, you know, labor intensive."

Conscious of being overheard, she had pitched her voice low. She was also blushing, unless the pink stain on her cheeks was due to fever. A slow, sweet relief rose inside Mitch.

"It does sound like a lot of hard work," he mused.

Still fiddling with the Kleenex, looking distinctly uncomfortable now, she nodded.

He reached for his scone, split it in half and buttered it. "Fortunately, I'm a workaholic."

The blush deepened. "Yes. But, I mean, this could be a lot of added pressure."

Adding a spoonful of jam to the scone, he bit in, chewed leisurely. "I work great under pressure."

She was bright red now. "Okay. Well, the, um, procreation part of the arrangement is negotiable."

"Good." Keeping his tone and actions casual, he pulled his dinner plate closer, feigning as much interest in the food as in the topic of discussion, though in truth every cell of his body felt tuned in to Elaine's slightest move, the subtlest change in her expression. "How about the rest of it?" he asked. "Is it all negotiable?"

She sat up straighter. The fidgeting stopped. Meeting his eyes, Elaine answered without hesitation, "No. No, I'm adamant about the rest of it. I won't get married unless I'm pregnant."

She didn't elaborate, and Mitch sensed it would be futile to argue. With words, at any rate.

So he nodded. "Fair enough." Tucking into the meal, he

advised her, "Maybe you better go shopping soon, just to be on the safe side."

"'Safe side'?" She shook her head. "What do you mean? Shopping for what?"

"A wedding gown." He spread a thick layer of ketchup over his cottage fries, the way he used to when he was a kid. Taking a big bite, he hummed then winked at her. "My guess is you'll be needing one sooner than you think."

Chapter Thirteen

Elaine went back to work on Wednesday, a different woman in some ways. Her job at Dr. Gussman's had lacked luster for some time. Originally it had been something to do so she could feel productive while she waited to begin her family. Now it was primarily a paycheck. There were days when she would watch the hands of the dentist's "Tommy The Tooth" clock inch in agonizingly slow notches across a giant molar.

But on Wednesday, after her dinner with Mitch the night before, Elaine felt like she was powered by electricity. Despite lingering cold symptoms, she had energy to spare.

Even Sue, Dr. Gussman's ever-peppy receptionist commented, "Are you chewing gum with caffeine?"

Elaine laughed. "Nope."

Sue sighed. "Too bad. 'Cause I was going to bum a piece. You look like you are seriously enjoying your filing."

Elaine laughed, but Sue wasn't far off the mark; she was enjoying everything today.

She'd gone home on her own last night after finishing dinner and chatting with Mitch. Just chatting. After his comment that she might need a wedding dress sooner than she thought, Mitch had changed the subject, discussing only light matters like Vicki's love of holiday decorating—"Watch out for spider-webs on the porch at Halloween. I almost strangled one year."—and M.D.'s health habits—"She thinks standing in line at McDonald's instead of using the drive-thru makes her part of the fitness craze."

He'd made her laugh, made her smile, made her heart jump around from sheer attraction. It jumped even harder as she arrived at the duplex at five-thirty, wondering if he'd show up unannounced tonight as he sometimes did. She wondered, too, (and who could blame her?), whether he'd want to get right to work on making that baby.

The thought of being Mitch's possible fiancée had the power to make Elaine feel as giddy as a young girl again. Which was why she tried not to focus on it, reminding herself, several times an hour when necessary, that if they married it would be because the timing was right. No declarations of love, no grand promises of forever. Rather they would marry with a settled, mature confidence. Nothing wrong with that.

Mature and settled was not, however, what she felt when she remembered that the next time she and Mitch made love they might also be making a child. When she thought about that she felt...

Yahoo! Knowing that she and Mitch were going to join their hopes and their bodies in the most incredible and daring collaboration of all made her feel sensuous and womanly, strong and alive and *connected*. In some ways, Elaine felt more deeply connected to Mitch than to any man she'd ever known.

Her heart hammered all the way to the door of her duplex. She wanted to take a shower, change clothes, do something with her hair.

"Elaine!" Vicki emerged from around the side of the house, heading toward Elaine at a trot. "Oh, thank goodness you're home. Thank goodness, thank goodness!'' She grabbed Elaine's arm. ''Come with me, please. I need your help.''

Vicki tugged her down the steps and around the house, giving Elaine no opportunity to ask questions. When they reached the azalea bushes, the same ones Elaine had once hidden in, Vicki came to an abrupt halt then took two slow, prowling steps and pointed. ''Look there,'' she said in what amounted to a loud whisper.

Elaine gazed at the bush. ''What are we looking at?''

''There,'' Vicki said, ''on the ground, hiding behind the leaves. Do you see her?''

''No.''

''For heaven's sake, she's lookin' right at us. Follow my finger.''

As Vicki pointed again, Elaine drew an imaginary line from the tip of the other woman's manicured nail to the ground beneath the bushes and, sure enough, she saw a pair of eyes, green eyes, staring back at her.

''It's a cat,'' Elaine said, unimpressed.

Mitch's sweet-as-pecan-pie stepmama nodded, close to tears. ''Just look at the precious little thing.''

So far all Elaine saw were two distinctly suspicious, unblinking eyes and a head that looked very much like a garden-variety gray tabby. Didn't Washington have pussycats? she wondered, impatient to get in the house and get changed in case Mitch stopped by.

''She's such a precious pumpkin,'' Vicki cooed, then she clutched at Elaine's arm in apparent concern. ''What are we gonna do?''

Thoroughly bemused by Vicki's sense of wonder and urgency, Elaine repeated, ''Do? I don't think you're supposed to do anything with someone else's cat. But if you want one of your own, maybe you could ask Mitch—''

''Me, have a cat? Oh, I couldn't, honey. I'm allergic. I can't even touch 'em, that's why I need your help. That precious pumpkin is a stray. She's skinny as a rail, except for her belly.

It's huge. She won't get near me, but when I put a plate of smoked salmon down, she darted out and gobbled it up so fast I thought she was gonna choke!''

"Smoked salmon?"

"I didn't have cat food. We can't let her starve, Elaine, and we can't let her run away. I bet she's been living on her own, trying to make do all by herself. She's gotta be so lonely and scared."

If Vicki was trying to press Elaine's buttons, she had her finger on all the right ones. "Still, she could be someone's—"

"She's got no collar. Besides, she's starvin' and she's scared of people. I think she's been alone a long, long time."

"Okay. I'll be right back. You stay here and watch her." For the first time, Elaine noticed Vicki's outfit—a pale blue, silk pantsuit. "You look great. Are you going somewhere?"

Vicki waved the concern away. "I've got time."

Hurrying to her apartment, Elaine eschewed primping in favor of gathering food and water for the cat. It was one thing to ignore someone else's plain gray tabby; no way could she ignore a sweet, starving, terrified kitty that, on top of possibly being pregnant, was so lonely she was practically crying.

Armed with a plate of tuna, a bit of cottage cheese for variety and a small plastic dish of water, Elaine jogged back to Vicki. "Is the cat still there?"

"Yes, and she's meowing so pitifully. I think she's saying," Vicki curled her fingers and raised her hands like little paws, "rescue me. Rescue me."

Unmindful of her white work slacks, Elaine knelt on the damp grass and began coaxing the stray feline out of her hiding place.

Forty minutes later, Vicki was in her apartment, scrambling a couple of eggs in case "Pumpkin" was still hungry. Elaine was crouched near the bushes, as still as she could be, while the cat mustered the courage to become acquainted. The little cat with the large tummy was obviously full of insecurities.

Twice she approached cautiously to sniff Elaine's knee, her big, watchful eyes trained on Elaine's face.

Engrossed in the shy getting-to-know-you dance, Elaine completely missed the arrival of Mitch and M.D. until the cat looked up, panicked and retreated to the bushes.

"Hey, what are you doing?" Mitch reached for Elaine's arm, helping her to a standing position. As she unfolded, her legs were barely able to hold her. "That grass is wet. It's been raining in Portland, or hadn't you heard?"

Lord. Was it so easy to turn her into a pillar of gelatin? One teasing grin, a strong hand beneath her elbow, and she was about to do the Jell-O wriggle right into his arms.

Was it her fertile imagination or had a new tenderness entered his eyes? "Hi," she said, sounding far too breathless.

Palms cupping her elbows, he gazed at her as if he had nothing better to do. "Hi, yourself."

M.D. cleared her throat with no subtlety whatsoever. "Newsflash… It's still raining. Could we go inside? Also, we have a reservation for seven." She tapped the round face of her oversized watch. "Elaine's going to have to change clothes."

Her faintly amused perusal made Elaine look down. Grass and dirt stained her white pants. "Where are we going?"

"I've been trying to call you for the past hour," Mitch said without complaint. "I'd have phoned earlier, but I couldn't remember the name of the dentist you work for. Do you have a cell number?"

"No, I don't have a cell phone. Why were you calling?"

"I'm taking M.D. and Vicki to dinner at Amadeus. I meant to tell you last night, but…" They'd had other things on their minds. "I hope you'll join us anyway."

Dinner with Mitch at one of the most romantic restaurants in Portland. Elaine smiled. "That sounds wonderful. I—"

"Here are the eggs. I scrambled them with a teaspoon of cream cheese and a hint of chives in case… Mitch, Emmy!

You're early." Vicki stood on the grass in her aqua sandals, carrying a plate with the eggs and a sprig of parsley.

"We're late," M.D. corrected dourly. "And getting later."

"Eggs?" Mitch inquired. "You remembered our dinner, didn't you, Vicki?"

"Of course. The eggs are for Pumpkin."

He looked at Elaine.

A jigger of adrenaline enlivened her heart. Pumpkin! The presence of Mitch and his tender eyes had driven the needs of the woeful, pregnant pussycat straight out of Elaine's mind. So much for maternal instincts.

Breaking away from Mitch, she hunkered down to peer into the bushes. "Pumpkin? Here, baby, baby. Are you still there?"

"Who's Pumpkin?" Mitch said behind her.

"If we lose this reservation, someone here had better make me filet of beef with port wine and wild mushroom sauce, because I've been thinking about it all day." M.D. did not sound like she was kidding.

"Pumpkin. Pretty sweetpea, where are you, baby?" Scanning the bushes, Elaine spotted the cat a few feet from where she'd been previously. "There she is!" Acknowledging the return of Elaine's attention, Pumpkin meowed piteously. Elaine held out a hand to caution the people behind her. "Nobody move, please. She's very skittish." Looking over her shoulder at Mitch, she explained, "Pumpkin is the name we gave a stray cat Vicki found. She looked like she was starving, and we think she might be pregnant. I can't go to dinner tonight. I'm sorry." More sorry than he knew.

"I'm not following. Why can't you go to dinner?"

"Because I was just getting her to trust me when you walked up." The misty drizzle left tiny beads of water on his hair. Elaine forced herself to stay focused. "I don't want her to run away. I want her to feel comfortable enough to come near us, so we can help her. I need to work with her some more. Do you understand?"

M.D. answered first. "Can we eat her? Because if not, I don't see what the big deal—"

Vicki stomped her foot. "Emmy!"

"Well, I'm hungry!" M.D. defended herself. "Why don't we go to dinner tonight and get the cat some therapy tomorrow?" She dug into the wallet-style handbag hanging near her hip. "I think one of my clients said she uses a pet shrink or psychic or something." She held a business card out to Elaine. "Call my office tomorrow. We'll get you the number."

Ignoring his sister, Mitch approached Elaine slowly. With a glance at the bushes to make sure he wasn't spooking the cat, he crouched. "How long is it going to take to make Pumpkin comfortable?"

Clearly he wasn't happy over the prospect of losing her to a frightened feline, but when she looked into his eyes, she saw humor and irony, rather than exasperation. "Don't wait for me."

Mitch glanced at his stepmother, and Elaine knew he was going to tell the others to go on without him. She could see the desire to stay with her war with his commitment to the others as she placed a hand over his. "Go to dinner with Vicki and M.D. Maybe you and I can visit Amadeus another night."

Clasping her fingers, he brought her hand to his lips. "Count on it." Removing his jacket, he placed it around her shoulders, over her protest.

Vicki placed the plate of eggs on the grass near Pumpkin's hiding place, and Elaine watched the others get into the car. She saw Mitch look back once, as if he were about to change his mind or hoped she'd suddenly change hers. Regret pierced her as the car doors closed, and the trio headed to dinner.

She locked gazes with Pumpkin. "You better be worth it, cat." Pumpkin mewed and took two tentative steps toward Elaine.

Mitch returned to the duplex around a quarter to ten, after dropping M.D. off at her place. Vicki dozed lightly in the pas-

senger seat, claiming the good wine and better food had made
her drowsy. Mitch didn't mind his stepmother's uncharacter-
istic quietude; he was grateful for the time to think.

If asked, he wouldn't have been able to say exactly what
he'd eaten. His mind had been on Elaine all night. He'd felt
like a louse for leaving her; moreover, he'd missed her all
through dinner. Now, as he searched the windows for a light
to indicate she was still awake, he felt his anticipation rise. He
wanted to see her one more time tonight. Maybe all night.

He couldn't remember when he'd been such a slave to his
desires. "Like a schoolboy," he muttered.

"What, sugar?" Vicki's blurry murmur indicated she was
losing the battle to stay awake.

"We're home." Mitch pulled into the driveway.

"Home?" Vicki lolled against the headrest, then snuggled
more deeply into the seat. "Oh, good," she sighed without
opening her eyes. "Is Daniel still up?"

Mitch stared at his stepmother, as pretty in her late forties
as she'd been the day she'd sashayed into their lives. That she
still considered her "home" to be with his father both touched
and disturbed Mitch more deeply than he would have guessed.
What was the matter with Daniel that he couldn't hold his
marriage together after twenty-four years?

Calculating quickly, Mitch realized his father was now sixty-
six. Did Daniel want to be alone at this stage in his life? A
seed of discomfort took root in Mitch's stomach. He'd long
ago made peace with the knowledge that *he* would be alone in
the winter of his life. At least, he'd thought he made peace
with it.

Exiting the car quietly and moving round to the passenger
side, Mitch opened the door to place a gentle hand on Vicki's
arm. "We're here," he said, half-reluctant to rouse her from
the mental picture that was making her smile softly. He didn't
have a repertoire of comforting scenarios to trot out in the quiet
moments of his life. He'd always claimed he found a dose of
reality more bracing than any fantasy. But, of course, he'd

claimed a lot of things back in the days when he thought he knew himself. In the days before Elaine.

Vicki stirred, blinking her eyes as she reoriented herself. "Oh my, I must have dozed." She offered an effortlessly winsome smile. "I'm sorry, darlin'. I hope I didn't do something embarrassing, like drool or snore."

"I can't imagine you ever doing anything embarrassing," he said sincerely as he helped her out of the car. "You're still the classiest gal I've ever known, Vicki."

Even in the dark, Mitch could see the sudden sheen of tears on her cheeks.

"What a lovely thing to say." Vicki spoke in a hush. She gave his wrist a brief squeeze. "You're a good son, you know." She headed up to the house.

Mitch stood at the car a moment. He didn't know whether Vicki meant that he was a good son to Daniel or to her, or both, and it occurred to him for the first time in his memory that neither he nor M.D. had ever called Vicki "Mom." That nobody ever had, as far as he knew. Suddenly it seemed churlish and mean for him and M.D. to have deprived her of that, though it had never occurred to him before.

Closing the passenger door softly, he followed her up the steps, escorting her to her apartment, where they gave each other the usual peck on the cheek. He wanted to say something, but didn't know what. As she went inside, the moment to speak passed, though not the restless, incomplete feeling inside Mitch.

He hoped Elaine was still awake.

Retrieving the box of dessert he'd left in the car, Mitch knocked on Elaine's front door. A dim light glowed through the curtains, but he heard no movement or activity within.

He was toying with the notion of calling her on his cell phone, when he saw the note taped above the knob: *Mitch, come in. Burglars, go away. I have pepper spray, and I know how to use it. Love, Elaine.*

Removing her directive, Mitch grinned, though he had every

intention of reading her the riot act for leaving her door unlocked and then announcing it.

He called her name as he entered the apartment.

"I'm in the kitchen," she returned, but so softly he could barely hear her.

While the living room was comfortably warm, thanks to the wall heater, Mitch noticed a considerable drop in temperature as soon as he entered the kitchen. One look at Elaine, and he understood why. The door and the screen leading to the backyard were wide-open. Seated on the linoleum floor, her back against the wall and her jean-clad legs stretched in front of her, Elaine wore a bulky sweater, scarf and heavy wool socks to defend against the late-night, autumn chill. As Mitch entered the kitchen, she smiled up at him.

"Shhh," she instructed quietly then pointed. The rattiest gray tabby cat Mitch had ever seen sat in a sphinx-like position by Elaine's feet. The cat's eyes were closed, and its body swayed gently as it breathed, as if the sad-looking animal longed to curl up and snooze deeply, but was fighting the impulse.

"She's just nodding off," Elaine whispered. The cat was so thin its spine made a bumpy ridge beneath its fur; its belly, however, was oddly swollen. "I don't want to wake her. Isn't she a little doll?"

A doll from a thrift shop, maybe. "How long have you been here?"

"I'm not sure. But long enough for my knees to lock. What time do you have?"

"It's ten-thirty."

"No wonder I'm sleepy. I've probably been here since seven-thirty. I had to coax Pumpkin inside. I think enclosed areas make her feel trapped."

Mitch couldn't believe what he was hearing. "You've been here with that door open for three hours? Why?"

Using hand gestures to remind him not to disturb the kitten, she answered, "I couldn't let her stay outside. It started to rain really hard."

Mitch wanted to lift Elaine to her feet, wrap his arms around her, kiss her until she was dizzy. Instead, he crouched down. "How long do you intend to cat-sit?"

"I'm not sure. I don't want her to run away, but I know I can't pick her up yet. She's not ready for it. And when I try to shut the door, she freaks."

Mitch envisioned years of kitty psychotherapy if it turned out that Pumpkin was here to stay. As quietly as he could, he sat against the wall, next to Elaine.

She looked at him. "What are you doing?"

"I'd say my behavior falls under the heading, 'If you can't beat 'em, join 'em.'" He handed her the white foam box.

She opened it, gasping when she saw a slice of dark chocolate cake layered with whipped cream and cherries. "I love black forest cake!"

Mitch nodded. "I know."

"How do you know?"

A silky lock of hair that had fallen from her ponytail tempted him to brush it gently, slowly behind her ear. "You hum when you eat Cherry Garcia ice cream," he said as if the information were private, intimate. Slipping his hand behind her neck, Mitch stroked her jaw with his thumb. "Within ten feet of a brownie, you begin to quiver." His thumb brushed lightly across her lips. "Like you are now."

Elaine's breath grew labored. "Well." She swallowed hard. "I love cake," she whispered.

"Mmm-hmm. Crying shame I didn't bring a fork. Can't get up to get one, either. I might disturb the cat." He shook his head as if he felt very, very guilty. "It's damned unfair of me to tease you like this. You really, really want that cake, don't you?"

Elaine wasn't sure what the game was, but she wanted to play; he could tell.

"Yeah. I want that cake." A little smile hovered around her

mouth, the lush mouth he was having a hell of a time not kissing. But kissing was so predictable.

"I'm a fair man," he murmured. Dipping a finger into the whipped cream that topped the chocolate confection, he pulled up a fluffy pillow. "It's my fault you have no fork."

Elaine's eyes widened; her smile broadened in delight as his finger moved toward her mouth. Mitch could see the tiny pulse beat at the base of her throat. "What do you expect me to do?" She laughed.

"Whatever you want." As he brought the whipped cream closer to her mouth, Elaine parted her lips. Mitch felt his own level of anticipation skyrocket. Her tongue darted out, and suddenly he was the one quivering.

By the time she finished the whipped cream, Mitch's temperature was rising, and he wondered whether he could handle the game he'd started. He reached for more cake, but Elaine held the box away from him. When he looked at her quizzically, she told him, "You said I can do whatever I want."

Dipping in, she scooped up a button of cherry-spiked whipped cream and moved toward him. Mitch opened his mouth, but Elaine shook her head. "Un-uh. You had dinner." Mischief danced in her eyes. "This is *my* dessert."

He waited, wondering what she was going to do, never guessing she would paint a sweet mustache above his lip. Or that she would slowly, methodically kiss it off.

Placing her small hands on either side of his head, she held him still, controlling the moment, or trying to. By the time she licked the last dab of whipped cream from the corner of his mouth, Mitch was half-crazed with desire for something much sweeter than cake.

Taking the box off her lap before she could come up with any more ideas, he tossed it aside, overriding her protest by distracting her with a kiss as deep and sensuous and unabashedly sexy as any he'd ever participated in.

It wasn't long before they were both mindless enough to forget where they were. Cradling Elaine's head, Mitch dipped her back until they were lying on the linoleum. Neither of them felt the cold.

Neither realized they had disturbed Pumpkin's nap, either. Fortunately, the little cat wasn't particularly bothered at the moment. While her new mistress enjoyed a different kind of indulgence, Pumpkin stuck her head in the abandoned dessert box and developed a taste for whipped cream and cherries. It was heaven on earth in Elaine's kitchen that night.

Chapter Fourteen

"So Kevin is a daddy and Stephanie is finally the Madonna she wannabe." Gordon wagged his head as he brushed butter over a layer of phyllo dough for the spanikopita he was assembling. Stroking the pastry brush back and forth, he raised a shaggy brow at Elaine. "And you are not crumbling, not suicidal?"

"Nope."

"I've got a pint of Chunky Monkey in the freezer."

Grating a brick of sharp cheddar for the beer-cheese dip she was bringing to her father's sixty-eighth birthday party that afternoon, Elaine smiled. "Don't want any."

Gordon curved a wrist onto his hip. "Dang, you really are okay."

"Told you. I'm not upset. I know my baby's coming."

"Then why haven't you picked out a donor? What's that about?"

Adding a bottle of beer to the mixture of cheeses in the

enameled pot, Elaine stalled for time. "Do you have any Worcestershire?"

Usually she told Gordon everything, but she hadn't told him yet about the agreement she'd struck with Mitch.

Hunting in Gordon's fridge, she found the Worcestershire sauce and added a couple tablespoonfuls to the pot. Unfortunately, she couldn't stall him forever. Gordon was her best friend. He would know she was hiding something, and she didn't want to be accused of lying by omission.

"Actually, I have decided on a donor," she admitted. "In a manner of speaking."

"You spring that on me now?" Gordon practically yowled, "when my hands are full of phyllo and I can't even hug you?" Holding a sheet of the fragile dough, he set it quickly atop the pan of spanikopita and began the buttering process so it wouldn't dry out. "What do you mean, 'In a manner of speaking'?"

"Mitch is going to be the donor."

Gordon ripped a hole through the top sheet of phyllo. He stared at Elaine. "Lawyer Mitch? Mitch the Eel? Vicki's stepson Mitch?"

"Yes to all three of them," she said wryly. "But he's not an eel. He's…very nice."

"Nice. Nice Mitch is going to father your child?" Clearly, the information did not compute. "How did this happen? He didn't even win Pin the Tail on the Donor. What did you do, just come right out and ask him?"

"No. As a matter of fact, he brought it up."

Frozen with amazement, Gordon ran the very real risk of ruining his spanikopita.

"You'd better keep buttering that," Elaine cautioned.

Gordon pinched the edges of the tear together, added another sheet and began stroking melted butter across the top, shaking his head the entire time. "There is obviously a great deal you have not told me. Since this is about your life and not mine, I will try to get past the gnawing sense of betrayal." He looked askance at Elaine. "What's happening between you and Mitch?"

"Nothing's happening." Elaine had never lied to Gordon before. She felt guilty, but not guilty enough to fill her friend in on all the details. "He's reached a point in his life where having children sounds good to him, and I want to have children, so this is a practical solution. It's not romantic. It just…makes sense."

"Uh-huh. I'm glad it makes sense to someone. I could use more clarification."

Fortunately, Elaine's new cell phone rang before she had to wriggle out of giving Gordon his clarification.

Leaving the pot of cheese dip warming on the stove, Elaine pulled the small, purple-faced phone from her purse.

"You got a cell phone, and you didn't tell me?" Gordon stabbed the pastry brush into the butter. "We're experiencing a trend here."

Ignoring him for the moment, Elaine answered her phone. When she heard the voice on the other end of the line, she made a quarter turn away from Gordon. "Hi. How did you get this number?"

"You left it on your phone machine." Mitch's amused voice sent chills along her arms.

"Oh. Right. Right." She'd purchased the phone and a service contract when she found out that Pumpkin would have to stay at the vet's at least a couple of days. Telling herself it was important that the vet be able to contact her any time, Elaine had tried to ignore the little voice that teased, *"Yeah, and Mitch said he'd tried to get hold of you, but you didn't have a cell phone. Now you can talk to him anytime, anywhere."* Because she wanted to say, "Nuh-uh," to that ornery voice, she hadn't rushed to give Mitch the number. She'd merely left it on her phone machine.…

"So you have a cell phone," Mitch said. On a wireless, he sounded very much like a purring lion.

"It's new. You're my first caller."

"I'm honored."

"*I* don't know the number," Gordon complained behind her.

"Where are you?" Mitch asked.

It was at least seventy degrees in Gordon's kitchen, so Elaine tried hard not to shiver. Was it only Mitch or did everyone sound tantalizingly intimate on a cell phone? "I'm at Gordon's," she said. "We're in his kitchen. Cooking."

"Mmm. What are you doing this afternoon?"

"This afternoon?"

"There's a French Master's exhibit at the art museum. How do you feel about Monet?"

"I love Monet. Are these museum pieces or private collections?"

Gordon cleared his throat as if a boulder had lodged there, no subtlety whatsoever. "Excuse me? I hope you're not making plans for *this* this afternoon. We're celebrating your father's birthday."

Elaine covered the phone with her palm. "I know that."

"And I know you're talking to Mitch!"

"We're discussing an art exhibit," she hissed, hoping to silence him. "It's not a big deal."

"Sure." Gordon scoffed. "Those French Impressionists are so *practical*. Give my regards to Cezanne. I'll give your regards to your father."

"I am not going to the art museum!"

"Lainey?" Mitch's voice resonated from the earpiece.

Gordon arched a brow. *Lainey?* he mouthed, giving her a smug you-don't-fool-me-sister look before turning back to his food.

Elaine returned the phone to her ear, feeling vulnerable and exposed in a way she couldn't define. If Gordon knew she and Mitch were considering marriage, he might tell Vicki; they'd become pretty chummy of late. Elaine didn't think she could bear picking her way across this rocky slope with Mitch while everyone watched. While everyone *hoped*.

"I'm here," she said into the phone. "I can't go to the

museum today, I'm afraid. We're having a thing for my father this afternoon.''

"A thing? What kind of a thing?''

"A little birthday gathering, nothing fancy. It's not a mile-stone birthday, but when he turned sixty several years ago, he said he wanted a party every year for the rest of his life just in case it turned out to be his last, so it's become a family joke. Generally the birthdays get more juvenile each year. Last year we went to The Family Fun Center.''

There was a brief silence on the other end of the line. "Do you have room for one more?''

It was Elaine's turn to pause. "You want to come to my father's birthday? It's not at the Fun Center this year.''

Mitch laughed. "That is a disappointment, but I'd still like to join you.''

Elaine cringed. "What I meant was, we're not going any-where. It's going to be a family potluck. Dull. Really. Our family gatherings are very dull.''

Having snuck up behind her, Gordon grabbed the phone and said to Mitch, "Yeah. The July Fourth limbo contest only lasted forty-five minutes. It's getting duller every year.''

"That's not true!'' Elaine snatched the phone back and pro-tested into the receiver. "That's not true. My family is very sedate.''

"Why are you acting like this?'' Gordon asked, watching her closely.

She made a slicing motion across her throat, indicating he should stifle himself or suffer the consequences.

"I don't need to be entertained, Elaine. Is there some reason you'd rather I not join you?''

Two or three dozen reasons. "No, no.'' How was she going to get out of this without telling the truth? That Kevin had usually found any excuse he could not to attend family func-tions with her. That going to her father's party with Mitch would bring her way too close to her dream of family, and the closer she got the more she could be hurt.

With no reasonable way out, she told him she'd meet him there, gave directions and hung up. If Mitch was bothered by her lack of graciousness, he didn't show it.

Oy gevalt. In a couple of hours, her parents were going to meet the man with whom their daughter planned to make a baby—before she was married to him—the same man who had represented her snakelike ex-husband during their divorce. That wasn't going to sit well.

To make matters worse, Gordon was watching her with a best friend's X-ray vision. The pastry on his spanikopita could crack like the Mojave Desert; he obviously didn't care anymore. He wanted information.

Well, she didn't want to give it! She didn't want to tell anyone anything yet. She wanted to quietly…quietly…go about her business with her heart tucked safely in her chest, not hanging out on her sleeve where everyone who knew her could see it break, if it came to that. If she was going to risk her dreams, her faith, one more time, she wanted to do it without an audience.

With an arm wrapped around her middle, the other bent so that the elbow rested on her opposite wrist, she pressed the knuckles of one fist against her chin. "I'm sorry that I hurt you by not telling you what Mitch and I are planning, but it all happened very recently."

Gordon remained immovable. Sniffing eloquently, he examined a thumbnail.

Elaine was a sucker, just a darned sucker for his you-wound-me pose. "All right, I haven't told you everything. But let's forget about it for today. Can't we just spend some fun, relaxing friend time cooking together and then hanging out at the potluck?" She flapped her hand at him. "Forget all that other stuff."

Gordon drummed his fingers idly on the counter.

"You know, Gordy, you could put me first today. That would be a really nice gesture. I mean, I'm under stress here.

We've still got a lot of cooking to do, and we're falling be-hind.'' She waited. ''Say something. Say anything.''

''Your cheese dip is scorching.''

''Is he a good lover?''

''Gordon!''

''What? I'm asking because I care. About you.''

Driving along Macadam on the way to her parents' house in West Linn, Elaine was too irritated with herself to enjoy the beautiful scenery. ''I told you, *no details.*''

She had spilled a few of the beans to Gordon, just a few, hoping to assuage his feelings before the potluck. She hadn't wanted the tension between them to inspire additional questions from her parents and Mitch. Her mistake had been in believing she could dole the information out in manageable portions without his colorful commentary and further probing.

''I've said all I'm going to,''. she stated with brutal finality. ''We made love, he *may* be the father of my baby, and that's it. End of story. We're two people who are ready to have a child, but we're not married. It's not so weird these days.''

''And you're not getting married?''

''I told you, no.''

She had not, however, mentioned her deal with Mitch: when the stick turned blue, the rings went on.

''You're going to be discreet and circumspect today, right?'' she asked. ''No stray comments. I don't want to have to dodge any bullets. Or explain this to anybody else. I don't want my family to suspect anything other than that Mitch and I are dating *very casually.*'' She eyed Gordon as he lounged in the passenger seat, tray of still-warm spanikopita on his lap. ''Please don't make me sorry I told you, Gordy.''

Gordon turned to her, sober as a judge behind his Bolle Rhodia sunglasses. ''Once again, you wound me.''

''For a large man, he limbos surprisingly well.''

Elaine didn't even bother to glance at Gordon. She could

hardly take her eyes off of Mitch, who was at that moment waging a heated battle against her brother for the title "Limbo Champion of West Linn." The flexibility of his body amazed her…and incited all sorts of shocking ideas. The flexibility of his personality rendered her utterly speechless. Who was that unmasked man?

Barney Rozel's sixty-eighth birthday party was in high gear in the Rozel's lush backyard. The "dull family gathering" Elaine had described to Mitch actually included several neighbors and good friends. Lanterns were strung across the patio; the trees were sprinkled with twinkly lights. The Jamaican Chicks Marimba Band, to which Elaine's mother had belonged for several years, was hammering up a storm of infectious music as people danced, limboed and gobbled the vast and eclectic array of food. But of all the people having a fabulous time, Mitch appeared to be having the most fabulous.

What the devil had got into the buttoned-down, upright, eminently dignified lawyer?

"I'm getting another coconut shrimp before they're gone. You want one?" Gordon asked as he pushed away from the patio door, where he and Elaine watched the action.

"No, thanks." Confusion put butterflies in her belly, leaving little room for food.

As Gordon left, Elaine reflected that she had originally intended to catch Mitch outside her parents' house for a quick briefing on how they should define their relationship for her family: casual, nonsexual, dating a few weeks if anyone asked—that was how she'd intended to present the situation. But he'd already arrived and entered the house by the time she and Gordon showed up.

Mitch had been chatting with her uncle Hank and cousin Holly when Elaine walked in. Though Elaine would have chosen to stand at a platonic distance, Mitch had held out his arm, drawing her cozily against his side. Holly's eyes had widened, Uncle Hank had smiled, and nothing Elaine had said or done since then seemed to convince anyone that she and Mitch were not a hot item.

Elaine couldn't even convince herself.

Snuggled against his side while they chatted with her relatives, she had felt more at home, more *right* than ever before.

Now, standing alone, she watched her nieces and her cousins' children, and she couldn't stop herself from imagining her own children joining the mix. Nor could she keep from visualizing Mitch at her side, watching them, too.

And in her visualization, she and Mitch were not platonic and they were not casual; they loved each other. She didn't even picture the ''in love'' part; she pictured the loving. The trusting. The forever.

A medley of cheers and groans went up from the crowd watching the limbo contest. Her brother had knocked down the bar. With exaggerated reluctance, he named Mitch the winner. The same shiny paper crown they'd used for two years running was plopped atop Mitch's head and a cold beer thrust into his hands.

When he sought her out and walked toward her, he wore the crown and a triumphant smile. He paused briefly along the way to pick up a glass of iced tea, and when he stopped in front of her, holding the drinks and grinning at her, wearing a paper crown her mother had bought at the Ninety-Eight Cent store, Elaine's heart nearly stopped.

Oh, no. *Oh, no.* He was going to make her want it all.

''Your brother is a ferocious competitor. I've faced lawyers with less determination.'' He handed her the iced tea.

Accepting the drink, she fiddled with the straw while she tried to collect herself. ''Well, he likes the crown. It's going to be a tough year for him without it.''

''Too bad.'' Mitch pushed the crown so that it slipped over his forehead at a rakish angle. ''I won it in a free and fair competition. I deserve an award. Unless you can think of another one.''

The suggestiveness was not entirely playful. His gaze moved from her eyes to her lips.

She'd kissed him before, but always privately. Not in front of her family. Not with twinkly lights and music and stars and the laughter of children swirling around them. If she kissed him here, it would be real. Sex happened in private. *Relationships* happened in front of parents and neighbors and friends.

All she had to do was stand on her tiptoes to touch her lips to his. Physically the gap between them could be closed that easily. The emotional gap was another story.

She wasn't sure why he was willing to expose their relationship to public scrutiny.

She wasn't.

"I think the crown looks good on you," she said. "You should keep it."

Awareness flared in Mitch's eyes. He understood her decision and accepted it with little change in expression, accommodating her by changing the subject. "You have a great family. I've never been to a birthday celebration quite like this. Outside of college."

"Oh, terrific."

"It's a compliment."

"How does your family celebrate birthdays?"

"For the last decade? With cards. Before that, Vicki would attempt to make things festive." He took a sip of beer.

Elaine tilted her head, listening to his tone more than the words. It was amazing; the lighthearted limbo king was gone, replaced by the contained lawyer.

"And before Vicki?" she asked, realizing she knew next to nothing about his early life.

After spending an evening with Elaine's family, Mitch wasn't sure he wanted to tell her what life was like for him and M.D. Nothing in his background justified a faith that he could create a family as happy as this one.

When he'd seen Elaine sitting on her kitchen floor, indulging with seemingly infinite patience and care the neuroses of a scrawny alley cat, he'd thought two things: *Kevin, you imbecile,* and *God, don't let me blow this.*

He'd stopped short of making love to her that night, even though his body had ached. Something had stopped him, though. At the time he'd thought he was out of his mind; now he was glad he'd exerted some control. When Elaine refused to kiss him a moment ago, he understood that she did not want to expose their relationship before her family and friends. She'd hung way back during the limbo contest, and earlier, she'd stiffened when he drew her near. She still thought they could end the relationship cleanly, with no one the wiser, if she didn't get pregnant.

But now Mitch knew he wanted more than the experiment they'd agreed upon; he wanted to be part of all this. It scared the hell out of him, but that wouldn't stop him. The question was, what was stopping Elaine? Shifting to stand beside her, Mitch sipped his beer and surveyed the party, which hadn't slowed a bit. The children were doing the limbo now, encouraged from the sidelines by their parents. Elaine's mother had accepted a cold drink from her husband, but was once again standing behind her marimba, joyfully hammering away while her spouse stood by, clapping his hands.

She'd asked what celebrations were like in his family before Vicki arrived on the scene.

"Not like this," he answered. "Before Vicki and after, the Ryders were…dignified. My father didn't like big displays, and he worked a great deal. He rarely remembered birthdays or anniversaries. Since I was older than Em, I'd write our birthdays on his desk calendar. I'd leave a list of 'suggested gifts,' too. We usually made out pretty well."

His smile held no bitterness, but Elaine felt angry for him nonetheless. If her family ever heard that story they'd help her throw him the biggest, baddest birthday celebration he'd ever seen, every year, whether he wanted it or not.

She stopped short of expressing the thought. First they had

to get pregnant. Then they had to stay pregnant. Then they could think about gatherings.

After, that is, they worked out the prenuptial agreement and all the other safeguards they would need in the event that their relationship didn't work.

She raised her iced tea glass, but the coldness of the drink seemed to magnify the coldness she suddenly felt inside.

An hour later, Elaine's father had blown out the candles on his birthday cake, and Elaine and Gordon were in the kitchen, making to-go packages of food for the guests who were starting to leave.

"It was a good party this year," Elaine said as she put plastic wrap around the remains of her cousin Holly's famous peanut butter-banana cream pie. "Dad seems happy. I didn't see him, though, as I was clearing the table. I wonder where he went?"

"In his study, I think," Gordon said, helping himself to a grape as he composed a fruit plate. "I walked by on my way to the bathroom and saw him in there playing with his new camcorder."

Elaine and her brother had gone in together on the digital camera, though the other guests had been told no presents were allowed. Since the party had become an annual event, only family was permitted to bring gifts. "He wasn't alone, by the way," Gordon added, popping another grape and speaking around it. "In case you're interested."

"Oh, no. He and Mom aren't making out again, are they?" Last year he'd been caught feeling her mother up behind the batting cages at the Family Fun Center.

"Your mother is teaching Uncle Hank to play 'My Dog Has Fleas' on the marimba. Your father is in his study with his camcorder...and Mitch."

Gordon must have dropped his voice an entire octave when he said, "and Mitch." If not for the ominous tone, Elaine might not have shivered. "So what's wrong with that? They seem to be hitting it off."

"I'll say."

Elaine pulled the plastic wrap too tightly across Holly's pie. The top squooshed. "All right," she said. "Give it to me straight."

"Well, I'm no expert," Gordon demurred, "but it looked to me like Mitch was pulling a Ryan."

"Pulling a Ryan." Elaine shook her head. "I'm sorry. This is supposed to mean something?"

Gordon rolled his expressive eyes. "Well, apparently it means you have forgotten six weeks of the most exciting TV of our lives. Ryan and Trista? *The Bachelorette?* Popcorn and hankies?"

"Oh, yeah."

Though Elaine had still been married when the show aired, Kevin had already taken to spending evenings "at work" or "with clients," so she and Gordon had made a date every Wednesday to make popcorn and watch the reality TV show that promised true love in six weeks. Like instant riches and instant weight loss, the concept had seemed too good to be true, but then Ryan got down on one knee, Trista cried and the Cinderella complex was born again.

"So what's 'pulling a Ryan?' Oh, no!" She clapped a hand over her mouth. "He's not—" Elaine glanced wildly around the kitchen, making sure no one was within earshot, and then lowering her voice to a hiss, anyway. "Mitch isn't asking my father if he can marry me?" Abandoning the to-go plates, she ran to Gordon, grabbing him by his shirt. "Why do you think that?"

Surprised, he put his hands atop hers. "Take it easy. They seemed to be deep in conversation, that's all. I was partially playing with you. I'm sorry." He drew her close, patting her back.

A breath of relief escaped in a whoosh. "Don't scare me like that."

Rubbing his hand in a circle between her shoulder blades, Gordon said, "I haven't seen you that frightened since *Food Monthly* misprinted the recipe for Holiday Bon Bons in their Christmas issue."

"They left out an entire can of sweetened condensed milk. I had a right to be upset." Giving Gordon's arms a grateful squeeze, Elaine stepped away from him.

"So what scared you so badly this time?"

Though she'd told herself the details of her agreement with Mitch were classified information, this evening had changed things. Suddenly Mitch seemed less predictable than he had even a couple of days ago. His desire for family kept growing. And as it did, her fantasies grew, too.

"We're not supposed to get married unless I get pregnant," she confessed to Gordon, who narrowed his eyes.

"You said—"

"I said we weren't getting married, which is true. For now. But Mitch made me agree that if I do get pregnant and we have a baby, we'll get married and stay married for a year. Then we can reevaluate."

"This is all very gothic."

"No, it's not. It's practical."

"Do you love him?"

"Shhh." Gordon had asked the question without lowering his voice. Elaine looked around, making certain they were still alone. "No. But I'm sort of…infatuated with him." To effect the appearance of a casual conversation, she went back to packaging leftovers. "I don't want to love him, and I don't want to marry him. Not unless it's for the sake of our child."

"Why don't you want to love him? I mean, if that's the natural progression of things?"

"Because. When you love someone who likes you a lot, but doesn't really *love* you and isn't *in* love with you, there's a piece of you that just never feels settled. It's like craving cherry cheesecake for days then eating a lemon drop and thinking you're going to be satisfied. Part of you stays hungry. I don't want to stay hungry. I don't want to look at someone day after day and always wish for more. Like in *Jerry Maguire*. Remember? Renee Zellweger fell for Tom Cruise, and he married her because the timing seemed right, but he wasn't in love with her and she couldn't stand not being his cherry cheesecake, so they split up and her heart was broken.''

"You're afraid your heart's going to be broken?" From the corner of her eye, Elaine saw Gordon watching her like the best friend he was, no shred of glibness or humor marring the compassion.

She tried to shrug, but her shoulders felt too heavy. A damned, dratted tear dropped onto her Aunt Suzanne's to-go plate. "I want to be the cheesecake. I want to be the thing someone is so hungry for that nothing else will do. I deserve that this time, Gordy."

Because Gordon agreed with her, all he could do was sigh.

Chapter Fifteen

The Monday after her father's party, Elaine was scheduled to pick Pumpkin up from the vet's. She arranged to leave work a bit early and was walking along Salmon Street in downtown Portland, heading toward her car, when her cell phone rang. Digging through her purse, she hoped the call was from her doctor, not the vet. She didn't want any new delays to keep her from bringing home her sweet kitty, but moreover she was hoping to squeeze into her doctor's schedule today.

All weekend she'd been feeling strange twinges in her pelvis. The same thing had happened last month. Most likely she was experiencing PMS, but taking into account a few other odd symptoms she'd noticed in recent months, Elaine wanted to chat with her doctor, just to be on the safe side.

Pressing the answer button on her cell phone, she held the slim unit to her ear. "Hello."

"Where are you now?"

Elaine stopped walking. "I'm downtown, on my way to the parking lot where my car is. And you?"

"Also downtown." As usual when they spoke by cell phone, Mitch's voice had a sexy, suggestive quality that made goose bumps rise along her arms. "Maybe we should rendezvous."

"It's only three-thirty. You're going to ruin your reputation as a workaholic."

"True." His sigh was exaggeratedly mournful and self-pitying.

Smiling, Elaine began walking again. She'd tried to pump her dad for information about his conversation with Mitch on Saturday night, but all Barney said was that Mitch was a fine man who'd given him good advice about his camcorder warranty. Elaine's mother, sister-in-law and cousin Holly had, on the other hand, taken turns calling her (and then in all likelihood each other) on Sunday. To a woman, they thought Mitch was a dreamboat, and they wanted all the romantic details—when Mitch and Elaine had met, how they'd met, did it seem serious? Elaine had edited heavily, but satisfied their curiosity.

"I have to pick up Pumpkin, anyway, and then hopefully my doctor will squeeze me in for an appointment, so I don't really have time for—"

"Why are you seeing your doctor?"

"I...uh, it's personal."

"We're trying to have a baby together. *That's* personal."

True, but they hadn't been trying very hard lately. When he'd said goodbye Saturday night, he'd kissed her on the cheek. And they'd been standing next to his car by then, with no one watching.

"It's a woman thing," she said, expecting his curiosity to be satisfied. She'd never yet met a man who wanted to discuss women's health care. But Mitch was not faint-hearted.

"And?" he prompted.

"And I'm having a little pain. It's probably a PMS symptom."

"When you get your appointment, call me back."

"Mitch, I am not—"

"Call me," he ordered. "Or I'll keep calling you. Hang on

a second." She heard a woman's voice, addressing him in the background. He responded, "Thanks. I'll be right in." To Elaine, he said, "I've got a meeting. Call me."

"Mitch, if you have a meeting—"

"Call, Elaine. I'll be expecting it. Use my cell number."

She scribbled down the numbers he'd given her once before and said goodbye. Almost immediately the phone rang again. This time it was the nurse in Elaine's doctor's office, and after listening to Elaine's symptoms and to her new pregnancy plan, they made an appointment for five-thirty that evening.

Pausing on the street corner, Elaine shook her head at the phone as she dialed Mitch's number.

"Have you been seeing my wife?"

Because Kevin Lowry worked in the same office as Mitch, it was not unusual for the men to run into each other during the week. Outside of business, they chatted casually, but were not the best of friends and never had been. They had never lingered in the conference room, for example, after office meetings. Until now.

It was four-thirty, and Mitch wanted to have one last conversation with his secretary then get out of here, but while the others were heading back to their own offices, Kevin had pointed first at himself, then at Mitch mouthing, "I...want... to...talk."

So now they were faced off, Kevin standing in front of the double doors he'd closed, and Mitch sitting against the table, arms folded, a thin smile playing about his lips. He tilted his head as if he wasn't sure he'd heard properly. "Are you asking whether I'm dating your *ex*-wife?"

Kevin, a tall, slender man with thinning hair and light eyes had trouble maintaining his poker face. His cheeks flushed red. "Under the circumstances, that's splitting hairs, isn't it, Mitch?"

"The circumstances?"

"You were my legal counsel during the divorce. Dating a

client's spouse—ex-spouse," he supplied before Mitch could correct him again, "calls your ethics into question, I think, Mitch."

What, Mitch wondered, were the ethics of punching Kevin in his smug face? "Do ya think?" he said in lieu of a solid hit, but Kevin missed the irony.

"Yes, I do," he said, "not to mention the ethics of dating the ex-wife of a partner in your firm." He took a step forward, his face growing redder by the minute. "Hell, man, you've been to my house on Christmas!"

"Yeah, put that way, it does seem kind of bad," Mitch agreed, controlling himself for the moment. "Although not as bad as cheating on your wife. You forgot to disclose that to your attorney, by the way. Also to the spouse in question."

"I didn't start seeing Stephanie until Elaine and I were over," Kevin insisted through a tightly clenched jaw.

"Over." Mitch nodded slowly, considering the word. "Apparently a relative term."

Kevin moved his suit jacket aside to put his hands on his hips. "You *are* dating her," he concluded, the anger behind his eyes clearly telegraphing his displeasure. "Have you slept with her yet?"

The energy with which Mitch pushed away from the table propelled him forward until he was practically nose-to-nose with his former client. "You lost the right to ask that. Move on, Kevin. She has."

"With your help, apparently." The depth of Kevin's bitterness stopped Mitch from flinging the lighter man aside and striding through those double doors.

"You're remarried," Mitch pointed out, curiosity and disgust warring inside him. "You and your wife just had a baby. Shouldn't you concentrate on making *this* marriage work?"

The discomfort on Kevin's face might have engendered sympathy if Mitch had less to lose.

Running a hand over his close-cropped hair, Kevin admitted, "I married Stephanie because she thought she was pregnant. It turned out to be a false alarm. The first time. She agreed to wait awhile after that, but…''

He didn't finish the sentence, so, silently, Mitch finished it for him: *But she wasn't willing to let you call the shots. Like Elaine was.* The difference apparently between Kevin's second wife and Elaine was that Elaine made her choices honestly, with respect for others. The way she did most everything. He doubted there was a sly bone in her body.

Kevin fiddled nervously with his tie. ''I haven't told anyone else that I suspect Stephanie…''

Mitch felt his entire body fill with revulsion and a kind of detached pity. ''They won't hear it from me.''

Kevin nodded, relieved, but after several moments of awkward hesitation he ventured, ''I don't mind if Elaine knows.''

Mitch's jaw clenched as understanding dawned. His disdain for his colleague increased tenfold. ''You left her, you have a kid with someone else…and now you want her back?''

''People have regrets, Mitch. They make mistakes.''

''Yeah, they do. And some people, apparently, never learn from them.''

''You arrogant—'' Kevin swore rudely. ''Elaine and I were together since college. You think she's over us? Don't kid yourself.'' He glanced at the doors behind him and lowered his voice. ''She's been seeing an old friend of ours lately. Digging for information. Ask yourself why.''

Mitch moved forward until he was practically nose-to-nose with his new nemesis. ''I'm not kidding myself, Lowry. I'm just not stupid enough to think Elaine would wait for you to come crawling back.''

Without giving Kevin a chance to respond, Mitch strode past him, shoving the double doors open and walking swiftly through the executive suites, unmindful of the senior partner who called his name. But with every determined step he took, Mitch felt the seed of doubt Kevin had planted take root.

The waiting area of the Portland Women's Health Care Cooperative was still bustling at 5:55 p.m. Children read books or played with toys in the center of the room. Women, mature and young, pregnant and not, filled every chrome-legged chair.

Elaine had chosen a seat close to the reception desk and was reading a magazine with a grinning baby on the cover. Absorbed in her article, she didn't look up until Mitch was standing in front of her. The first thing she saw was the flower he held, a long-stemmed pink rose wrapped in cellophane. Extending it toward her over the top of her magazine, he said, "Sorry I'm late."

Late? Elaine hadn't expected him at all. She had phoned as requested, answering his questions about the time and location of her appointment, but she certainly had not expected him to show up. He was the only adult male in the waiting room.

Lowering the magazine, she accepted the rose, aware of the glances they received from her fellow patients. "Thank you." She enjoyed the fragrance briefly then murmured, "Are you planning to stay? I mean, this has nothing to do with the baby."

Bending toward her, Mitch whispered back, though his whisper seemed to parody hers, "Do you mind that I'm here?"

"Well—" She glanced around the room. "Not if you don't. You weren't thinking of coming into the examining room, were you?"

He pursed his lips then shook his head. "I'm not feeling that need."

They smiled at each other.

Elaine felt ridiculously buoyant. A tickly warmth stirred inside her. She'd attended her doctor's appointments alone since she was old enough to drive. She wasn't particularly brave when it came to needles and paper gowns and diagnoses; visiting the doctor alone was merely something one did as an adult. With Mitch here, the nervous knot in her tummy began to untie. That he cared enough to show up made her feel…nonsensically cherished.

"There's nowhere to sit," she told him, preparing to get up so at least they'd both be standing, but a nurse emerged from the inner office and called the name of a very pregnant woman two seats down. Without being asked, the ladies next to Elaine shifted so Mitch could sit near her.

He seemed big and out of place in the femininely appointed and female-inhabited room, but if he was uncomfortable at all he didn't show it. Within moments, he was flipping through a dog-eared copy of *The Baby Book* and asking Elaine if she'd ever heard of "this family bed idea."

Trying not to smile, she nodded. "I may have run across the concept once or twice."

There followed a discussion—with several other women chiming in—about the merits and drawbacks of sleeping with one's baby. Mitch was a full participant, asking questions, offering opinions, quoting from the book on his lap. As the women nearest them were called in to their appointments, other women from across the room came over, and new discussions were started: stroller or sling? Cloth diapers or disposable?

After a time, Elaine grew quiet. She couldn't speak; she was too busy trying to decipher this new Mitch.

This was what she wanted. The feeling turning every part of her warm and cozy. Maybe another woman would fall in love over a trip to Paris or standing under the moon on a Caribbean cruise. Not her. She fell hook, line and sinker in a gynecologist's office during a debate over nature vs. nurture.

She fell in love when the man in her life absently reached over to hold her hand as he listened intently to a woman explaining the benefits of baby wearing....

She fell in love when she knew for certain Mitch Ryder would be not merely her husband, but her partner in life....

"Elaine Rozel?"

Using her maiden name, the nurse called her to her appointment.

Elaine stood on wobbly legs. Standing with her, Mitch winked and squeezed her hand. "I'll be here."

She looked into his eyes and felt her heart stop, just long enough to appreciate the fact that it started to beat again when he smiled.

Elaine Joanne Lowry née Rozel fell in love when suddenly in an OB-GYN's waiting room, the world made absolute, perfect sense.

Looking into Mitch's eyes, she returned the squeeze before letting his hand go. "I'm counting on it."

"So call the office tomorrow, and we'll schedule you for an internal ultrasound at Providence. Think you can take a couple of hours off work later this week if they can get you in?"

"That soon?" Sitting up on the examining table, her bare legs dangling beneath the atrocious paper gown covering her thighs, Elaine stared at her doctor. "Do I *have* to do it that quickly?"

Elaine's doctor, a tall, attractive woman in her mid-forties with an air of confidence that was usually quite reassuring, scribbled on a chart as she spoke. "Your next cycle's about a week away. I'd like to get you in before it starts if we can. The sooner we find out what's going on, the sooner we can identify and deal with anything that might prevent you from getting pregnant."

"Do you think it's that serious? It's just a few cramps. Maybe if I laid off the Ben & Jerry's for a while—"

"I felt a lump of some sort, Elaine." Aretha turned and looked at her patient with a smile that was both calm and firm. "It may not be impressive at all, but let's find out what it is."

"Lump?" A few minutes ago, while performing the examination, Aretha had said she felt "a little thickness" that was "probably nothing." Now Elaine had a lump? "Aren't all lumps impressive?" she asked, feeling queasy. Well, a little more than queasy, actually; she thought she might do something projectile on Aretha's camel suede pumps.

Making a face, Aretha removed her glasses to rub a spot on one of the lenses. "I hate the word lump. What I found is something indeterminate. And you're probably right, it's probably just cramps. Ordinarily I'd wait a cycle and see if it resolves on its own. But when a thirty-seven-year-old patient who wants to have a baby comes in complaining of pain in her pelvis, and I feel something…whatever it is…I've got to follow up. Right?''

Put that way, Elaine felt a little more calm. "Right.''

"Okay. So we'll make an appointment tomorrow. And don't worry. Relax. Go out to dinner.'' Aretha replaced her glasses. "Have a little Ben & Jerry's.''

"So that's all it is? A case of cramps?'' Mitch twisted a wine opener into a bottle of chardonnay.

"Garden variety.'' Elaine knew that wasn't *exactly* what Aretha had said, but she didn't want to make a big deal of anything, and she definitely didn't want Mitch to take more time off work or to insist on coming along for her internal ultrasound. Besides, seeing Aretha had soothed her worries… and gave her something new to ponder.

Their sojourn in the doctor's waiting room had been relatively brief, but profound. There was no denying that she wanted Mitch. Day and night. For lovemaking, for conversation, for the million tiny decisions made during a day and the few huge decisions made during a lifetime—she could imagine him now as her partner in all of it. What amazed her was that she wasn't afraid.

The pop from the cork made her smile. Maybe they'd start saving wine corks in cheesy gallon jugs they could put on their coffee table so when their friends came over to play Bunko twenty years from now, Mitch could tell them, "Yep, we've been together long enough to have opened nine hundred and thirty-seven bottles. We're shootin' for two thousand.''

"What's funny?''

Over the bowl of lettuce she'd been tearing, Elaine looked into Mitch's inquisitive, unbeatably sexy eyes and felt a rush of pure, heart-thumping affection. "You would never say shootin'.''

"I beg your pardon?''

Leaving the sparkling granite counter in Mitch's kitchen,

where she was certain that few meals had ever been prepared, Elaine walked to the kitchen table. Plucking the bottle of wine from his hand, she set it in the pewter wine holder he'd unearthed from a cabinet and moved into him. Very, very close.

"I'm not hungry," she said, nevertheless eyeing the buttons on his shirt as if she'd like to eat those.

Surprise sparked deep in Mitch's eyes. With a glance at the wine bottle, he cocked a brow. "Not thirsty, either?"

Slowly, Elaine wagged her head. "Hmm-mm." With a feathery touch, her fingers found the closed top button. Thankfully, he'd already discarded his tie; she had never been good with ties. "How about you?" she asked, easily loosening the shirt another notch. "Are you thirsty?"

The sudden dryness in Mitch's throat suggested he was parched, but no wine would quench this thirst. For days, he'd held off making love to her again. When a glance from her, a smile, a frown—hell, when the mere thought of her—had made him clench with the need to bury his body deep inside hers, Mitch had denied himself the privilege.

And now he knew they should talk. Kevin's words gnawed a hole in his gut when he thought about them.

Elaine started on the next button. The brush of her cool, small knuckles against his chest was enough to make every muscle in Mitch's torso contract. He wanted to cover her hand with his, stop her, at least until he could be sure he was in control of himself.

So far, their relationship had been unconventional in the extreme. He wanted to woo Elaine, to court her before making love again.

Elaine spread Mitch's shirt open and bent her head to his chest. She twirled a finger in his chest hairs, traced a tiny circle on his skin as her lips nibbled their way across his chest. If they didn't talk, someone was bound to get hurt…maybe him.

Her teeth found his right nipple, and her tongue darted out. Intending to reach for her hand, he grabbed her buttocks instead, which was less effective as a halting maneuver. Still, he managed to rasp, "We need to talk."

Against his chest, Elaine shook her head. "Don't wanna."

Keeping one hand on her rump, he buried the other in her hair and urged her head up. Her lips were parted; her eyes heavy-lidded, but alive with desire and challenge. It took every ounce of Mitch's strength to growl out, "You're a conventional woman. You need marriage."

Brows lifting at the word *conventional,* Elaine discovered that if she wriggled her left hand into his shirt just a couple of inches, she could stroke both his nipples at the same time. "We covered this already."

Letting go of her head, he slid his hand down the side of her neck, her collar, her shoulder, en route to grasping the hands that were driving him crazy. Unfortunately, he dropped his focus and grabbed her breast. "We got it wrong. There's a...pattern to follow. Marriage first. We're not following the right pattern."

Elaine traced figure eights around his nipples. "I'm following a pattern."

He placed his hand atop hers. "Most people marry *before* they get pregnant."

Elaine bit him through his shirt. Mitch gritted his teeth against a groan.

She was making this unnecessarily difficult. Filling his hands with her, he forced himself to speak. "I'm thinking about you...what's good for you."

"Thanks." Reaching up, she pulled his head toward hers and stood on her toes so their lips met. "Now shut up," she murmured, initiating a kiss that threatened to render him speechless for life.

In one swift, conversationless move, Mitch pulled Elaine against him, pressing his hips firmly into hers. The devil with "convention." If he wasn't inside her within the next thirty seconds, he was going to embarrass himself in his own kitchen.

Getting them to the bedroom was the tricky part. Elaine partially solved the problem when she wound her arms around his neck. While they were still kissing, he reached for her legs, drawing them up, surprising her so that she had to hang on to him tightly.

With her arms and legs wrapped around him, their lips and tongues dancing as he walked, Mitch carried Elaine to his bedroom for the first time.

Kicking open the door, he moved immediately toward the bed, allowing her legs to slide down until she found her footing. He didn't intend to leave her balanced for long, however. Pressing a knee between her thighs, he parted her legs, pulling away just enough to reach for her, letting her know he, too, meant business. In his mind, whether they made a baby tonight was incidental to the need that made his blood pound and his sense of urgency roar to life.

As he cupped the feminine mound that only a thin cotton panty protected, Elaine's head arched back. Her eyes, wild and passion-dazed, met his. With his knee spreading her legs a bit farther, she was forced to clutch his arms for balance. Eschewing niceties, Mitch moved over the top of her panties to explore her more boldly. Elaine groaned, pressing down into his hand, and Mitch admitted that courting season, brief as it had been, was already over, at least until they'd had enough of each other.

And there was no telling when that would be.

Lifting her again, he laid her on the mattress and followed her down. If he'd meant to slow his pace, the mere sight of Elaine made such control all but impossible. Her creamy bosom rose and fell rapidly beneath the smooth bodice of her dress; her hazel eyes were half-closed with passion. The lips he would never, ever tire of parted as she breathed.

Easing the hem of her dress up her smooth legs, Mitch lowered his body to hers.

Two days of walking on air made Elaine feel giggly and energetic. After she and Mitch made love Monday evening, they had dinner on his patio, drank wine in the Jacuzzi, ate dessert sitting cross-legged atop his bed and made love again, this time under the covers.

And they'd talked. They'd talked about movies and vacation sites, their favorite architecture and what they loved about living in Portland. Elaine shared her dream of having a little cottage somewhere on the Northern Oregon coast, with a porch swing, a white picket fence and a gray poodle named Sophie. Mitch revised the vision, swapping Sophie out for a golden retriever named Jack. Neither of them mentioned marriage.

Until around midnight.

Just as Elaine was gathering the shards of her self-discipline and preparing to go home, Mitch grabbed her, tumbled her back into the bed and placed one of his big, warm hands on her tummy as she tried to wriggle away. "Marry me, and you can stay all night. Think it over... A king-size bed in a heated town house or a long drive in a cold car?" Circling her belly button with the tip of his finger, he whispered into her ear. "Choose." Using his tongue to give her ear the same treatment her belly button was receiving, he told her again, hypnotically, "Choose, Lainey, and then plan to stay tonight anyway. Because I'm not letting you out of this bed until I absolutely have to."

He'd started kissing her again, and to the best of her recollection, no more words had been spoken. None intelligible, anyway. She'd gotten up at an ungodly hour to shower then run home, change into her work clothes and apologize profusely to Pumpkin, who had spent her first night home alone in a bed near the floor heater in the kitchen. Elaine had phoned Vicki early in the evening to ask her to check on the cat. She hadn't mentioned to her neighbor where she was or why, but she realized belatedly that if Vicki had caller ID, she would know exactly where Elaine spent the night.

Mitch had needed to catch up on work Tuesday night, and Elaine had needed to cuddle Pumpkin and catch up on sleep, but they planned to meet tonight for dinner.

Perhaps Mitch would mention marriage again, and if he did,

she did not intend to play hard to get. She wanted to marry him. Never had she experienced such passion and desire. Never had she felt the safety and comfort and peace she did with Mitch. Their conversation interested her every bit as much as their lovemaking, and now, when she thought of marriage and Mitch in the same context and her daydreams took flight, she let them.

She was so happy, that taking two hours off work to keep her ultrasound appointment felt like no hardship at all. And dropping into her doctor's office to get the results was fine, too, because she wanted to ask Aretha about prenatal vitamins—folic acid and extra iron and calcium and all the rest. If marriage was right around the corner, becoming a family couldn't be far behind.

For the first time in years, seeing women with round, pregnant bellies and mothers with young children made Elaine feel excited, not sad. It was a wonderful gift to feel like part of the parenthood club, not a curious and yearning bystander.

"Thanks for coming in again, Elaine." Aretha entered her private office with her lab coat flapping. Sitting behind her desk, across from Elaine, she removed her glasses, rubbed her eyes and admitted she'd like to do the same to her feet. "Only Wednesday, and already it's been a long week."

"Maybe you need to take Wednesdays off," Elaine suggested, only partly teasing. "Try golf or in-line skating."

"If I took Wednesdays off, I'd try napping." Sipping what appeared to be a cold coffee, Aretha grimaced. "How are you feeling?" she asked Elaine. "Any more pain?"

"Mmm, a couple of twinges today. Not a big deal, though."

Aretha pulled a file Elaine assumed to be hers from a stack on the upper left corner of her desk. With her elbows on the desk and her hands braced on her forehead as if she were shading her eyes, Aretha reviewed the contents of the chart. Tipping her hands, she looked up at Elaine. "Actually, dear heart, it's a bigger deal than we originally thought."

Chapter Sixteen

True to form, Portland's ephemeral autumn sunshine gave way to gray clouds and a chilly wind by the time Gordon was due to get off work Wednesday evening. Elaine huddled on a bench outside her friend's northwest office, waiting for him to emerge from the old brick building. She had no idea how long she sat there. A college-age student on Rollerblades skated by; a woman asked the time; a man wanted change. In each instance, Elaine simply stared, unable to muster the energy to respond.

Suspected POS, Polycycstic Ovarian Syndrome, complicated by endometrial hyperplasia. It was a wonder, Aretha said, that Elaine hadn't complained more about symptoms. Some women were very lucky when it came to pain, the doctor concluded. *Yeah, lucky,* Elaine had agreed. And in truth, the only pain she felt at the moment was in her soul.

Probably, Aretha had said, they would do a laparoscopy, to confirm the diagnosis. It was a fairly invasive procedure, but Elaine didn't even care about that right now. All she cared about was Aretha's summation of the impact the diagnosis could have on Elaine's intention to have a baby: "The likelihood of conception is in question...chances of a full-term pregnancy compromised..."

Likelihood of conception is in question...full-term pregnancy compromised...

Round and round the words went in Elaine's head, until there seemed to be no meaning to any of it, anymore. Except for a miserable sinking sensation, she was numb.

Then Gordon came out of his office, thank God. Thank God. And she called out to him, the hoarse croak of a drowning person, and he said her name in surprise and walked over, and immediately, as she rose from the bench, he held out his arms.

Elaine huddled in the familiar bearlike embrace, but refused to cry, knowing that if she started now, she wouldn't stop for a long, long time. She needed her wits about her.

For the next hour and a half, anyway.

Mitch bounded up the porch steps to the duplex. He carried two bouquets of flowers plus wine, ice cream and a gift bag from Victoria's Secret. Making a pit stop at Vicki's, he tucked one bouquet under his arm so he could rap on the door.

Having made a personal commitment to show more appreciation for his stepmother, do a few more of the things he imagined a son might do, Mitch figured he'd start tonight by dropping off a bouquet of roses before he headed next door for his date with Elaine.

At 7:00 p.m. the sky was darkening and moths flapped around the porch light. Winter waited around the bend. In the past, Mitch had considered winter to be an inconvenience. Now he imagined long evenings in front of a fireplace and even longer weekends. Elaine had changed his perspective on just about everything.

When Vicki opened the door, Mitch thrust the bouquet in front of her. "For you, dear lady," he said, "compliments of the Ryder siblings.'' He'd have to remember to mention to M.D. tomorrow that he'd picked up the bouquet.

Vicki blinked her large blue eyes several times in surprise. ''Why, Mitch. Why, my goodness—''

''What the hell…?'' From behind his flustered stepmother, a distinguished gentleman in his sixties appeared. Eyeing Mitch, the man said, ''I thought that was you. But you sounded like one of the Knights of the Roundtable. What's got into you?''

''Oh, Daniel!'' With a backhanded swat to his chest, Vicki admonished her husband. ''Don't ruin a lovely moment.''

Looking genuinely perplexed and more than a bit disgruntled, Daniel Ryder gestured to his son. ''Get in here. I need your help.''

Stunned to find his father in Portland without any warning, Mitch opened the screen door and entered his stepmother's duplex. She gave him a warm hug. He and Daniel hadn't seen each other in months, maybe closer to a year, but they shook hands rather than embracing. They always had.

''I'm surprised to see you here,'' Mitch admitted. ''I thought Colt vs. Switzer was about to go into closing arguments.'' Colt vs. Switzer was a huge, high-profile case for which Daniel was the litigating attorney.

''It is,'' the senior Ryder confirmed gruffly. ''I have no time for playing games, which is why I'm damned disappointed in you and frankly surprised by your disloyalty.''

''Disloyalty?''

''Yes. Encouraging Vicki to live in Portland. She lives in Bellevue, damn it!''

So that's what this was about. Daniel had come to take Vicki home. Mitch was amazed. He hadn't thought Daniel would cave in so quickly. And for Daniel, the mere fact that he'd come to get Vicki was the equivalent of ''caving in.''

''I didn't exactly encourage—'' Mitch began.

''You rolled out the red carpet!'' Daniel barked. ''Look at this place. Now I want you to talk some sense into your stepmother. You deal with divorce every day. It's not pretty. Tell her.''

Mitch turned to Vicki. "Divorce is not pretty."

Lifting a brow, she gave him a subtle wink. "Thank you for that information."

Obviously Daniel expected more from his son in the way of support. "Tell her she's got to come home, for God's sake."

Vicki made a sound of utter disgust, looking very much like she was prepared to leave the room. Mitch waited until he had her full attention then told her, "If you go back to him, you're crazy."

It was hard to tell which of his parents was more stunned. Before Daniel's blood pressure shot into orbit, Mitch asked his father, "Have you given her a reason to go back?"

"What the hell is that supposed to mean?"

"Do you even know what it would take to get her back? Have you asked?"

Vicki looked at Mitch with gratitude and at Daniel with challenge. "No, he hasn't."

Daniel began to perspire. "I don't believe this. Has your sister turned on me, too?"

Mitch shook his head. M.D. would probably be as appalled by the need for communication and the honest expression of feelings as Daniel was. Gently, he advised his father, "Just ask her, Dad."

Both Mitch and Vicki waited, wondering what the proud, stubborn, difficult man they both loved would do now that his back was finally against the wall, where it probably should have been years ago.

Shaking his head, Daniel swore, but Mitch could see him struggling to accept the inevitable. Wiping his brow with the back of his hand, he asked in a low tone Mitch had never heard from him before, "What do you want, Vick? What would it take to make you come home?"

The challenge in Vicki's eyes softened to satisfaction. Holding her stepson's flowers, she bent her head to inhale their aroma, taking her time to consider before answering. "I've already told you what I want in my life, Daniel. Family."

"I'm sixty-four, Vicki, I can't give you—"

"Oh, yes you can. 'Family' can mean a lot of different things. For now, let's just say it means love. That's where we'll start. I'm not coming back to you until you promise to tell me, 'Vicki, I love you,' every single day. And I do not mean over the phone, via fax or by memo." She took several steps until all that separated her from her husband was the bouquet of roses. "You've got to look me in the eye and say the words. But only if you mean them."

Unconsciously it seemed, Daniel reached up to hold his wife's arms. He appeared older and more tired than he usually did, but less forbidding, too. His expression was profoundly serious when he opened his mouth to speak then halted, glancing over at Mitch. "Do you have to be here for this?"

Vicki turned to smile at her stepson. "Maybe not the first time."

But Mitch was hardly listening. *You have to tell me you love me…every single day.*

Damn it. Had he said the words to Elaine? Had he even said them to himself *about* Elaine? No, on both counts. Rather, he'd done his best to maneuver her over to his way of thinking without giving her what she needed most—the promise of family the way Vicki defined it. Her definition sounded like the truest Mitch had ever considered: *Let's just say it means love.* That was the family Elaine wanted…and needed. A family that sprang from love, not merely the willingness to have children.

"Look, I've got to go," he said apologetically, paying little attention to the fact that they wanted him gone. With the words *I love you* ready to burst off his tongue, he had to see Elaine now, this minute.

Leaving his father and Vicki, Mitch practically barreled through the screen door and sprinted down the porch to Elaine's. He knocked with as much restraint as he currently possessed. Receiving no response, he banged on the door more forcefully.

She was supposed to meet him here around seven. Mitch checked his watch—it was ten after the hour. He waited several more minutes…though not patiently. Moving around the back of the house to see whether she was inside, taking a bath or a nap, he realized that the house was dark. It appeared she hadn't been home yet at all, which seemed strange given that she'd told him she was getting off work early; she was always punctual.

Ten more minutes of waiting, and that was it; Mitch's patience was exhausted. Returning to Vicki's, he reached up to tap on the frame of the screen, but the scene inside stopped him. His father and Vicki were wound in an embrace so passionate, they were practically one person. Mitch's first impulse was to leave; his second was to grin. It was his third impulse, however, that won out. Now that his father and stepmother's relationship was ironed out, Mitch needed to cement his own, and he needed help.

When he cleared his throat, Daniel jumped. Vicki appeared more composed, though in the ambient lighting, Mitch could see her blush.

"I hate to bust in," Mitch apologized, "but have you seen Elaine? She was supposed to be here half an hour ago."

"Elaine? Oh!" Still clasped against Daniel's chest, Vicki put both hands to her mouth. "I completely forgot. I am so sorry, sugar."

"Who is Elaine?" Daniel asked, and Vicki started to explain, but Mitch interrupted.

"What did you forget, Vicki?"

"That Elaine called earlier."

"Who's Elaine?" Daniel said.

"My next-door neighbor. Mitch is sweet on her, but he doesn't want anyone to know it yet. Elaine wants a baby, but she's divorced, and guess who her ex-husband's divorce lawyer was, by the way?"

''Not Mitch?''

''Yes. Won't that be a funny story to tell your grandchildren?''

''Hilarious.'' Daniel eyed his son darkly.

''Vicki, what did Elaine say?'' Mitch had no intention of hashing out the ethics of his relationship with Elaine right now. And maybe he'd never do it; you had to be there.

''Let's see.'' Vicki tried to think back. ''She called around six-thirtyish, I'd say. And she asked me if I'd mind watching Pumpkin for a few days. Of course I said I wouldn't mind a bit, partly because I wanted to irritate your father. He seemed to think I'd pack up and leave the moment I saw him standin' on my porch.'' She tweaked Daniel's chin, and he did, indeed, look irritated when she mentioned Pumpkin. He was also staring at his wife as if he'd like to eat her up.

Bemused but happy for his parents, Mitch was more concerned now about his own romance. ''Vicki, did Elaine say where she was going? Did she mention coming home first?''

''Mmm, no to both questions. Although she did say she'd see me when she got back, so I suppose that means she's not planning to come home tonight. I thought maybe she was going somewhere with you.''

The first warning bell sounded in Mitch's head. Elaine knew he had to catch up on work, so she wasn't planning a trip with him. And if not with him, then where…and with whom?

''Oh, one other thing,'' Vicki remembered. ''She was with Gordon when she called.''

''How do you know it was Gordon?''

''Who is Gordon?'' Daniel, who liked to be in control of most situations, was having some trouble with this one.

''I heard a man's voice.''

The second warning bell clanged. Immediately Mitch thought of Kevin and felt as if someone were wringing his gut like a rag. ''How do you know the man was Gordon? Did you recognize his voice?''

"No. But I heard him ask if Elaine wanted nutmeg on her latte. Most men never think about nutmeg."

Daniel looked at Mitch and frowned. Mitch frowned back and added a shrug. He turned to Vicki. "Do you know Gordon's number?"

The muscles in Elaine's calves ached as she hiked across the all-but-deserted beach. Sand and water seeped into her canvas deck shoes, chilling her bare feet. The physical discomfort didn't bother her.

After a sleepless night and two hours of walking, the only fatigue she felt was of the spirit.

Yesterday evening, Gordon had given her the keys to his family's cottage in Canon Beach, usually one of her favorite places in the whole world. During the summer, the beach hummed with tourists and art festivals; it teemed with color and life. In the drizzly fall and winter seasons, however, the small coastal town offered the peace and relative quiet Elaine craved so she could think. Even the gray sky and intermittent rain made turning inward seem natural.

In one week Elaine would turn thirty-seven. Some women had babies in their forties. But rarely women with POS. With or without the additional complications Elaine had, many women with POS never had babies at all.

Keeping her head down as she trudged through small hills of sand, her hands stuffed into the pockets of an oversized windbreaker Gordon had lent her, Elaine felt as helpless and sick as she had when Aretha first broke the news. Perhaps the beach had been the wrong place to come. She'd never yet shuffled through sand without imagining children filling buckets and taking turns burying each other so that only their giggling faces stuck out. She'd imagined their noses shiny with sunblock and their warm, cuddly bodies at the end of the day as she snuggled with them, one child under each arm, atop a big bed in a cottage by the sea.

Now it seemed that someone else's simple reality might remain her impossible dream. The thought of Mitch did not console her.

What was the use of marriage? *What was the use?* She had no glue with which to hold a marriage to Mitch together. Her love and the presence of children might have done it; they could have had a chance. Now...

Elaine shook her head, pulling a tight fist from her pocket to backhand a tear from her cheek. She'd cried enough last night and this morning. It hadn't helped anything.

She should have phoned him before she left, but selfishly she didn't want to see him or even hear his voice. The dream had been in the palm of her hands; now it was gone, and she couldn't bear to think about it.

Elaine began to feel the fatigue from her long walk and sleepless night as she turned up the cobbled path to the cottage. She intended to drink a glass of water then find the vacuum and start cleaning. Her intention was to busy her body so her mind would calm.

The moment she entered the house, however, her plans drifted away. She felt like Mama Bear arriving home after Goldilocks had reorganized the house. This was not the same purely functional living room she had left.

The newly adorned room looked like a Hallmark store.

Mylar balloons floated on strings tied to chairs, lamps, even a vase on the coffee table. Long-stemmed pink and yellow roses bloomed from the vase and in a tall crystal container on the dining table. Stuffed animals sat on the sofa, like children lined up for a school photo. A toy dump truck and a large doll rested against the leg of the coffee table.

Elaine ventured farther into the room to pluck a stuffed bunny off the sofa. Its stitched-on smile and glassy eyes looked oddly hopeful. "Baxter." She recognized it as the comfort toy she'd slept with for years.

Her parents were here. But why would they—

"You're back."

Elaine turned. *Mitch.* He stood in the cottage's open doorway, panting as if he'd jogged to get here. Moving into the room, he put hands on this thighs, trying to catch his breath and speak at the same time.

"I went to Haystack Rock. Gordon said that's where you like to walk."

Unease that bordered on nausea churned inside her. "Gordon. Gordon told you I was here?"

Mitch shook his head. "He was loyal. Wouldn't tell me a thing. Even when I challenged him to an old-fashioned fist-fight."

"So who—"

"Your mother. I waited here an hour, but when you didn't come back, I got antsy and then when I didn't see you on the beach, I was afraid you'd get back before I could explain." Strengthening, he gestured to the room he had, apparently, decorated.

"I walked in the other direction," Elaine murmured, lowering herself to the edge of the sofa.

Mitch crossed to her and knelt on the floor. "When Gordon wouldn't tell me anything, I went to your parents. I didn't know where else…" He pressed his lips together, shaking his head. Unbelievably, she saw moisture in his eyes. "They're great people."

Elaine had phoned her mother to cancel a lunch date for Saturday and wound up crying, telling her mom about the diagnosis. Suddenly the balloons, the stuffed animals and the children's toys made sense. They also made Elaine unaccountably angry. "I can't believe she told you!"

"Why didn't *you* tell me?"

"Because I wasn't ready yet."

"When would you have been ready? You told other people." A note of challenge added an edge to Mitch's tone. It didn't make Elaine feel guilty at all; it made her more stubborn.

"I told Gordon and my mother."

"Why?"

"I've known them forever."

"And?"

Frustrated, Elaine tossed her bunny to the side. "What do you mean?"

Rising, he stood over her. His eyes were dry again, but sparking with emotion. "You trust them. That's the difference. You don't trust me, yet."

Elaine rose, too. "I don't know how you can say that after what we agreed to. This has nothing to do with trust."

He reached for her shoulders. "Yes, it does. You *shouldn't* trust a man who can't say, 'I love you.'" Holding her gaze when she wanted to look away, he told her, "I went to your parents because they know how to love, and I need to learn. I don't know how to be a family man, Lainey. How to be the best man for you. So I asked for help."

Realizing he had her full attention now, he let go of her shoulders, using only his honesty to hold her. "Your mother said she thinks you settle for what's good enough. Don't. Don't settle. Not for me. And sure as hell not for Lowry." He growled the last sentence.

Confusion swirled in Elaine's mind. She couldn't process what Mitch was telling her fast enough to make sense of all of it. "Kevin?" She hooked onto the last thing he said. "What has Kevin got to do with it?"

"Lowry gave me a message for you." Mitch's jaw became so tense he could barely open his mouth enough to emit words. "I talked to him at the office. He wants you to know his marriage to Stephanie isn't going well. And that—" He paused, his jaw contracting even more tightly. "He hasn't forgotten what you two had together."

Mitch stood as still and straight as a marine, waiting for her response. Elaine felt her own muscles tense, but from the attempt to not laugh.

"Well, that's Kevin. Unhappy with what he's got and mourning what he gave up. I feel bad for his baby, but Stephanie is a pretty tough cookie. I'm sure she'll bring him around.''

Kevin was no longer Elaine's burden. The weight of her own problems was enough.

"These toys. Why—"

"You don't care about Kevin, anymore?"

Making a face, Elaine waved a hand. What was the point of wasting a minute on that? "Did my mother tell you what the doctor said?"

"You're over Kevin." Pure satisfaction relieved the tension in his face.

Elaine shook her head. He wasn't getting this.

She took a step back and circled around the coffee table, nearly tripping over the dump truck. "I may not have children." She refused to sugarcoat anything. "Ever. Aretha, my doctor, found all sorts of things wrong. These balloons, these toys—" She raised her chin. Forced herself to speak the awful truth. "I won't be using them, Mitch, so if you've decided you want kids, you'd better look—"

Mitch moved around the table before she finished the sentence. He put his hands on either side of her face. "Here. I'm looking for my family right here. Where are you looking?"

Elaine's eyes filled with tears. The words that would have thrilled her two days ago only made her ache today. "I'm not looking anymore."

As Mitch continued to hold her, neither his touch nor his gaze wavered. "Yes you are."

She shook her head.

"Change your definition of family," he said forcefully. "I have. 'Family' is you and me. Your parents and my parents. M.D. and Gordon." He took a breath and said words that were blatantly unfamiliar to him. "Family is love. It took me thirty-six years and two months to realize that. Thirty-six years on my own and two months with you."

Elaine took his hands and pulled them away from her face. Briefly, she held on tightly then forced herself to let go and turn away. Walking to a small table and chairs, on which he'd tied the most balloons, she fingered one of the long ribbon strings for a moment then closed her eyes. Mitch wanted her. He wanted to be part of the life she already had. The knowledge swelled her heart. And broke it. Perhaps in this moment more than any time before, she realized how very close she had come to living her dream.

With her eyes still closed, she whispered. "Family is children, too."

Very soon, she felt Mitch's presence behind her.

"I didn't fill this room with toys to torture you." He waited, but she said nothing. Rather than touching her again, he requested, "Lainey, look at me."

Knowing he deserved her compliance after everything he'd told her, she turned and opened her eyes. What she saw was a man determined to overpower concern with confidence.

"Loving you I've had to let go of what I thought I knew about myself. And the way I thought I was going to live my life."

Pushing a lock of beach-mussed hair behind her ears, he said more softly, "I love you. There must a lot of ways to bring children into a family, but they all begin with love. We can have that. Can't we, Lainey?" He moved closer, delving his fingers gently into her hair. "Say the words. Turn us into a family."

Epilogue

"Marigold Desiree. *That's your name?*" Gordon leaned back in his deck chair and laughed, his still robust chest and belly bouncing with humor.

A full five years after meeting M.D. Ryder, he'd finally discovered her given name.

"My mother had a keen sense of the absurd," M.D. said, directing a scowl of patent displeasure at her brother, who was carefully seating himself in the chair next to Gordon's. "I can't believe you told him."

Mitch offered an apologetic shrug, but appeared distinctly unguilty. "Had to happen someday. Besides, I feel like I'm in *The Wizard of Oz* when the kids call you Auntie Em."

"So you'd rather they call me Auntie Marigold? Not a chance." Leaning forward, she pulled her niece from Mitch's lap.

Four-year-old Libby Ryder went easily to her aunt's arms and planted a smacking kiss on her lips. Wry, unsentimental M.D. melted visibly under her niece's charm.

"Who do you love best?" M.D. murmured to her winsome niece.

Libby's answer was swift and sure. "Daddy!" she crowed, cannoning back to her father's lap.

"Sorry." Mitch shrugged, though in truth he wasn't the slightest bit sorry. The past five years had been the best of his life. Leaning back in the chair, his daughter nestled against him. Mitch sighed audibly as he surveyed his backyard.

Vicki stood with Elaine's dad at the BBQ, tending the beef ribs while Mitch's father, Daniel, followed his two-year-old grandson on a tour of the garden to look for the ladybugs that routinely sent Nate into gales of laughter. Elaine's mom came out of the house, carrying a bowl of coleslaw and a book of sheet music for her marimba.

And then Elaine appeared. Mitch's heart did a drum roll. In a pale green dress that set off her freckles, she was even more beautiful to him now than she'd been on their wedding day. Over her shoulder she wore a baby sling, inside which slept their newest addition, Isabella.

After checking with Vicki to make sure the food was under control, Elaine turned toward the group on the deck. She made sleepy eye contact with Mitch, and they grinned. Having three kids in five years didn't give them much time for rest, but they wouldn't change a thing.

Conceived first in their hearts, each of their two elder children had been born in a different country. Libby had come to them via Guatemala and Nate from Korea. They'd been discussing—only discussing—increasing their ranks again when Elaine had mentioned that she wasn't feeling well. She'd been tired, had indigestion and was moody and had wondered aloud to Mitch if she was starting menopause. Merely uttering the sentence had brought a torrent of tears despite her protests that the idea didn't bother her that much. Mitch had sent her to the doctor over more protests and Elaine had returned home with a dazed smile on her face and a prescription for prenatal vitamins in the diaper bag. Isabella had joined the family six months later, to everyone's amazement.

Well, not everyone's. Mitch hadn't been as surprised as the others. A miracle was a miracle, after all. Now they had three.

Loving Elaine had changed his life.

For one thing, he was no longer a divorce lawyer; now Mitch belonged to a family practice. Within the next year, he planned to move into adoption law.

Settling into a chair, her sleeping bundle held against her by the sling, Elaine reached out to stroke her elder daughter's arm. "Why don't you help Grandma Laura play her marimba?"

The dancing dark eyes of their daughter lit with joy. "Okay!" She squealed as only a little girl can. Elaine caught a quick kiss before Libby skipped off to join her grandma in their favorite activity.

Between the white deck chairs, Mitch and Elaine caught hands.

"So is this the last one?" Gordon nodded toward Isabella.

"For a while, anyway," Elaine said, her free hand absently stroking Isabella's downy head.

"But we never say never," Mitch added, winking at his wife.

"True. But I would like to sleep eight hours at a stretch at least once before we do it again."

"You two are certainly prolific," M.D. commented wryly, sipping an iced tea.

Her sister-in-law nodded. "I know. Mitch jokes that we start another child—one way or another—every time I say, 'I love you.'" She looked at her husband, and her sleepy face transformed to pure bliss. "Right?"

"Works like a charm," he agreed.

Five years after saying their *I do's*, Elaine's heart was still the first thing Mitch saw when he looked in his wife's eyes.

Her expression reminded him that all his miracles began right here, with the miracle of being loved by her.

Squeezing Elaine's hand, he felt contentment well inside him, and he smiled. "Works like a charm."

* * * * *

SPECIAL EDITION™

**Coming in November to
Silhouette Special Edition
The fifth book in the exciting continuity**

THE PARKS EMPIRE

DARK SECRETS. OLD LIES. NEW LOVES.

THE MARRIAGE ACT

(Silhouette Special Edition #1646)

by

Elissa Ambrose

Plain-Jane accountant Linda Mailer had never done anything shocking in her life—until she had a one-night stand with a sexy detective and found herself pregnant! *Then* she discovered that her anonymous Romeo was none other than Tyler Carlton, the man spearheading the investigation of her beleaguered boss, Walter Parks. Tyler wanted to give his child a real family, and convinced Linda to marry him. Their passion sparked in close quarters, but Linda was wary of Tyler's motives and afraid of losing her heart. Was he using her to get to Walter—or had they found the true love they'd both longed for?

Available at your favorite retail outlet.

If you enjoyed what you just read,
then we've got an offer you can't resist!

Take 2 bestselling
love stories FREE!
Plus get a FREE surprise gift!

Clip this page and mail it to Silhouette Reader Service™

IN U.S.A.	**IN CANADA**
3010 Walden Ave.	P.O. Box 609
P.O. Box 1867	Fort Erie, Ontario
Buffalo, N.Y. 14240-1867	L2A 5X3

YES! Please send me 2 free Silhouette Special Edition® novels and my free surprise gift. After receiving them, if I don't wish to receive anymore, I can return the shipping statement marked cancel. If I don't cancel, I will receive 6 brand-new novels every month, before they're available in stores! In the U.S.A., bill me at the bargain price of $4.24 plus 25¢ shipping and handling per book and applicable sales tax, if any*. In Canada, bill me at the bargain price of $4.99 plus 25¢ shipping and handling per book and applicable taxes**. That's the complete price and a savings of at least 10% off the cover prices—what a great deal! I understand that accepting the 2 free books and gift places me under no obligation ever to buy any books. I can always return a shipment and cancel at any time. Even if I never buy another book from Silhouette, the 2 free books and gift are mine to keep forever.

235 SDN DZ9D
335 SDN DZ9E

Name _____ (PLEASE PRINT)

Address _____ Apt.# _____

City _____ State/Prov. _____ Zip/Postal Code _____

Not valid to current Silhouette Special Edition® subscribers.

Want to try two free books from another series?
Call 1-800-873-8635 or visit www.morefreebooks.com.

* Terms and prices subject to change without notice. Sales tax applicable in N.Y.
** Canadian residents will be charged applicable provincial taxes and GST.
  All orders subject to approval. Offer limited to one per household.
  ® are registered trademarks owned and used by the trademark owner and or its licensee.

SPED04R   ©2004 Harlequin Enterprises Limited

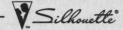

SPECIAL EDITION™

presents

an emotional debut

THE WAY TO A WOMAN'S HEART

(SSE #1650, available November 2004)

by

Carol Voss

It had been two years since her husband's death in the line of duty, and Nan Kramer was still struggling to raise her children in peace. But when her son flirted with crime to impress his friends, family friend and local cop David Elliott came to the rescue. David had always believed that cops and families didn't mix, but he couldn't ignore the sparks of attraction that ignited whenever he was around Nan—and neither could she. Could they overcome the odds and find happiness together?

Don't miss this beautiful story—only from Silhouette Books!

Available at your favorite retail outlet.

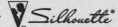

SPECIAL EDITION™

presents

bestselling author

Susan Mallery's

next installment of

 Watch how passions flare under the hot desert sun for these rogue sheiks!

THE SHEIK & THE PRINCESS BRIDE

(SSE #1647, available November 2004)

Flight instructor Billie Van Horn's sexy good looks and charming personality blew Prince Jefri away from the moment he met her. Their mutual love burned hot, but when the Prince was suddenly presented with an arranged marriage, Jefri found himself unable to love the woman he had or have the woman he loved. Could Jefri successfully trade tradition for true love?

Available at your favorite retail outlet.

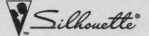

COMING NEXT MONTH

SPECIAL EDITION

#1645 CARRERA'S BRIDE—Diana Palmer
Long, Tall Texans
Jacobsville sweetheart Delia Mason was swept up in a tidal
wave of trouble while on a tropical island holiday getaway.
Luckily for this vulnerable small-town girl, formidable casino
tycoon Marcus Carrera swooped in to the rescue. Their mutual
attraction sizzled from the start, but could this tempestuous duo
survive the forces conspiring against them?

#1646 THE MARRIAGE ACT—Elissa Ambrose
The Parks Empire
Red-haired beauty Linda Mailer didn't want her unexpected
pregnancy to tempt Tyler Dalton into a pity proposal. But the green-
eyed cop convinced Linda that, at least for the child's sake,
a temporary marriage was in order. Their loveless marriage was
headed for wedded bliss when business suddenly got in the way
of their pleasure....

#1647 THE SHEIK & THE PRINCESS BRIDE—
Susan Mallery
Desert Rogues
From the moment they met, flight instructor Billie Van Horn's
sexy good looks and charming personality blew Prince Jefri
away. Their mutual love burned hot, but when Jefri was suddenly
presented with an arranged marriage, he found himself unable to
love the woman he had—or have the woman he loved. Could Jefri
successfully trade tradition for true love?

#1648 A BABY ON THE RANCH—Stella Bagwell
Men of the West
When Lonnie Corteen agreed to search for his best friend's long-
lost sister, he found the beautiful Katherine McBride pregnant,
alone and in no mood to have her heart trampled on again. But
Lonnie wanted to reunite her family—and become a part of it.

#1649 WANTED: ONE FATHER—Penny Richards
Single dad Max Murdock needed a quiet place to write and a baby-
sitter for his daughter. Zoe Barlow had a cabin to rent and needed
some extra cash. What began as a perfect match blossomed into the
perfect romance. But could this lead to one big perfect family?

#1650 THE WAY TO A WOMAN'S HEART—Carol A. Voss
Nan Kramer had lost one man in the line of fire and wasn't about to
put herself and her three children through losing another. Family
friend—and local deputy—David Elliot agreed that because of his
high-risk job, he should remain unattached. Nonetheless, David had
found his way into this woman's heart, and neither wanted to send
him packing....

SSECNM1004